PLAY IT AGAIN

—

AIDAN WAYNE

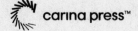
carina press™

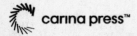

ISBN-13: 978-1-488-05377-1

Play It Again

Copyright © 2019 by Aidan Wayne

Recycling programs
for this product may
not exist in your area.

www.CarinaPress.com

Printed in U.S.A.

PLAY IT AGAIN

Chapter One

The door to Rachel's room opened and closed, followed by the sound of footsteps.

Dovid winced. He knew what was coming. It was February third. Which meant—

"Dovid," Rachel sing-songed, "guess what time it is?"

Dovid groaned, refusing to lift his fingers from his book. "No. No, no, no, come on, we've done this every year since we released that stupid video."

"Exactly. It's tradition now."

"Watching it one more time isn't going to matter to the view count," he tried, just like he had every year for the last five years.

"Doesn't matter," Rachel said, plopping down next to him on the couch. "It's still one of our highest viewed videos, and do I need to mention that it's the one that went viral and got us popular in the first place?"

"Ugh." Dovid marked his place and set his book down on the arm of the couch. "Fine then, just play the damn thing."

Rachel didn't say anything, but then there was the oh-so-familiar click of a mouse button and—

"Psst. Dovid. Dovid, wake up."

Dovid sighed. Rachel had come into his room at

three am to bother him. They'd hit on the idea together, but being woken up after a night of illicit drinking was much less fun than it had initially sounded.

"Rachel? What...what time'sit? What d'you want?"

"I needed to ask you about your name, remember?"

Dovid groaned, because he knew what was coming next. He knew a drunk, heavy-sleeper, and thus only half-awake, eighteen-year-old Dovid was sitting up in bed and fumbling for his glasses because he knew he was being filmed and his glasses were an important accessory even at fucking three am, and asking, *"Wha' about my name?"*

"Well... I heard another person call you David yesterday."

On the couch, present-day Dovid bristled indignantly. And video-Dovid was doing the same thing. *"I know,"* he mumbled. *"Fuck him."*

"Why? What's the big deal?"

"Because it's my name," Dovid whined. Whined. Present-Dovid groaned. *"And it's not that fucking hard."*

"Yeah?"

And here it went. *"It's so simple. It's just two syllables. 'Do-vid.' Two vowel pronunciations. 'Do-vid.' It's one of the simplest things to do! Everyone knows how to say 'duh.' It is an integral part of human language. Everyone knows how to say 'vid' because there isn't a person on the planet who can't say 'video.' Combine them. 'Duh' plus 'vid.' 'Duh-vid.' 'Dovid.' It isn't! That! Hard!"*

Dovid sank down into the couch. Video-Dovid was just warming up.

"And just why is 'David' supposedly so much easier to pronounce? Because it's more mainstream? What makes something mainstream? Why can people get

'Schwarzenegger' and have that be mainstream? It's not fair. My name is so much easier. It is, isn't it?"

"It's easier than 'Schwarzenegger,' sure," Rachel said, in unison with her video-voice. He could tell that they were both trying not to laugh.

"See? Well, no, I mean, I can't—" at that, at least, Dovid's lips quirked. Even at three am he still managed to make blind jokes *"—but you can. And so can so many other people. And that's an expression too, that's dumb. Just because I can't see* really *doesn't mean I can't see a stupid point. Like how easy my name is. It is easy, isn't it? Wait, you just said that. So did I. Anyway, David isn't a dumb name, but it's a different name. Than mine. Because I'm Dovid. Duh. Also 'vid.' And that's my name. It's so easy!"* A pause. *"And I'm awake now, thanks a lot."*

"I'm sorry."

"Ugh."

"You can go back to bed if you want to."

"No, I can't," Dovid whined. Again. *"I'm going to be kept up about the injustice of name usage and its varying pronunciation properties. Also, I am really awake. Ranting woke me up. Now what am I supposed to do? Rachel, I have a test in... What time is it?"* Video-Dovid slammed his hand on the clock next him.

In an even, British accent, the clock chimed out, *"The time is three fifty-eight."*

"Rachel. Rachel, Rachel, I have a test in the morning. And I'm awake. Why did we decide to do this?"

"Because you thought it'd be something funny to put on YouTube."

"Was I right?"

"It was pretty funny, yeah."

"Great." **A** pause. *"I'm going to take a shower, I think."*

"Okay."

"That means you should stop filming and also that you should go away."

A laugh. *"Okay. G'night."*

"Shut up."

"There," present-Rachel said as the video ended. "That wasn't so bad, was it?"

"Baby me sounds like such a brat."

"Adult you still sounds like that," she pointed out.

"Excuse you, my voice definitely evened out."

"I meant about the name thing."

"Oh, shut up and finish your little ritual."

She laughed. "Aaaannd our current view count for that video is two million, seven hundred and forty-three thousand, six hundred and eighty-nine views."

"Fucking…when did we break six hundred thousand?"

Rachel nudged him. "Like last week. Weren't you paying attention?"

"I don't have your compulsion to track the current view counts of all our most popular videos," Dovid grumbled. "Also, I hate that video."

"You thought it was a good idea at the time," she said, voice still colored with laughter.

"We came up with that idea while we were drunk! And we weren't allowed to tell anyone that because we were both underage and we *still* can't tell anyone because Mom and Dad never found out."

Rachel patted him solemnly on the back. "A secret we will take to our graves."

"I *hate* that video."

"Oh, you do not, stop it. That video is what helped

your rise to YouTube success and fame. And you're known for way better stuff than 'Angry Blind Teen Rants about His Name.'"

"I also shouldn't have given you video-naming privileges."

"I name all of your videos. I'm the creative one, remember? You'd be nothing without me."

Even if it had been someone else, Dovid still would have bristled. He hated being reminded that sometimes he had to depend on others. That he wasn't ever going to be quite as independent as he wanted to be. With Rachel, Dovid sighed but smiled. "Yeah, I know."

Pretty much since they were born, Rachel took her "seventeen minutes older and thus the big sister" job very seriously. Even more so when she was old enough to realize that Dovid wasn't a typical child.

Or no, because Dovid *had* been a pretty typical child. Just that, thanks to medulloepithelioma—a type of incredibly invasive cancer—he grew up missing two parts a typical child possessed, after they were removed in order to get rid of the cancer entirely.

Rachel learned early on that having a little brother without eyes meant she'd be acting as his eyes (and insisting on doing so) whenever the chance arose and sometimes when it didn't. Rachel was the one who tried to beat up the kids who teased him, who helped navigate clothes shopping, and who, amazingly, didn't mind doing most of the cleaning in their shared apartment.

And yet she did it all without being suffocating. They were just Dovid and Rachel Rosenstein, living and working together in Seattle, documenting their lives (well, mostly Dovid's; Rachel hated being on camera) for a living, and getting along surprisingly well even after all these years. Which was pretty good considering their whole dynamic existed because of those things.

"So, hey," Rachel said, bumping shoulders with Dovid on the couch. "Are we still on to review that restaurant today?"

"Yeah, I talked to the owner again this morning. They're comping meals for both of us and he asked that we order more than we'd typically eat so that we can review as many dishes as we can."

Rachel rubbed her hands together, the sound familiar. "Awesome. I'm going to eat so much dessert."

"You always say that."

"And it's always true," she said solemnly.

"And yet you refuse to be on camera to talk about said desserts, so I also have to eat a little bit of everything and, I don't know if you noticed, Rachel, but I do try to maintain a certain physique for my viewers."

"Okay, one, of course I try not to notice, you're my baby brother. Two, saying it like that makes it sounds like your viewers are watching you for an entirely different reason, and three, it's February— you'd freeze without a shirt on anyway."

"One, I'm not your 'baby' brother, I'm like fifteen minutes younger than you—"

"Seventeen!"

"Not the point. Two, you've *read* me some of that fanfiction—against my will, I might add—so you know even better than I do that some of our viewers watch me exactly for that reason, and three, I'm not saying I'm going to pose without a shirt on, duh—"

"Vid."

"Rachel."

"What?"

Dovid groaned. "I don't know why I put up with you."

"Because you love me. We already established this."

"Yes to the stupid restaurant. We're going to eat lots of food and desserts, and then you're probably going to sneak some video of me working out later because you always do."

"Can I help it if I need to give the fans what they want?"

"So you do admit some of them want me for my body," he said triumphantly.

She patted him on the shoulder. "Don't worry. I'll help keep your virtue intact."

"Oh no you fucking won't, if I don't want said virtue. You'll make yourself scarce, like a good sex-repulsed aroace."

"Ick. True."

He laughed and stood up. "Okay, I'm ready to get ready for food if you are. Wanna grab the camera and we'll mic me up?"

"Already grabbed. Is that what you want to wear?"

Dovid ran his fingers down the front of his shirt. It was a nice cotton blend, and according to where he'd found it in his closet, was a faded grey plaid print. He was wearing a black tee underneath. "Yeah, sure. We don't have to film 'Dovid decides what to wear before he goes out' every time I leave the house."

"Yeah, but it always helps solidify the time skip."

"Let me mic myself up, woman," he said, holding out his hands for the gear.

* * *

"We ready?"

"Yeah, hang on, checking sound…okay, yeah, we're good."

"Awesome. Should I do the clap?"

"Yeah, go ahead."

Dovid clapped his hands, waited for Rachel's answering finger snap to signal she was ready, counted to five in his head, and then opened his mouth.

"Hey, guys! This is Don't Look Now with Dovid and Rachel. I'm Dovid, Rachel's behind the camera, and today we are reviewing The Sweet Spot, a cafe bistro specializing in desserts. They have other food," he added, "but mostly Rachel is interested in the desserts."

"Dovid, come on, eyes on the prize."

"I don't even have eyes. You can't tell me what to do."

"Dovid."

"Okay, okay. Anyway, yes, The Sweet Spot. As always, I'm going to review on the three things I find most important when picking an eatery." He held up three fingers. "One! The atmosphere. The sounds, the smells…is it an appetizing place to eat? Obviously, I can't comment on the decor, but that's Rachel's job to show you. Two! The food. Duh—Rachel, don't say it!" He heard her snort, then cleared his throat. "The food. Since that's a huge part of any place to eat. And three, accessibility. Is there a weird stoop at the door that I have to be aware of? Are the tables and chairs spaced far enough apart that I can get around easily and by myself? What about the restroom? Though for that one, we didn't get a private meal at this place, so I can't actually show you the restroom, sorry, guys, but I will, of course, describe in detail. All that and more, coming up." He stopped talking, waiting for Rachel.

"Camera's paused," she said a second later. "Ready to head over?"

Dovid nodded. "Yup. Let's do this."

Due to the busy, populated, and close-together store-front setup of downtown Seattle, they often weren't able to film right outside of the building they were visiting. Today, for instance, they were positioned across the street, The Sweet Spot in the background. So Dovid had to go back down the block to the crosswalk, cross the street, and then pick his way along using his cane until Rachel let him know he'd reached the right place.

She filmed b-roll with his mic off as he walked. "Okay," she said after a few minutes. "Door's about two steps to the left." Dovid nodded, then turned his mic back on. When he wasn't doing a video and had Rachel or someone else by his side, he often let them just hold the door open so he could go on in. But this was, again, partly about accessibility.

"Okay," he said as he got to the door and felt for the handle to open it up. The door swung inward. "First of all, there's no bump or anything on the stoop, it's all smooth. Nothing to trip on or get a wheelchair stuck on, so that's a plus." He put his arms out on the doorway. "And the doorway's a decent width. A chair shouldn't have a problem. So far so good."

Once he got into the actual cafe though, the problems started. Especially since he heard Rachel's quiet "uh-oh." He pushed on, tapping forward.

"Hi," from a female-sounding voice. "I'm Bernice. How many am I seating today?"

"Two," Dovid said.

"And would you like a booth or table?"

"Booth, please."

"Okay! Just follow me." And then an uncertain pause.

Dovid wasn't going to count that as a strike against

the cafe. "If you could talk to me and walk slowly, I should be able to follow you just fine."

"Um, okay, sure. What should I talk about?"

"Anything you want. Something you find interesting. Or tell me about your favorite foods here."

"Alright, uh, sure." The hostess launched into a mini-speech about the cafe's specials, focusing on a couple different desserts that were house favorites. Dovid followed along with his cane.

But he kept bumping into chairs. The tables were very close together, and it was hard to navigate with a cane. And a wheelchair certainly would have an even harder time. Bernice was walking pretty fast too. Dovid found himself trying to hurry up to follow her, and he actually bumped into a chair—with someone sitting on it.

"Excuse me!"

"Sorry, sorry," he said, pulling his hand back. "I didn't see you."

A falter, probably as the stranger took in his glasses and cane. "Oh, uh, that's okay."

"Sorry," he said again, before finally being seated at the booth Bernice led them too.

"I'm really sorry about that," Bernice said. "I didn't think…um."

Dovid nodded, accepting the apology. "Thanks for showing me to the booth."

"You're welcome. Your server will be with you momentarily."

"Okay."

As soon as Bernice's footsteps faded, Dovid turned so he was sitting straight in his seat.

"Am I facing the camera?"

"Yeah, and it's on the tripod. Go ahead."

Dovid counted to six in his head to give Rachel editing leeway, then said, "So that was a negative for The Sweet Spot. The aisle was plain too narrow for me to get through easily on my own. Which also means it'd be even harder to have someone side-by-side leading me along. And I don't know exactly how wide the aisle was because I couldn't see it, but it really didn't seem like a chair would be able to maneuver comfortably either. Now, our hostess might not have been thinking and there was a wider path she could have shown us, but I can only judge what I got." He waited a few more seconds then, to Rachel, "We've got to edit out the part where she shows her face, and play music over her talking. I don't want her to get into trouble."

"We might have to edit out most of that bit, or cut the video around the parts she's in. I tried to film mostly you though."

"Can you sort of fuzz out her back or something?"

"Yeah, I can censor her. That shouldn't be a problem."

"And we've got to slow-mo me bumping into that guy."

"You sure that wouldn't be kind of…in poor taste?"

Dovid tilted his head. "You think so? I don't. It sucks that I ran into someone, and it's going to have some people up in arms. I think putting an effect on it would make it a little more lighthearted."

"Maybe… Oh, oh, here comes the server. Turning the camera back on."

"Hi, there. My name is Anthony, and I'll be your server today." There was the sound of something being set down in front of him on the table; probably the menu. "Can I start either of you off with something to drink?"

"Do you guys have a braille menu, by chance?"

"Oh, um. I... I can certainly check. Would you like anything to drink while I go do that?"

"I'll just have water to start with, thank you."

"I'd like lemonade please," Rachel said.

"Got it. I'll be right back with your drinks and a new menu." Anthony's footsteps moved away from the table.

"Still filming?" Dovid asked.

"Yeah, go ahead."

"Okay," Dovid said to his future-viewers, "if we're invited to a place to review it, the staff is usually briefed ahead of time, especially given my situation. The places are also usually proud to boast that they're properly accessible, but at this point I'm sort of guessing that the owner invited me knowing about my restaurant reviewing and not about the blindness. You know as well as I do that most of the places that invite me personally have introduced a braille menu. I'm sort of skeptical that this place has one. That's not necessarily a negative against them, but it's kind of confusing. How do you even know about my channel and not know I'm freaking blind?"

"Here we are," Anthony said, setting two heavy objects on the table. "Water for you, and a lemonade for you. And I'm so sorry, but I asked and I don't think we have a braille menu. But, um..."

Dovid squashed a sigh and tried to sound polite. "Yes?"

"Are you guys Don't Look Now? If you aren't and don't know what I'm talking about just forget I said anything, but I—"

Now Dovid grinned. "Hey yeah, we are. You a fan?"

"Yes! I watch you guys with my sister. She's going to freak that I met you and that she didn't. Oh my god, am I going to be in one of your videos?"

"Yup," Rachel said, and it sounded like she was grinning too.

"Oh my god, that is so awesome. Could I, um, I'm so sorry to fan out over you, you probably just want to eat in peace, but could I have a picture?"

"Sure," Rachel said. "I'll take one of you and Dovid together. You have a phone?"

After Anthony had his picture taken with Dovid, he cleared his throat. "Right, um, yes, well. Thank you so much. And now I will be your very dignified server. And oh god, I'm so sorry we don't have a braille menu, I know that's like, one of your big deals."

"It's not your fault," Dovid said. "Rachel'll just read me everything like she usually does when this happens."

"I could recommend you something too, if you want?"

Dovid raised an eyebrow at Rachel. Bernice had already listed off a bunch of recommendations, but that had been mostly for background noise. Besides, at this point, Dovid was way more partial to Anthony than he was to Bernice.

"Yeah sure, go ahead." He smiled. "What do you think we should try?"

Anthony suggested two sandwiches, a pasta dish, and three desserts, including something called the Cookie Monster Madness Milkshake.

"We'll take one of everything you just said," Dovid told him. "Rachel, is there anything else you want to try?"

"Oof, I wish, but no, that's already a lot of food. I'll be content with three desserts."

"Oh yeah," Dovid said. "Could I also have some coffee?"

"Sure thing," Anthony said. "I'll bring that to you now."

Dovid smiled again. "Thanks a lot."

"N-no problem."

Once Anthony's footsteps had retreated again, Dovid turned to Rachel. "I like him," he announced. "He's cute."

"You only like him because he just fanboyed all over you," Rachel said, the laughter clear in her voice.

"That did add to the cuteness factor, yes, but—"

"But you like his voice."

"I do like his voice," Dovid said.

"This is totally going into the blooper footage."

"Aw, no, don't be mean. He's nervous enough as it is."

"I won't show him, I'll just find a creative way to highlight that you thought your server was cute."

Dovid shrugged. "Okay, sure. Anyway, read some of the menu out loud to me? We still need the voice-over for the menu pan."

"Right, sure. Oh, wait, hold up. Your crush is back."

"I brought you your coffee," Anthony said, setting two things down on the table with a click. "Cream and sugar are next to the coffee."

"Thanks."

"You're welcome. And, um, your orders will be up soon. Anything else I can do for you right now?"

"That's all," Dovid said, after Rachel stayed silent. "Thank you."

"You're welcome!"

Dovid moved his hand on the table until he reached the mug and placed it in front of him. Then he grabbed the creamer and sugar and set it to the side. He drank his coffee black, for the most part.

"Alright," he said to Rachel. "We've got a window without interruptions. Read to me?"

"Sure thing." Rachel read down the menu, and Dovid had to admit that the cafe had some really interesting and tasty sounding dishes. He also liked the creative names of them all.

"The menu is fun," he told the camera, once Rachel was finished. "And I admit to being partial to the staff. Or rather, our server seems great." Rachel snorted. Dovid continued, knowing she'd fix that in editing. "We ordered a total of six dishes. Way more food than even Rachel can eat—"

"Hey!"

"Do you deny it?"

A sigh. "No."

"Right, then. Way more food than even Rachel can eat, but since our meal is being comped, we wanted the chance to try as many things as we thought we could stomach. So, entrees first, then desserts, and we'll tell you what we think."

While they waited for their food, Rachel went to take whatever footage she wanted of the rest of the inside of the cafe. Used to this, Dovid waited in the booth and drank his coffee, absentmindedly going over what other things they could do for their next video. Restaurant review was a pretty well-liked subject, but the next video set to be released was another segment of Don't Look Now's "Day in the Life with Dovid" and he had been drawing a blank on what he should be doing or talking about.

Maybe it was time to make another video on dealing with lack of creativity. He got away with those once or twice a year. It gave Rachel freedom to be really wacky with her editing too. Then again, Rachel usually had ideas of her own when Dovid drew a blank.

"I'm back," Rachel said, sitting down again in the booth across from him. She knocked into his leg with her foot. "And just in time; here comes our food, I think. I'm getting footage of all this."

"Here we are," Anthony said as he placed several different sounding items down on the table. "The Fish it Were True Tuna Sandwich, the Eat Your Vegetables, Yes All at Once Mediterranean Sandwich, and the Grown-Up Mac and Cheese. I thought I'd maybe give you some time before I brought out the desserts? Unless, um, unless you did want them brought out now too—"

"This is fine," Rachel said easily. "I'd rather wait on the desserts, especially that milkshake. It'd be totally melted by the time we got to it, and that doesn't make a good camera shot."

"Okay, yeah. Just signal me when you want those desserts, okay?"

"Sounds good," Dovid said, smiling. "Thanks."

"Right! Um, enjoy your food."

"We will."

"How old is he, you think?" Dovid asked once Anthony had left again. "Too young for me? Too old? He didn't really sound like he could be too old."

Rachel kicked him under the table. "You're not trying to pick up our waiter. We're still reviewing. Focus."

Dovid sighed heavily for theatrics' sake. "Fine, fine. Take your shots and macros. I'll just sit here and wait to eat my food."

Rachel, of course, took her sweet time taking all the video and still shots for the food, moving plates and dishes around. Another reason why it was good they hadn't been given the milkshake from the get-go; it really would have been totally melted by the time she was done. "Alright," she said several long minutes later. "Tripod's all set up again. I'm ready for you."

"Food?"

"Already divided it," she said, tapping the plate in front of him. "Tuna's on the right, veggie's on the left, and be careful, these sandwiches are *stacked*. Mac and cheese is at three o'clock."

"Got it," Dovid said, once he felt out everything. "Clap?"

"Clap."

He clapped, and then it was finally time for him to have fun again, instead of waiting like a lump while Rachel got fancy with her camera.

"Alright, guys," he said. "Why don't we go with tuna first?" He took a bite of the sandwich and his eyebrows went up over his glasses. "Okay, I wasn't expecting that, but the tuna is warm. It was probably warmer before Rachel took her billion macro shots—" Rachel nudged him under the table "—but it's good. Not too much mayo which is nice. I hate it when mayo just oozes out of a sandwich. There's lettuce in here too, pretty classic and something I happen to really enjoy with tuna." He took a couple more bites. "It's also got cheese, melted. Probably one of the reasons why the tuna itself isn't cold. The bread is just this warm, buttery toasted goodness. Definitely a win for me." He set the tuna sandwich down and picked up the veggie, carefully holding the whole thing together. It was a pretty big sandwich. "Okay, now the entree for all the vegetarians out there. This is the Eat Your Vegetables, Yes All at Once Mediterranean Sandwich, and the name is a mouthful, but the sandwich feels like it's going to be one too. It's a hefty sandwich. Here goes." It took him a few tries to get a bite in, and he could hear Rachel giggling behind the camera.

"Okay," he said once he'd managed to finish his giant mouthful, "that is a good sandwich. According to the menu, it's got zucchini, yellow squash, red and green peppers, and cheese. All the vegetables are really good. They're grilled I think? And seasoned really nicely. The peppers are sweet, so the grill and cheese make a nice contrast. And the bread itself is…wow. I think they said they make all their bread in-house, right?"

"Right," Rachel said. "That's what our hostess told us."

"Yeah, and it tastes like it." He took another bite, chewed, swallowed. "Rachel, this is really good, you've got to try this one. I thought the tuna was good, but this is way better."

There was a pause while Rachel presumably took a bite, then, "Oh yeah, wow, that's great."

"Right?" He nodded. "So far the food is a win for me." He reached for the last dish, trading the bowl of mac and cheese for the plate of sandwiches. "Okay, last of all is the Grown-Up Mac and Cheese. It's shell pasta, four cheeses, baked so there's a nice crust on it." He found the spoon in his little bundle of utensils and tapped the top of the pasta. "Yeah, hear that? That's a baked cheese crust. And it's supposed to have chopped broccoli and hot dog pieces in it? Not sure how the hot dog makes it grown-up, but I guess the broccoli is supposed to even it out or something. Anyway, this dish can also be made vegetarian, since you can ask them to leave the hot dog out. And now for the moment of truth."

He used the spoon to break the top cheese layer and scoop up some of the mac and cheese, cupping his hand underneath it automatically as he took a bite.

"This is good too! Though at this point, I'm not surprised. The broccoli and hot dog are both chopped really fine, so they add flavor and a bit of texture without being too ostentatious. The pasta has just the edge of a bite to it, which, as you know if you've watched this channel, is how I personally feel pasta should always be made. The cheese is seasoned and look, look at this." He took another scoop of pasta and lifted it above the bowl. "Rachel, am I right in saying that there are strings of cheese there?"

"Yeah, and they look delicious. Finish talking so I can try some."

Dovid snickered. Rachel took forever with her macro shots while Dovid had to wait to eat; Dovid took time describing the food so Rachel had to wait. Perfect system. "Okay, so yeah, strings of cheese. So, what I mean is that the cheese isn't this creamy, almost liquid sauce that a lot of mac and cheese is. This has different cheeses and textures. So yeah, definitely not your classic mac and cheese. But really good. I like this a lot."

"Okay, okay. Now gimme."

He snorted, but gestured at the bowl. "Alright, fine, I guess you can try it."

The next few minutes were just them eating a little more and talking. They'd pick and choose what dialogue bits and pieces to use during editing, but they'd found their audience really liked a more authentic "sit and chat" episode. Which was fine with Dovid. It was nice (and super cool) to be able to just be himself for a living. He was always going to be thankful.

"Alright," Dovid said, before he ate his way to being full. "We still have three desserts to try. Don't fill up. Unless you *want* me to eat all of them by myself."

"Dovid, I will always have room for dessert. It's like you don't know me at all."

Dovid reached for the mac and cheese bowl again. "Did you eat all of this?" he asked incredulously.

"You helped!"

"I had like four bites."

"Shut up, shut up, I'm going to find Anthony and ask for our dessert."

Dovid laughed as Rachel got up. He mentally started going over his end-of-meal review while he waited. So far, the food was a definite win, service was decent, food came fast. All in all, a great cafe…for someone who was able-bodied.

As it was, the food was good, and he was looking forward to the desserts, since they were going to be great, if the entrees were any indication of quality. But there were lots of good eateries around that had good food and were way more accessible. Wider places to walk or crutch or wheel, and braille menus offered, if the clientele was blind like Dovid was. And while Anthony was a great server (he'd come by to refill drinks, but had made sure to wait for a lull in conversation because "I didn't want to interrupt you guys if you were filming"), Bernice hadn't really known how to deal with Dovid. This was going to be sort of a mixed review.

"He said it'd only be a few minutes," Rachel said as she took her seat again.

"Sounds good. Camera's off for the moment?"

"Yeah, what's up?"

"What's your opinion on this place?"

"Ah, figuring out the end-of-meal review, huh?"

"Yeah. I mean, the food is great. The service was… mixed. Anthony seems really genuine, so I think he would have been fine even if we weren't a show he's a fan of, but Bernice did…not do a very good job dealing with a blind guy."

"Yeah, there's a wider aisle on the other side. I discovered it looking for Anthony."

"Seriously? Why'd she take me through the fu—freaking tables, then? And is it wide enough for a chair?"

"Only if no one's actually sitting at the tables. It's still pretty narrow. And I've got no idea why she led us the way she did. I had some trouble navigating, and I'm sighted."

"Yeah." Dovid sighed. "Sucks, because the food's really good. I'd come here again. But I wouldn't bring Marissa. Can you imagine? A blind guy and a wheelchair user trying to navigate this place?"

"Yeah. Damn."

"Um," from next to them. "I—sorry to interrupt, but I've got your desserts."

Dovid smiled, because Anthony deserved one. "Thanks a lot."

"Hang on," Rachel said. "Let me turn the camera back on and get you putting the stuff down on the table."

"O-okay."

There was a definite smile in her voice when she said, "Okay, ready."

"Right," Anthony said setting down a plate with a click. "Here's the Bad for You and We Don't Care Brownie. The Lavish Lemon Meringue Pie—" another click "—and, of course, the Cookie Monster Madness Milkshake."

"Thanks a lot, Anthony."

"Enjoy!"

"We will," Dovid said.

"Right after I get more footage," Rachel said.

Dovid groaned and sank down in his seat.

Chapter Two

"Hello, everybody! I'm Sam, and welcome to another episode of Let's Play Dire Straits." Sam made sure everything was recording as he wanted, and then continued. "So, we last left off in the game on the precarious hill, trying to survive while the wind and rain beat down around our character. I'm going to work on constructing a hut to protect ourselves, so we don't succumb to the weather and meet our untimely demise."

Sam liked his Let's Play YouTube channel. He didn't have very many followers at all, only about four hundred, but he had conversations with quite a lot of them on a weekly basis when he uploaded his videos. That was one of the reasons he liked doing YouTube, really. It was very difficult for Sam to meet new people; large groups overwhelmed him, and he was too shy to approach individuals. But thanks to YouTube, he was not only able to share his love for a game he really enjoyed, but he was able to talk to others about it. Exchange tips, tricks, and suggestions. That was the part of YouTube he enjoyed most.

"Oh dear, it looks like one of the big birds doesn't like the fact that we've taken her egg. Let me just skip away from her and move over a couple of screens…" In-game, the bird gave up on chasing Sam's character and turned around. "What? You're giving up? Just like that? Oh, that's disappointing. I've taken your young! You're a bad parent. I'm genuinely disappointed in this bird now."

He played through the game, recording for about an hour, like he always did. He talked through the good parts, the hard parts, and added his own little narrative touch. Or tried to. He'd had a few comments saying that they liked his play style, but they really liked what they deemed his "adorable silliness." Sam wasn't quite sure what it was about him that was adorable, but then again, it wasn't as if they were able to see him through the screen. He didn't use any of those fancy videos. He was just a disembodied voice playing a fun little top-down 2D survival adventure game.

"Alright," he said, after he finished up the hour, "that's it for today, everybody. Thank you so much for listening in, and this was Dire Straits."

He cut the recording, watched over the video to make sure there weren't any audio or video issues, and then it was time to render the footage so he could upload it to YouTube.

Rendering could take forever, so while he waited he went to make himself a cup of tea, and then brought up the Kindle Unlimited app on his phone to pick a new book to read. He'd finished his last one on his break at work that day. He always read during his lunches. Always read whenever he had the chance, truth be told. Another reason why he didn't know very many people; he was the type who kept his nose in a book more often than not.

Books were easier than people.

Then again, with his job being IT, there were often good reasons he came home having exhausted his social-skill quota for the day and was only up to playing some games or reading a book before crashing. Books and video games also didn't yell at you, or snidely act as though you were a waste of space.

Sam sighed. That all came with the job description of dealing with frustrated and angry customers. He didn't mind doing the actual computer work, but talking on the phone gave him enough anxiety as it was. Never knowing whether a call might turn nasty made him dread it every time he was given a ring.

But again, YouTube was different. He'd only really just started uploading videos about a year ago, after getting the idea in his head when his brother said something along the lines of "You play that game all the time, why not just do a let's play for it?" and given him a mic headset. Sam hadn't done anything about it for ages, but the idea had rattled around until finally he found himself using spare bits of time to research how to record and upload videos.

Now he played his games like he usually did, but he had a specific "YouTube only" file that he played and recorded every Friday night after he got home from work. He rendered it right after, then set it to upload, and by the time he was ready for bed, the video was live and he could tag it and put it out there in the world.

The really nice part about it all was that, when he woke up Saturday morning, he usually had at least one comment or two from his followers. That was always such a pleasure to wake up to.

He always responded too. It was easy, with so few comments. But his small group of followers were loyal. He saw the same usernames in the same comments and conversations. It was a total delight, really.

He picked his book and settled in to read, but it was

only a few minutes later that his phone buzzed with a new comment from YouTube.

Hey, the person, Rachel R., had written. I was rec'd your channel a couple weeks ago, because I was looking for Dire Straits let's plays, and I might have binge-watched the entire thing. Just caught up now. Really enjoy what you do. Thanks for putting it out there! Looking forward to the next update.

Sam grinned and wrote back. Thanks! I'm so glad you are enjoying my videos. If you ever have any other questions or comments, please feel free to let me know. I'm always up for bettering my channel. (And good news I suppose, but I'm uploading another video tonight. It should be up in the next few hours.)

The reply wasn't immediate, but it did happen, just as Sam finished another page of his book. Awesome, good to know. Do you update regularly?

Yes, Sam replied. Every Friday night, circumstances allowing.

And then, Cool! I'll keep that in mind. You definitely just gained a subscriber.

Beaming, Sam checked the uploading video, and then returned to his book.

* * *

"Hey, Dovid," Rachel called from her bedroom. "Come here. You've got to check this out."

"I'm busy," Dovid called back, before salting the pasta water and dumping the spaghetti into the boiling pot.

"Dovid, come on!"

"I am *making dinner*, woman. Hold on." He set the timer for seven minutes and, only then, did he say, "Now, what is it?"

"I found something I think you'll like."

Dovid sighed. He wasn't going to get more than that until he actually went to Rachel's room to see what she wanted. He grabbed the timer and shuffled along, maybe taking his time, a little.

"Dooooviiiiiid."

"I'm coming, I'm coming. Geez. Now what do you want?"

"So, you know how I'm into Dire Straits?"

"That video game? Yeah." Rachel had discovered it back in January, playing it at a friend's house, and immediately fell in love. She refused to buy it, however, because, according to her, it would eat up every single bit of spare time she ever had if she actually owned the game. So instead she lived vicariously through Let's Players. Or tried to. She hadn't been having a lot of luck finding someone she wanted to actually listen to and watch play. "What about it?"

"I finally found someone."

"For what?"

"To watch! His name is Sam, and he's from Ireland, and he's got this awesome way of speaking and he plays really well. He's got like a year in-game where he hasn't died yet."

"That's great," Dovid said, trying for encouraging. "Glad you actually managed to find someone you could stand."

"You've got to listen to him."

"What? Why? I don't care about the game." He couldn't play it, couldn't appreciate it, and thus had little interest in it.

"No, you've got to *listen* to him. He's adorable. And his voice is adorable."

"Two adorables?"

Rachel grabbed his hand and pulled him closer. "Shh. Just listen to the first episode."

"Rachel, seriously—"

"Hello, everybody. I'm Sam, and welcome to my very first episode of Let's Play Dire Straits. I'm going to go right into it but first, for those who don't know, so Dire Straits is a top-down 2D survival adventure game. You have to gather food and resources and build bases to keep your character fed, healthy, and sane. As I've only started out and loaded up a new game with my player character, I'm just skipping about here, collecting grass and twigs and flint—"

"Just skipping about?" Dovid repeated dumbly.

"I know, right? And he talks like that all the time. He's got this utterly adorable way of speaking."

"I see." Rachel had been right. Sam… Sam definitely had a voice Dovid was interested in. Not that he'd tell her. She'd just get all smug about it. "What's his channel name?"

"Why do you want to know?" Rachel asked, voice sly. Damn it.

Dovid shrugged, trying for nonchalant. "If you're really all up in arms about me listening to this guy, I might as well do it on my own computer out of your way."

"Uh-huh." Rachel sounded like she was grinning, but all she said was, "His name is Playitagainsam."

"Right. Well, I guess I'll look him up. In between making dinner."

"It's just pasta," Rachel called after him. "It's not like it's so hard!"

"Says the person who managed to burn the pot last time she tried!" There was a reason—aside from the blindness—that Dovid was in charge of food prep and Rachel was in charge of sweeping and vacuuming.

Dovid went to his room, turned on his monitor and went to YouTube to find Sam's channel. When he'd found it, he went to the first episode of the Dire Straits series and set it to load while he went back to the kitchen to finish dinner, getting the broccoli he'd already chopped up and throwing it in a pan with salt, butter, and dill.

Once the timer beeped for the pasta, he drained it then got out the cheese, marinara sauce, and spices and stirred everything together, adding the spices to taste. He'd been making this particular dish for ages; it had been one of the first things Dovid had learned how to really cook. He and Rachel had dubbed the Dovid original "yummy pasta" back when they were kids.

He set the table and, by the time he was done, his fork easily went through the broccoli, indicating that it was ready. He brought all the food to the table, grabbed the pitcher of water from the fridge, and then went to get Rachel.

Over dinner they talked about the next video project. On top of sporadic videos whenever they felt like it, their channel released two videos regularly, Monday and Thursday. Usually one was a review of something and the other was some type of vlog. Over the years they'd both gotten a little looser in what they chose to release. They did "Day in the Life" videos, apartment tours (for their own place, as well as some other accessible apartments in the area), food reviews, and fan mail openings. Dovid got a lot of fan mail, mostly food, because he often said that he'd try anything once. People all over the world sent him stuff to try. He'd unbox something, Rachel would tell him what the package said it was, and then Dovid would try it.

Hands down the worst thing he'd ever eaten, on or off camera, was some salmiakki a fan from the Netherlands had sent. Dovid was *pretty* sure it had been sent with good intentions but it was still essentially punishment candy.

"I think we should just have another fan unboxing, or a question-answering session," Rachel said. "Easy, the fans like it, and not too hard to edit."

"We did just get in a lot of new fan mail," Dovid said. "Want to arrange for a livestream? We could do it Wednesday, and then upload it as our Thursday video."

"Sounds good to me."

"So how did you find this latest Let's Player?"

"Sam?"

"No, the other one you made me listen to."

Rachel snorted. "On a forum actually. I got sort of desperate looking around all of YouTube trying to trawl for someone I liked, so I turned to forums. I found this one obscure little thing that had a guy who recommended him. Tried it on a whim. I'm caught up to his videos now, which sucks a little bit, because it means I've got to wait for him to upload new ones. On the plus side, he does update regularly. That's every Friday night. Well, for him. It's Friday afternoon for us, with the time difference."

"Wait a second," Dovid said. "What do you mean you're caught up? He's got like fifty videos up, and you've only been into the game for like a month. And I know for a fact that you hadn't heard of this guy two weeks ago, because you were still looking for someone to watch."

There was a pause that went on a little too long, accompanied by a slight squeaking that told Dovid Rachel was probably shifting in her seat. "Wait," he said grinning. "Don't tell me you binge-watched his whole series."

"Okay, I won't tell you."

"He's that good, huh?"

"I just like how he plays the game, okay?"

"Right. Well, clearly he's this YouTube wonder. I really will have to give him a listen. Is he a top Let's Player or something?"

"Not even close," Rachel said. "He's got under a thousand followers. But he's super personable. I wrote him to thank him for the videos and he wrote back, like, instantly."

"Huh." So, he sounded like a genuinely nice guy too. Dovid sort of wondered why he didn't have that big a following then. He asked Rachel.

"Probably because Dire Straits is an Indie game, and it's pretty new. It's only been out a couple years. I don't know how big a following it has. Which sucks, because it's a damn good game."

"And you just burned through the videos of the one Let's Player of it you really liked."

"Oh, shut up."

* * *

After dinner, Dovid went to his room, grabbed his little "don't bother me!" sign from the inside of his doorknob and put it outside before closing the door. It was a system they'd developed for ease of communication. If the sign was up, the only reason the other person got disturbed was if the apartment was on fire. Not up and, well, usually they both left their doors open in their rooms anyway. But it was a just in case. Sometimes Dovid listened to stuff with his good headphones, which meant he couldn't hear knocking on his door. That often meant Rachel had to burst in to get him. Once he'd been listening to a horror podcast and she'd tapped him on the shoulder to get his attention. He'd stood up from the desk so fast he'd knocked her over.

Rachel was also free to wake Dovid up if the sign wasn't on his door, and vice versa. It just added a layer of privacy, which was especially important if Dovid brought someone home.

Right now though, it was mostly a means to actually watch Sam's videos to see what all the fuss was about, while also not letting Rachel know what he was doing. Just in case she felt like being smug.

He put on his headphones and settled down to listen. Each video was about an hour; quite long for a YouTube video. But it also meant that Rachel had burned through nearly fifty hours' worth of video in the last two weeks. In her free time. That was honestly hilarious, and Dovid planned on razzing her about it, now that he'd learned that new bit of information.

But he had to admit, Sam did have a great voice. He was *very* easy to listen to. And it helped that what he was saying was interesting. Dovid hadn't had a lot of interest in Dire Straits, but Sam clearly and genuinely loved the game so much, it was infectious.

"...now the funny thing about this biome is that the trees aren't exactly your ordinary trees, now are you? I'll show you. Watch, I'll try to chop it down, just get myself a little bit of firewood, and oop—there it goes! A painpine. These things can be nasty. Slow, but they're a sanity drain for as long as they're around you, and their hits really hurt. I'm going to just do a bit of dodging for now. One of the ways you can get them to de-agro is to plant pinecones. That'll appease them, I suppose

because you're planting more of their brethren? In any case—"

Before Dovid knew it, it had been an hour. And Rachel had been right, Sam was kind of adorable. It wasn't that late yet, and he had nothing else to do today. So, he set the next video to play.

"Hello, everybody. I'm Sam, and welcome to another episode of Let's Play Dire Straits. Last time we played, there was a bit of nasty business with the warthog village and I ended up having to kill quite a lot of them. Which, as you recall, was terribly sad on my part for a number of reasons..."

Dovid snickered. Sam had been brokenhearted that the warthog village had turned against him during the full moon. In part because he "hated the slaughter" and partly because the warthogs were useful non-player characters and killing them all meant he'd have to wait a few days for a respawn.

"—Ahah, bird! Look at that. You had no business eating those seeds, as they were clearly my seeds, and now you're dead. That's a pity. Although, you know, it's funny, I'm so abominably bloodthirsty in this game when it comes to farming for meat and butter and all that, but in reality I'm a vegetarian. I don't mind if other people aren't of course, it's not my job to regulate, but it's my own difference I'm making, yeah? I'm a gentle soul, really. I can't even squash bugs; I try to catch them and take them outside. No reason to harm a spider if there isn't need, after all. And they're such good bugs, spiders are. I mean arachnids. And sorry, there I seem to have gone off on a tangent. Back to the game—"

That had Dovid smiling. It sort of figured. The way Sam talked and described things—he even spoke softly—Dovid wasn't really surprised to hear that he was a vegetarian. Dovid wasn't one, though he did do his best to make sure he was eating as humanely as possible. He sort of hoped that might be something Sam would appreciate.

Not that that mattered in the slightest, of course.

A couple episodes later, and Sam was talking about how Dire Straits had *"Really gotten me out of the depths of despair, a little bit. Not the* Princess Bride *kind, but the regular kind. The doldrums, you know—"* And Sam totally got points for referencing *The Princess Bride.*

Sam cleared his throat. *"I might have mentioned before that I work in IT. And it's an alright job, pays the bills, there're much worse things out there to do, and I'm very fortunate that I get to sit in a cubicle in a climate-controlled building. But it's still taxing work, you know? Or maybe you don't. But people call in and you need to help them out and often they're cross because something isn't working right, and I have to ask questions that sometimes make them even more cross and, well, it makes me tired. Emotionally, I mean. It can be draining. And me, I'm not all that social at the best of times, so it zaps my energy, you know? But playing this game gave me something to play with. And experiment on and figure out, and it was something new and fun and exciting to look forward to. And so now I get to share that with you all as well. I really like that. I'm grateful I get to do this, you know?"* A laugh. *"For all of you who might be watching today."*

Dovid yawned, surprised he felt so tired, and then thought to check the time.

It was one in the morning. When did that happen?

And had he really just binge-listened to six hours' worth of Sam's let's plays?

Yes… Yes, he had. And he'd thoroughly enjoyed all

of them. Rachel had been right on two counts. One, Sam was absolutely adorable, no questions about it. His voice was wonderful to listen to, but what he said was equally as nice. Two, Dovid liked him. A lot.

Damn it, Rachel was going to be insufferable about this. But Dovid also couldn't bring himself to care. In part because he was so tired, but also because he was absolutely going to watch more of Sam's channel when he was more awake again.

But why the fuck did he only have like four hundred followers? What the hell was up with that? Sam was *great*. It was a fucking crime that the rest of YouTube didn't know about him.

But maybe Dovid could have a hand in changing that.

Chapter Three

"Hey, guys! This is Don't Look Now with Dovid and Rachel. I'm Dovid, Rachel's behind the camera, and today I wanted to talk to you about a YouTuber that I've discovered. Well, Rachel discovered him, fell in love with him—"

"I did not, tell them the truth. From the beginning!"

"Guys, if I had eyes, I'd be rolling them right now. But fine, fine. Okay, so you know how I mentioned a couple weeks ago that Rachel had gotten totally obsessed with this game Dire Straits? Of course, you do, but if you don't, the link is right here." He pointed to what would be the top right of a video screen, for Rachel to edit in later. "Anyway, she found a Let's Player, introduced me to him and, well, we both like him a lot.

"Now, first off, I want to go ahead and put it out there that I'm in no way sponsored by his channel. In fact, he doesn't even know I'm doing this plug. But he's got like four hundred and something followers and, frankly, I think it's criminal that more people don't know about him."

Dovid went on to introduce Sam's channel, talked a little bit more about the game for any new watchers, and then also told his viewers some key points about why he and Rachel got such a kick out of watching him.

The word "adorable" might have been thrown around a few times. But hey, Dovid told it like it was.

He wrapped up with the usual spiel about liking, commenting, and subscribing, mentioned the social media accounts he and Rachel individually ran that would be in the description below, and then ended with one last plug for Sam's channel, complete with the link in the description, as well as an "or just click here!" followed by another point.

"That was a really good take," Rachel said as Dovid took off his mic. "I'm barely going to have to edit any of it. Mostly I'll just need to throw on a soundtrack and slap on the video links."

"What can I say? I'm a professional."

"Yeah, yeah. I might have to cut down on some of the gushing though."

"Excuse you? What gushing?"

"Oh, Sam is *so* adorable. His voice is *so* nice. *He's* so nice. He's a *vegetarian* and cares about fluffy bunnies."

"He cares about *spiders*. I mean, probably bunnies too, but he specifically mentioned spiders. How can you not think that's cute?"

Rachel snickered. "I do think it's cute. I just also happen to think that you didn't, necessarily, need twelve minutes to expound upon his cuteness."

"It was really twelve minutes?" Dovid asked, his cheeks absolutely not going hot.

"Time stamp says eleven minutes, thirty-seven seconds."

"Wha— Why didn't you stop me?"

"Why would I have done that? You were on a total roll. It's just obvious that you're also in love with this guy."

"I'm not in love with a Let's Player you found on YouTube," Dovid said with dignity.

"Yeah, not *yet*."

"Don't you have editing to do? Go away."

"So you can watch more of Sam in peace?"

"Maybe," Dovid mumbled.

"Ha! I *knew* you'd like him."

"Gee," Dovid said dryly, "and here I thought you wouldn't figure it out. After I told you I wanted to plug him in a video. And then apparently proceeded to talk about him for eleven fucking minutes."

"Nearly twelve."

Dovid let out a self-sacrificing sigh.

"What episode are you even on, by the way?"

"Nine," Dovid said after a long pause. "I watched six episodes last night, and then one this morning while I exercised, and then two after lunch before we filmed."

"You watched nine hours' worth of videos in *two days* and you made fun of me when I got through fifty in two weeks?"

"I take it back, okay? I get it now."

"Clearly. And I seem to be missing something."

"Will you just go away?"

"Yeah, yeah. But you only get an hour before I'm dragging you out to the living room to start edits."

"Fine."

"Fine."

"Good-*bye*, Rachel."

Rachel laughed, but she left the room, footsteps fading. She didn't close the door behind her but that was to be expected.

Dovid immediately turned to his computer, went to the open tab with Sam's paused tenth video, and started it up from where he left off.

* * *

Sam woke up Friday morning to a billion and one messages and notifications on his phone, all from YouTube, some from Twitter.

He spent a moment blinking blearily down at his phone, startling as it buzzed several more times. More notifications from YouTube. Sam made the executive decision to ignore all of them as he got ready for work, because there was only so much social media one could deal with at six-thirty in the morning.

The thing was though, his phone kept going off. All through his commute and his arrival to work, it kept buzzing in his pocket, email after email and notification after notification. He had absolutely no idea what was going on, but he also knew he was absolutely unable to cope with it at the moment, so he made the decision to turn off his phone.

It was only on his lunch break that he turned it back on, because he did want to read, and he ended up scrolling through his email out of morbid curiosity. His Gmail didn't seem to be broken, but the sudden subscriptions and amount of comments from his YouTube channel was staggering. In the end, he just highlighted the whole lot of them and set them to delete, then went to YouTube itself to turn off channel notifications for the time being. The actual issue he would wait to resolve once he got home, before he started recording his next video.

He selected the fantasy novel he was in the middle of, eagerly losing himself in the story, ate his lunch, and went back to work, but the wonder of it all kept him distracted the rest of the day. It was fine when he was actually dealing with a client, but off the phone his mind drifted as he tried to puzzle out what might be going on. He hoped his channel hadn't glitched out or been hacked. He had all his recordings saved on a backup hard drive, but it would be no fun to have to reupload all of them, nor would it be what he'd want to do. It had been a year of work and comments and fun. He hoped he hadn't just lost it all.

It was a relief, more so than usual, once he got off work and went on his way home. Back at his flat, he took off his shoes, hung up his coat, and went over to the corner where he kept his computer. This was clearly not the sort of thing one could handle on just a phone.

His email was, thankfully, empty of new notifications once he'd logged on, but then it was time to make the big jump and check out YouTube.

Some of his tension left him once he looked at his channel and realized that nothing seemed wrong with it.

Except for the number of subscribers and comments.

"Thirty thousand?" he whispered in quiet disbelief. "Where did you all come from?" Looking for clues, he scrolled through the comments he had gotten. The top comments on his most recent videos were still from usernames he recognized, but even his old videos had a massive amount of comments now, particularly his first several.

You're pretty good, man! Thanks for the videos.

Dovid was right, he's adorable, isn't he?

Great video.

I'm a vegetarian too!

=DDD

DOVID I LOVE YOU AND YOUR STUFF

Anyone else here from Don't Look Now?

かわいい!

Thanks for the rec, Dovid!

whats the big deal hes just irish

I'm a DLN fan, and I see what they mean about your voice.

Definitely earned the three adorables from me.

"Adorable?" Sam asked, bewildered. And who was Dovid? What was Don't Look Now? Over half the comments mentioned one or the other or both. What in the world was going on?

When in doubt, Sam turned to Google for an answer.

"Dovid, Don't Look Now" immediately brought up a YouTube channel as well as a zillion other hits from everything to other social media websites to BuzzFeed. Feeling a touch overwhelmed, Sam went to YouTube first.

The featured video was "Let's Talk Let's Players."

Sam clicked it.

A young man wearing dark glasses was sitting in front of a wall covered in different colored dots arranged in various patterns. He was wearing a blue shirt that offset his tan skin and short, dark hair, and had arms that made Sam swallow just a little bit. *"Hey, guys! This is Don't Look Now with Dovid and Rachel. I'm Dovid, Rachel's behind the camera, and today I wanted to talk to you about a YouTuber that I've discovered. Well, Rachel discovered him, fell in love with him—"*

"*I did not,*" came a voice from behind the camera "*—tell them the truth. From the beginning!*"

"*Guys, if I had eyes, I'd be rolling them right now.*" Sam blinked. That explained the dark glasses he supposed. "*But fine, fine. Okay, so you know how I mentioned a couple weeks ago that Rachel had gotten totally obsessed with this game Dire Straits...she found a Let's Player, introduced me to him and, well, we both like him a lot.*"

"No," Sam whispered. "No way. No way."

"*Now, first off, I want to go ahead and put it out there that I'm in no way sponsored by his channel. In fact, he doesn't even know I'm doing this plug. But he's only got like four hundred and something followers and, frankly, I think it's criminal that more people don't know about him.*"

The video proceeded to go on (and on and *on*) about Sam's merit, his voice, called him adorable (several different times), and wound down with, "*so you all better go to his channel and show him some love. He really deserves it! Link here, as well in the description below. Don't forget to follow Don't Look Now on social media. All those links down below as well. As always, guys, see you later! Well, I won't—*" a grin, the grin of someone who had made that joke dozens of times and still found it funny "*—but you know what I mean.*"

The video ended.

Sam glanced at the time stamp. Thursday, around seven-thirty. With the obvious time difference, that was after Sam had been in bed himself and wasn't checking his messages.

He looked at Don't Look Now's subscriber count, and had to take a shuddering breath. Six million and some subscribers. Dovid was clearly a hugely popular vlogger on YouTube, and he'd just plugged Sam's channel. Sam's dinky little let's play channel, with fifty videos and a lot of rambling.

Dovid had called his rambling adorable, and said his voice was smooth and soothing.

Sam swallowed and looked at his notifications again. He'd gotten fifty new subscribers in the last fifteen minutes.

He had utterly zero idea how to handle this and a let's play video to record, because that's what his regular followers knew to expect.

Oh dear.

* * *

"Hello, everybody, I'm Sam, and welcome to another episode of Let's Play Dire Straits. Erm, we left off last episode trying to fancy up our base a little bit by moving some turf around and adding carpet, because I like the look of that, so I'm just going to wait til nightfall and go off to shear more sheeples for wool to make that and, ah, well, I suppose I want to welcome all you new followers to my channel. I admit to being a bit flummoxed here, that I suddenly have so many. But you're all welcome to watch of course, and I do hope you enjoy it. I, um, I'm going to go ahead and dedicate this episode to Dovid and Rachel from Don't Look Now, if that's alright. And, erm, Dovid, if you're watching this, I really, really hope I'm pronouncing your name right, because I did watch that particular video of you being mad when people did it wrong, and I know things can sort of get muddled with my accent, but I'm doing my best. Now, ah, in-game, as you can see here, I've gathered some more food from my farms; I'm planting corn mostly, because it's got the best shelf life for travel, and popcorn gives you sanity too, if you choose to actually cook the corn so..." He prattled on as he played, more than a little nervous with how many people he knew might be watching. It seemed so much more feasible when it was just the odd few hundred. Thousands and thousands were a bit much, in his opinion. It was just a silly little YouTube channel he did for fun. How was he supposed to live up to what Dovid had built him up as?

In the end, he tried not to think about it and just played. He enjoyed his game and making videos, and clearly that was what his viewers liked. He just was going to keep doing that, was all.

With this thought in mind, he recorded for the rest of the hour and went about his usual routine of setting the video to render while he went to read on his phone.

After a few minutes though, he got an idea into his head that he couldn't shake. Should he maybe send Dovid a message? Surely Dovid got hundreds of them a day—after all, Sam had gotten a ridiculous amount himself—but there was no harm, right? Just a thank-you.

No, no, Dovid probably got inundated with messages if the amount that Sam had gotten recently was any indication. There would be no point. Sam had already dedicated a video to him. If Dovid watched them regularly, and it seemed as though he did now, he'd get the thank-you from that. Right? Right.

God, he hoped he'd pronounced Dovid's name correctly. He'd even practiced saying it, making sure it didn't come out sounding like David by accident. A round 'uh' sound. He'd tried.

Sam made an attempt to put it out of his mind. He uploaded the video, kept his YouTube notifications turned off, content with just checking them Saturday morning via the website itself, and got himself ready for bed.

* * *

Rachel was taking a bath when Dovid got the notification that Sam had uploaded a new video. He loathed to wait to watch it, but he and Rachel had sort of made a pact that they'd watch the new ones together, just like they did when there was a series they were following together.

"Rachel, hurry up!"

"Why are you bothering me?"

"Sam uploaded another video," Dovid wheedled. "I want to watch it. And I don't want to wait for you."

"Suck it up, I'm relaxing."

Dovid slumped against the door. "Fine. But you're not allowed to take baths on Fridays anymore."

"Fuck you," Rachel called cheerily.

Grumbling, Dovid went to the living room with his laptop and tried to distract himself until Rachel finally, finally walked in. She immediately sat down next to him and put her head on his shoulder.

"Ack, stop it, your hair is dripping wet."

"Oh yeah? Well, who told me to hurry up?"

"You couldn't even put it up in one of those fancy towel things?"

"Actually, I brought a towel out with me to do just that," Rachel admitted, moving away from him, followed by the sound of fabric rubbing together. "I just wanted to bother you first."

"Rachel," Dovid whined. "I want to watch the video."

Rachel snorted. "I can't believe you made fun of *me* for liking Sam's stuff."

"Yes, yes, I take it all back. Can I hit play now?"

"Sure, go ahead."

"Hello, everybody, I'm Sam, and welcome to another episode of Let's Play Dire Straits." Dovid grinned and sat back on the couch. *"Erm, we left off last episode trying to fancy up our base a little bit by moving some turf around and adding carpet, because I like the look of that, so I'm just going to wait til nightfall and go off to shear more sheeples for wool to make that and, ah, well, I suppose I want to welcome all you new followers to my channel. I admit to being a bit flummoxed here, that I suddenly have so many."* Flummoxed. Sam had just used "flummoxed" in a sentence. God, but he was cute. *"But you're all welcome to watch of course, and I do hope you enjoy it. I, um, I'm going to go ahead and dedicate this episode to Dovid and Rachel from Don't Look Now, if that's alright. And, erm, Dovid, if you're watching this, I really, really hope I'm pronouncing your name right, because I did watch that particular video of you being mad when people did it wrong—"*

"Oh my god," Dovid said, mortified, pausing the video. "Oh my god, Rachel, he watched 'Angry Blind Teen.' Oh my god."

"What's the big deal? Almost everyone has watched that. It's our third most popular video."

"But *he* watched it. And he heard tiny angry me whine about my name!"

"You always whine about your name."

"But he didn't have to *know* that."

"Hey, I mean, he got it right, didn't he?"

Yes. Yes, Sam had gotten Dovid's name right. And Dovid really, really liked hearing Sam's voice saying his name. Probably he should be worried about that, to some degree. "I guess so," he managed to say. "It was nice of him to worry."

"Right? So quit making a fuss and let me watch the rest of the video. I've been waiting all week for this update."

Dovid pressed play again.

"*—and I know things can sort of get muddled with my accent, but I'm doing my best. Now, ah, in-game, as you can see here—*" Dovid let Sam's voice wash over him, listening with interest as he played the game.

"*—think I'm going to make another simulacrum next episode, because it's about time we made one of those. We do have the reincarnation stones as a fallback plan, but I'd rather keep those for emergencies. Besides, if we make a simulacrum, it'll be close to our base, or wherever I want to put it. It's much better to control where you come back to life, don't you think? Anyway, I think I've rambled on enough for one episode. Thank you all for watching, and I'll see you next time.*"

"That was fun," Rachel said, once the video was over. "And it was cool that he dedicated it to us."

"Yeah. I think I'm going to write him a thank-you."

"For the dedication?"

"Why not?" he said, trying to sound nonchalant. "I think it'd be nice."

"It's not a bad idea," Rachel said after a moment. "And he does try to respond to comments directed at him. Though," she added, "that might be hard for him to do now."

"Why?"

"Because he gained like fifty thousand followers since you plugged him yesterday," she said matter-of-factly. "And he might be feeling a little overwhelmed."

Dovid's heart sank. He hadn't really thought of that. He was a YouTube star; it was his livelihood as well as his hobby. More views were always better to him. But maybe for Sam…he had sounded pretty nervous at the beginning of his video. "All the more reason to contact him," he said after thinking about it. "If nothing else I can offer some advice in dealing with the increase in subscribers."

"Yeah, not a bad idea at all. Even if it's just an excuse for you to finally work up the guts to talk to him."

Dovid didn't bother to dignify that with a response. Instead he turned his laptop away from Rachel and tried to think of where to send his comment. He was worried about sending it through YouTube; it might get lost in all the sea of comments Sam was already getting. But Sam had mentioned a Twitter a while ago, hadn't he?

Dovid checked and yeah, it wasn't in the description box of the video, but it was in Sam's YouTube bio. He pulled up Twitter and went to Sam's page. Again, only a few hundred followers. Perfect. YouTube hadn't followed Sam to Twitter yet, though that would only be a matter of time. Dovid quickly opened up a DM and pondered a bit about what to say.

Dontlooknowdovid: Hey, this is Dovid from Don't Look Now (though you probably guessed from my username, haha.) I just wanted to say thanks for that dedication. It was really cool to hear that, especially since I'm a fan.

He left it at that. Hopefully Sam would reply and that would start more of a conversation. Dovid really hoped he did; he was dying to talk to him a little more one-on-one. He kind of wanted a little bit more of Sam's attention.

In order not to dwell too much about Sam's reply

(if there would be one), Dovid went to take a walk, his phone and earbuds ever present in his pocket.

He was on his way back when his phone beeped with his Twitter DM notification sound. Since it was freezing outside, he hurried back to his apartment in order to check the message, barring himself in his room, plugging an earbud into his laptop, and then setting the message to play.

Playitagainsam: Goodness, hello! And please, don't thank me; you're the one who mentioned me in your video in the first place—I should be thanking you.

Dovid grinned and hurried to type a response.

Dontlooknowdovid: It was well-earned, man. I really do like your stuff a lot.

Playitagainsam: Well, thank you. Thank you very much.

Dontlooknowdovid: On that note, are you okay?

Playitagainsam: What do you mean?

Dontlooknowdovid: Well, uh, you sort of got really popular really fast. I was wondering how you were doing.

Playitagainsam: Oh! Well, I won't pretend it isn't a little...overwhelming? But that's not to say I'm not grateful! I do appreciate you talking up my channel.

Dontlooknowdovid: It wasn't a hardship. I mean it, I'm a huge fan. I may have binge watched...almost all of your episodes. It's just, I meant what I said in the video; voices are hugely important to me. And I really like yours.

Playitagainsam: Oh, well, thank you.

A moment passed, and Dovid listened to the "message being typed" sound start and stop several times before Sam's next message beeped at him.

Playitagainsam: I'm sorry, I'm afraid I don't know what to say. I mean, I'm glad you like my voice, that you were able to get something from my videos.

Playitagainsam: Just, um...

Dovid swallowed. He hoped he hadn't done something to make Sam uncomfortable. Especially now that they were actually talking. He might have been fanboying a bit inside.

Dontlooknowdovid: Yeah?

Playitagainsam: Adorable? Really?

He had to laugh.

Dontlooknowdovid: Hey, man, I call them as I see them. Or don't see them, rather.

Dontlooknowdovid: (Sorry, I make a lot of blind jokes. I hope that doesn't bother you.)

Playitagainsam: Of course it doesn't bother me. I rather think you're entitled to make them, if you want to.

Dontlooknowdovid: I kind of figured you'd say that :) but I like to be sure. It bothers some people that I do. Ironically, it tends to be the sighted guys who get all up in arms about it. Other blind people are like "Yeah, whatever, you've only made that joke like fifteen times."

Playitagainsam: Oh. That's...a bit irritating, that sighted people try to police you like that.

Dontlooknowdovid: Aw, thanks for understanding :)

Dontlooknowdovid: Seriously though, you sure you're okay with all the YouTube stuff? I could offer some advice, if you wanted.

Playitagainsam: Oh gosh, um, that would be greatly appreciated actually. I'm afraid I don't quite know how to deal with it all. As of right now, I've just turned off all my notifications so they don't break my email, and I've been hiding from YouTube in general. And I feel sort of bad, because all the people who normally comment are getting a bit buried, and I would like to try to keep up that dialogue if I can, you know?

Dontlooknowdovid: No, I get it. It's going to be a little harder to be personal now. I didn't really think about that part for you. I'm sorry.

Playitagainsam: It's alright. I'll just, you know, adjust. Is there something you can recommend?

Dontlooknowdovid: You could always message the people you normally talk to and mutually friend them on Twitter. That's one way you could keep up communication.

Dontlooknowdovid: I will warn you that your new fans are going to be finding your Twitter too. But Twitter's a little bit easier to regulate over YouTube comments, since you can adjust it to filter your mutuals first on your feed.

Playitagainsam: That's a good idea. I wouldn't have thought of it myself. Thank you.

Playitagainsam: Oh! Since we're talking, I wanted to ask...did I get your name right?

Dontlooknowdovid: My name?

Playitagainsam: Yes. I wanted to be sure I pronounced it correctly. I was so worried I practiced it with my recording equipment to try to get it right since I know how important it is to you but I couldn't be sure.

Dovid buried his face in his hands. He was so cute. He was so *cute*.

Dontlooknowdovid: You did! =D thanks so much for putting in that effort. I appreciate it. It's always nice to hear that sort of thing.

Playitagainsam: Of course. I can only imagine how difficult it is to have a name people always get wrong. Now, there's not a whole lot you can do with Sam. So I'm a bit lucky on that front.

Dontlooknowdovid: I won't hold it against you. Now hey, so you know, I'm going to have a lot of people asking me about you, and you're going to have a lot of people asking you about me.

Playitagainsam: Really, why?

Dontlooknowdovid: Because, uh...well, I'm kind of a big deal, absolutely no meme intended. I mean that I have a big following! Not, um, not to brag or anything.

Playitagainsam: You have over six million subscribers on YouTube, I think you're allowed to brag at least a little bit.

Dontlooknowdovid: Haha, okay fair. But that's what I mean. A lot of people know who I am and are interested in my personal life. Which is kind of silly, considering how much of my personal life is actually up on YouTube. But I try to keep non-YouTubers out of it unless they explicitly don't mind, because it's not fair to them otherwise. But you *are* a YouTuber.

Dontlooknowdovid: And that just means that you're already a presence. So now that people know we know each other or, um, think we know each other, they're going to be curious.

Dovid winced. He'd only just realized how much he might have fucked up.

Dontlooknowdovid: Oh my god, I never really considered the ramifications of this for someone who might not be interested in popularity I am so sorry. Fuck, I'm basically the worst.

Playitagainsam: You're not the worst at all. I don't really MIND that more people know about my channel, I just, you know, might need some adjustment time. And your advice on how to handle things would be really helpful, so thank you for offering.

Dontlooknowdovid: Of course I'll help! This is all basically my fault. I am so sorry.

Playitagainsam: It's okay.

Dontlooknowdovid: Right, okay, yeah, wow. Sorry. Uh well. Yeah. So people are going to be asking you about me, or even about you. You are never under any obligation to answer questions you don't want to, ever. And anyone who bothers you can be reported or marked as spam. You ever have trouble with something, just let me know. I'll usually know how to deal with it.

Playitagainsam: Okay. That would be lovely.

That would be lovely. Really, world? Really? This was how Sam was reacting to Dovid basically fucking up his life? God, he was ridiculous.

Playitagainsam: What should I do if they ask me about you?

Dontlooknowdovid: Hahaha, you can literally tell them whatever.

Playitagainsam: But I don't know whatever. I only just met you now.

Dontlooknowdovid: Alright, fair point. If you really want to reply, you can just tell them we're friends and that you'd prefer to have our privacy respected. That usually works for most people, and the really crazy ones you can ignore or report.

That was okay, right? To have Sam tell people they were friends.

Dovid hoped they could be friends. That would be really nice.

He maybe liked Sam too much, for only having had watched his videos and the conversation they were having now.

Then again, he'd watched almost fifty *hours'* worth of footage of Sam. That had to count for some sort of insight to who he was as a person.

Dontlooknowdovid: If they ask me about you, that's what I'm going to say. That I'd prefer to have your privacy respected.

Playitagainsam: Alright. That works for me, then.

Dontlooknowdovid: Okay, good. And again, I'm really sorry about this. I guess I didn't even think.

Playitagainsam: You already apologized to me plenty :) no worries. I'll handle it as best I can. And…maybe ask you some questions, if that's okay?

Dontlooknowdovid: No, yeah, of course! You can ask me anything you'd like. Whenever. Just DM me, and I'll answer when I get the chance. I might be busy shooting something or doing a review or whatever, but I'll always answer.

Playitagainsam: Haha, don't think you have to be at my beck and call. I'll be content with whenever is convenient for you. You must be very busy working.

Dontlooknowdovid: No busier than you. YouTube IS my full-time job, so that's what I do with my time. You're the one who has a grown-up job.

Playitagainsam: I rather feel that being a full-time YouTuber is just as much a grown-up job as someone stuck in IT. You have to master so many different skills! I barely can keep up a Twitter account along with YouTube, and all I do is one let's play a week.

Playitagainsam: And I think it's wonderful that you're doing something you obviously love so much.

Dontlooknowdovid: Wow, um, thank you.

Dontlooknowdovid: Coming from you, that means a lot.

Playitagainsam: Coming from me?

Dontlooknowdovid: Sorry! It's just, okay, so I sort of binge-watched your channel and like half of your videos in like a week? And Rachel—that's my sister, if you don't know who she is—already ragged on me about being able to down that many hours of footage in a

week, don't worry. But after watching them all, I just…
you seem like a really great guy?

Playitagainsam: Oh. Wow. Well, thank you. I really appreciate you saying so.

Dovid bit his lip. He didn't want to make this weird. He just wanted to keep talking to Sam and not make this weird.

Dontlooknowdovid: So IT. How did you get into that?

Playitagainsam: Oh, it's not all that interesting a story.

Dontlooknowdovid: Tell me anyway?

A moment's pause.

Playitagainsam: Well alright, if you'd like.

Dovid smiled.

Chapter Four

"Hi, everybody, I'm Sam, and welcome to another episode of Let's Play Dire Straits. Last time I talked about us trying to mine the riverbed for runes. The riverbed, for those of you who don't know, is another level of the game. It's very treacherous; all sorts of new monsters and things just waiting to try to kill you. It's a great challenge! I always have a lot of fun in the riverbed. But in order to go mining, we do have to prepare. I want a good bundle of supplies to take down with me in my pack, which means we'll be wanting to make food, take some pre-crafted shelters and firepits, all the comforts of home, you know?"

Sam yawned, trying to cover the sound from the mic. "Goodness, excuse me. It was a long day at work and I was up rather late last night reading." And talking to Dovid again. "Excuse me one moment while I take a sip of tea, here." This time he moved the mic away from his face to drink, moving it back after he set his mug back down on his desk. "Mm, delicious, delicious tea. Anyway—oh! I almost forgot, I'm sorry, I wanted to welcome all my new subscribers. There are, well, there are quite a lot of you apparently. Thank you to those who watched my other videos and decided to stick with me, as well as all my subscribers who have been with me for a while. You're all lovely people, and I'm glad I'm able to provide some semblance of entertainment."

He talked and played his game, and was almost half an hour in before he remembered that he had some questions he'd meant to answer. He sometimes had subscribers ask him questions and he tried to respond to them in comments or in video when he could. Now, with so *many* new comments, he wanted to maybe try to give some of his older followers a little more attention.

"Right, sorry, let me just kite this lamprey eel for a moment, there you go—ahah! Beat you." He grinned and reached for the pad of paper he'd jotted his notes down on. "Anyway, Meganbeginagain, I wanted to reply to your comment about our pet vulture Clarissa McBeakbird. Because first off, it's always nice to see a familiar icon and username. Yes, she is still laying eggs as far as I know, but I haven't fed her in a while. And oh dear, that sounds really awful to say aloud, isn't it? I'm sorry, Clarissa! I'll go home and feed you right away. Or, well, not right away; I'm still in the riverbed. But soon, I promise. So, erm, yes, with the latest patch, the pet birds don't die if you forget to feed them for a while, they just stop laying eggs. You have to start feeding them regularly again, and then after a couple days they'll start producing eggs again.

"So you all know," he added, "pet bunnies *can* die now, if they're left alone too long and aren't fed. That's half the reason why I haven't tried to get one. I'm away from my base so often now, doing advanced quests and building, and I can't stand to think that I might accidentally let a creature starve to death. Even if it was a virtual creature. I'll admit it, I did play about Neopia when Neopets was a thing, and I couldn't ever bear the thought of my pets starving and my not tending to them, but I also didn't want to put them up for adoption in case their *new* owners ever stopped playing the game and forgot about them. So I gave the entire account to my little cousin, who likes the game very much and keeps it up as a hobby. I still might check in with her once in a while, just to see how they're doing."

He cleared his throat, feeling a little silly. Somehow he always tended to go off onto tangents like that. Oh, well. His viewers stuck around for a reason, he supposed. "But back to the game, I also wanted to address selkiesummers's question about why I'm not just farming sheeples. That is to say, why I'm not creating sheeple farms, as opposed to just leaving them in wild herds—"

Before he knew it, his hour was up. It had been a good run, he thought. Even if he had been a bit silly in what he talked out that wasn't in-game. Then again, he was always like that, and people still watched him.

Slightly more people, now, actually.

Anyway, he didn't have to reason why; he'd just continue to make let's play videos. Speaking of, he set his video to render, pulled up the cozy mystery novel he'd just started, and settled in for a usual Friday night.

* * *

Dovid buried his face in his hands. Sam cared about his virtual Neopets so much that he had made sure they'd gone to a good home and he *still checked on them*.

God, he liked Sam so much.

This was such a problem.

Rachel nudged him. "Would you stop pausing the video every time you think he does something cute?"

"I can't handle him. Rachel, I can't handle how cute he is."

"So, let me watch in peace, and you can watch some other time and stop interrupting."

"Nooo, I need you for support."

"Support for *what*?"

"He's talking to me, Rachel! We are exchanging conversation. And he's so nice, and genuine, and—"

"And cute, yes, you have said. Multiple times. We've covered this. You have a massive, massive crush on a Let's Player who lives in Ireland."

Dovid didn't even try to deny it at this point. "Hey, you like him too."

"Yeah," she said. "But I'm not head over heels in love with him."

Okay, that he'd deny. "That's an exaggeration."

"Sure."

"I just like him a lot."

"Uh-huh."

"Rachel, Rachel, I want to talk to him more. What can I do? Am I allowed to just DM him? Will he think that it's weird?"

"I don't know. I mean, you've already talked to him. I can't see there'd be anything wrong with saying hi. You could let him know you watched his video and whatever."

That was a great idea. He could do that. "I could do that."

"Yes, you could. Now, in order to tell him the truth about watching his video, you need to finish it. By which I mean let me watch his damn video now."

Grumbling, Dovid pressed play.

* * *

Dontlooknowdovid: Hey! Just wanted to let you know that I watched your recent video. I thought it was great. You really know what you're doing in the game. And it was cool to learn that thing about sheeple farming. Also liked how you talked to some of your fans in-video. I do that too, and it's always appreciated, from what I've found.

The reply came early Saturday morning, around eight o'clock. Dovid was half asleep when his phone beeped, and he fumbled trying to find it and set the message to play. It was only once it started that he realized the DM was from Sam, and that made him sit up, now more alert.

Playitagainsam: Thank you very much! I'm glad you liked it. It wasn't too much, you don't think?

Dontlooknowdovid: Too much? No, of course not. Your videos are always really genuine sounding. I really like listening to them.

Playitagainsam: Oh, I'm so glad to hear that. And if you don't think they're too much, I'll defer to your YouTube experience.

Dontlooknowdovid: Anytime.

Dontlooknowdovid: What are you up to today?

Playitagainsam: Nothing too exciting, I'm afraid. I'm quite a boring person, actually.

Dontlooknowdovid: I've got a hard time believing that :)

Playitagainsam: Really! I've spent the day drinking tea and reading, and playing more Dire Straits. I have a few personal runs that aren't YouTube related. I went out for a walk to my grocery store as well, though it was too cold to really enjoy being out of doors.

Dontlooknowdovid: See, that sounds like a nice day to me.

Playitagainsam: I do find it quite nice, yes. After a workweek, I tend to use my days off to decompress, when I'm not running errands. It can be hard, being on with other people all the time.

Dontlooknowdovid: I won't pretend I know exactly how that feels—I'm definitely an extrovert, and my whole life is about letting people see exactly who I am. But I can get needing to take a break from it. Some days I'm just tired, you know? I don't feel like filming.

Dontlooknowdovid: Or I guess it's more that I don't feel like letting people in.

Playitagainsam: I think that's perfectly reasonable. It sounds exhausting quite honestly, bringing people "with" you everywhere you go! I couldn't imagine being in front of the camera like that, much less all the time.

Dontlooknowdovid: You sound like Rachel. She wouldn't be caught dead in front of the camera.

Playitagainsam: How in the world did she become half of a YouTube duo then?

Dontlooknowdovid: It's actually half her fault. She had to make a presentation for class about an underrepresented minority. Which, I mean, her twin brother is LITERALLY BLIND. I'm not sure what her teacher was expecting.

Dontlooknowdovid: Anyway, she'd always liked making videos on her phone and stuff—she's a Snapchat/Instagram wiz, so she decided to film the presentation instead of doing a PowerPoint. And guess who was the star guest speaker?

Playitagainsam: I can't imagine.

Dontlooknowdovid: Hahaha, right? Anyway, we had a lot of fun, and then sort of came to the conclusion at the same time that we should just keep making videos like this; stuff that lets the world see that I'm just your average guy. I'm just missing a couple of parts.

Playitagainsam: I'd hardly say you're average.

Dovid had typed you're sweet and was about to hit send before he came to his senses and erased it.

Dontlooknowdovid: Thanks, man! 'Preciate it. But no, yeah, we got a pretty good response, and had a pretty loyal, if small audience. Then we got it into our heads to film "Angry Blind Teen" and— Can I tell you a secret?

Playitagainsam: Sure, if you want to. I won't tell.

Dontlooknowdovid: We were so, so drunk when we filmed that. Our parents had gone away for the weekend and we thought it'd be a good idea to see what it was like to get drunk off our asses. But we were underage at the time, and then it went viral on YouTube and we REALLY couldn't tell people we were drunk. Our parents still don't even know. And everyone on YouTube who's watched that video just thinks I'm a big whiner. Which is true, I sort of am, but being drunk didn't help.

Dontlooknowdovid: You are now the third person on this planet privy to this information, by the way. Counting Rachel and me.

Playitagainsam: I won't breathe a word.

Dontlooknowdovid: :)

Dontlooknowdovid: So yeah, after "Angry Blind Teen" got people actually looking at our videos, our popularity skyrocketed. It was like…we'd been making these really great videos, but now people knew they existed. Rachel was having a blast filming and figuring out sound and shots and whatever, and we both had a good time deciding what to film for our videos and editing them together.

Dontlooknowdovid: We always say that Rachel does the heavy lifting, and I'm the pretty face.

Playitagainsam: Oh I'm sure that's not true.

Dontlooknowdovid: Aw, you don't think I'm pretty?

Shit, flirting, this was probably flirting territory——

Dontlooknowdovid: But no, it's kind of true, haha. She's definitely a huge driving force behind everything.

I'm just the guy who invites people into his life. She's the one who makes it possible for them to really look and listen. I mean, I've got a hand in editing and everything, but filming is a lot easier when you've got someone telling you where to point your face xD

Playitagainsam: Hahaha. Alright, that makes sense. But sounds to me as though you're both very important. And both very good at what you do.

Dontlooknowdovid: Thanks. We try.

* * *

"Hey, guys, this is Don't Look Now with Dovid and Rachel. I'm Dovid, Rachel's behind the camera, and today we're going to be baking chocolate chip cookies! Well, I'm going to be baking them. Rachel is going to follow along with the camera and not get anywhere near the oven. Or any of the ingredients. Rachel's kind of a mess in the kitchen, guys."

Sam watched, grinning, as Dovid listed all the ingredients and took his viewer through a step-by-step instruction on how to make chocolate cookies, with the addition of all his little tangents and stories. Rachel's only job really was to hold the camera; Dovid even had a talking scale that told him how much of each ingredient he was measuring out, so he didn't have to worry about that sort of thing. And meanwhile, Sam hadn't even had any idea that talking scales existed.

He wondered what else he took for granted, as a sighted person.

Well, that was half of why he had started watching Dovid's videos. And besides being educational and fun, he seemed like such an interesting person, and genuinely very nice, if how he was interacting with Sam (and on his channel in general) was any indication. Sam had only watched a few episodes here and there, picking things sporadically based on title or presumed content, but he'd enjoyed all of them. Dovid had a wonderful personality, as did Rachel, and Sam had a lot of fun watching their dynamic. No wonder they appealed to such a wide audience.

It also, well, it also didn't hurt that Dovid was in no way difficult to look at.

Which…was that fair on Sam's end? He couldn't help that he found Dovid attractive. That had just…happened through talking to him and then watching his videos. And then even more talking, because Dovid talked to him, and acted as though it was no big deal.

That was indeed a big deal to Sam. That this famous YouTube star would even give him the time of day, much less express interest in Sam's own videos and then offer advice on how to deal with a sudden onslaught of popularity. Sam couldn't summon up the courage to initiate conversation that didn't have to do with YouTube questions, and, well, he could admit, at least to himself, that he might have started wracking his brain to come up with said questions as of late, but Dovid didn't seem to mind at all. He often kept talking to him after the question had been answered. Asking Sam about his day, or talking about his own.

Dovid had even started asking Sam questions about whatever he was reading at the moment. Asking for recommendations and then, a couple days later, striking up a conversation about the book because he'd started to read it himself. Sam had begun to start making sure any new books he chose to read had audio versions out.

Sometimes Dovid got stuck on a video and they

brainstormed together. Dovid made Sam feel as though his ideas and opinion were worth listening to.

Which did not, exactly, help Sam's crush.

Chapter Five

Dovid wasn't doing anything much, just planning out another video on his computer, when his phone beeped with a Twitter DM alert. He plugged in an earbud to check the DM and was very pleasantly surprised.

Playitagainsam: Hi, Dovid. I know it's the middle of the day for you, but I wanted to ask your advice on what to do about Twitter? Only I seemed to have gained quite a lot of followers very quickly, after I released my last video. Obviously it's not vital! But if you have a chance and don't mind a bit of a chat, it'd be appreciated.

Dovid hurried to respond.

Dontlooknowdovid: Hey! Of course. I'd love to talk to you. What's up?

Playitagainsam: Oh, hello! How are you today?

Great, now that he was talking to Sam.

Dontlooknowdovid: Pretty good :) Yourself?

Playitagainsam: Can't complain, can't complain. And

I'm sorry to bother you, I just… Twitter has exploded a little bit, on my end.

Dontlooknowdovid: You're not a bother. Please don't worry about it. And okay, yeah, the YouTube mass followed you to Twitter?

Playitagainsam: I'm afraid so. And it's so odd, because I took my Twitter information out of my YouTube profile, like you suggested. I've only put my Twitter information up in a few of my videos. Sporadically, you know? Because I use it so seldom, I forget. So some of my new subscribers must have watched…a lot of my videos and found the links.

Dontlooknowdovid: I'm sorry. I sort of knew they would.

Playitagainsam: It's alright. I mean, you did warn me. I suppose I just wasn't expecting quite so many of them. I'm abysmally boring on Twitter, and only just got active recently, to talk to people I knew from before the craze. Like you suggested.

Playitagainsam: And it was working very well, these last few days. But then, ah…

Dovid went to check. Sam's three-hundred-fifty-ish Twitter follower count had jumped up to almost four thousand. And he was nearly at one hundred thousand subscribers on YouTube now.

Dontlooknowdovid: I get it. It's overwhelming. Just remember—you don't owe any of them anything. It's up to you how many people you let into your life like that. Hell, you could even make your Twitter invite-only, if you wanted to. That might make things easier.

Playitagainsam: Oh no, I'd feel so bad.

Of course he would. Because Sam was too good for this world.

Dontlooknowdovid: That's fine too! Just try to keep it in mind that that's always an option for you. So if things do ever get too overwhelming, feel free to lock your Twitter for a little while for a breather.

Playitagainsam: Okay. Thank you. I'll try to remember that. And I suppose, after the initial panic, it isn't all that bad. And most of the comments have been very nice.

Dontlooknowdovid: That's good! That's great.

Dontlooknowdovid: Though please tell me if you ever get anything nasty. Especially if it sounds like it's from one of my fans. Block ANYone who makes you feel bad. And if you give me usernames, I'll have them blocked on mine and Rachel's Twitters too. They know I don't allow that shit. Or they should.

Playitagainsam: Thank you. I really do appreciate it :)

Dontlooknowdovid: Of course. Now wait, what time is it for you? Isn't it like midnight?

Playitagainsam: Not quite. It's around eleven. I should be asleep honestly, but I'm almost done with reading

Defiant Truth—it's quite unfair you can listen to it faster than I can read it by the way, and then the Twitter notifications happened and I'm afraid I'm prone to easy panicking when it comes to social interaction so I immediately thought of you.

Sam had thought of him. Sam had panicked and thought of *Dovid*. This was the greatest day of Dovid's life.

Dontlooknowdovid: I'm really sorry you panicked, but I'm glad you felt comfortable to come to me about it. I'm always here if you need something.

Playitagainsam: Goodness, well, thank you.

Dontlooknowdovid: Of course. You going to bed now?

Playitagainsam: Technically I'm already in bed. I'm just not asleep yet. But yes, I probably should try to sleep now. Work tomorrow and all that. Even if I want to finish this book!

Dontlooknowdovid: I get it—why do you think I read it so fast? But Defiant Truth will be there for you in the morning :) I hope you have a good day at work. May all your calls be easy to deal with and all your clients be even-minded and polite.

Playitagainsam: You know, I couldn't ask for a better thought for tomorrow. Here's hoping! And you have a good rest of your day.

Play It Again

Dontlooknowdovid: Thanks. Good night.

Playitagainsam: Talk to you later :)

Playitagainsam: Oh dear, I'm sorry, I didn't mean to assume that we'd be speaking again. You've already been such a help.

Dontlooknowdovid: No, no, I hope we do talk again. Say hi whenever you want. You don't have to wait until you've got a social media issue, you know :) I like talking with you. I… If you don't mind, I'd like to keep up a conversation.

Playitagainsam: Oh! Well, sure, of course. I'd really like that.

Dontlooknowdovid: Me too :)

Dontlooknowdovid: But later, because I really don't want to keep you up too late. Have a good night.

He nearly added a heart emoji before he caught himself.

* * *

Dontlooknowdovid: Hey, Sam. I'm not entirely sure when you get off work, but it's like ten am for me, so I think it's like six for you? (I think before we figured out that you're eight hours ahead of me.) Anyway, just wanted to say hi and ask how things were for you at work. Wanted to know if my good wishes actually bore fruit.

Dovid sent the message off and then proceeded to try to forget about it. Sam would answer when he could.

Or if he wanted to. And he might not feel like it, which was also entirely fair.

And Dovid was a damn YouTube star; you'd think that he'd be better at this whole online communication thing.

Playitagainsam: Good morning! Thank you for thinking of me. The day went alright.

Dontlooknowdovid: Aw, just alright?

Playitagainsam: I might have had an...interesting experience today, is all.

Dontlooknowdovid: Oh yeah? Anything you can talk about? Or want to talk about? I'm all ears.

Dontlooknowdovid: (literally; I use a text-to-speech function)

Playitagainsam: That's very interesting! And, well, if you really want to hear it's...a bit NC-17.

Dovid frowned. That didn't sound good.

Dontlooknowdovid: What? Are you okay?

Playitagainsam: Just some secondhand embarrassment. I, well, you see, I was using TeamViewer to recover some files for a client.

Playitagainsam: And, well, I found...quite a lot of porn. On his work computer.

Playitagainsam: And far be it from me to judge someone on their, um, porn habits? But it was all rather filthy and kind of vile and we both sort of kept talking as though I wasn't scrolling through pages of the files trying to find the non-porn ones I was looking for. It was just very awkward. Sort of colored the rest of my day.

Dontlooknowdovid: Oh my god, I am so sorry. I mean, I'd probably find that hilarious if it ever happened to me, but I'm so sorry it was so awkward.

Dontlooknowdovid: Though in order for it to happen to me, I would have had to click a file so it started playing and I heard the noises to clue me in on what was going on. Which would be even MORE awkward.

Playitagainsam: Goodness, I can imagine it would be. I'm very glad that I didn't do that. That scenario makes my experience seem not so bad. At least I only had to scroll past file names and thumbnails. And aside from that, it was a very mild day in terms of work.

Dontlooknowdovid: Glad to hear it. :)

Playitagainsam: What about you? Anything exciting going on today? Less traumatizing?

Dontlooknowdovid: Hahaha, exciting no, less traumatizing maybe. I'm spending the day editing with Rachel. We just did a Day in the Life video—we do those every so often—and those are fun but they require massive editing. And I've got to make the music for it too, once we decide on what footage to use.

Playitagainsam: Wow, that sounds like a lot.

Dontlooknowdovid: It can be. But I love it, you know? We both do. Makes it all worth it :) Well, that and the fact that we also get paid. That helps make it worth it too!

Dontlooknowdovid: Hey, speaking of, I noticed that your videos don't have ads or anything. You've totally broken the 10,000 view minimum to put them up. Have you thought about maybe monetizing your channel?

Playitagainsam: I hadn't thought about it at all. You... really think that's something I could do?

Dontlooknowdovid: Oh yeah, for sure. Your videos are getting a couple thousand views each right now, as people work their way through them, and I know your latest few all had a bunch of views.

Playitagainsam: Thanks to you.

Dontlooknowdovid: I don't know about that. I might've been a push to get you popular, but the fact that so many people stayed to watch you and subscribed means that you're rising on your own merit. Which is awesome!

Dontlooknowdovid: Anyway, getting that many views per video means that you have the option to put up ads and get paid for it. I could show you how to set that up, if you wanted. It's not that hard at all.

Playitagainsam: You don't think my viewers will mind? I know many people don't like ads.

Dontlooknowdovid: You'll have the people who use ad blockers, and that's something you can't help. But a lot of people whitelist the artists they like, specifically so they can add to their income. Just something to think about.

Playitagainsam: Goodness. I can't say I really consider myself an artist.

Dontlooknowdovid: Why not? You make content. People like your content. Sounds like being an artist to me :)

Playitagainsam: I suppose that's true.

Playitagainsam: You really think people won't mind ads? I certainly wouldn't be averse to the extra income, but I don't want to come off as greedy.

Dontlooknowdovid: Do I come across as greedy to you?

Playitagainsam: Oh no, of course not!

Playitagainsam: I'm so sorry, I didn't mean to imply you were. That's not what I meant at all. You're an artist making a living.

Dontlooknowdovid: Right. Exactly. And you could be too.

Playitagainsam: Oh. Well. I suppose you're right.

Playitagainsam: Alright, I'd like to give it a try. There's really nothing to lose, is there?

Dontlooknowdovid: There you go!

Dovid proceeded to walk Sam through enabling ads on his channel and set them as "per view" as opposed to "per click." Sam was very appreciative all throughout, and Dovid tried to make it clear that he wasn't expecting anything from Sam for doing this. That he just wanted to help, because he liked him. Which was all true.

He really hoped Sam liked him back. It seemed like he did. He kept up the conversation. But Sam was also *nice*. Was Dovid imposing and not aware of it?

Dontlooknowdovid: And that's all there is to it. Now, I should probably get to editing before Rachel busts down my door. But don't be a stranger, yeah? Say hi whenever you feel the urge :)

Playitagainsam: Why thank you. And I'll be sure to.

Awesome.

* * *

Dovid's phone beeped with an incoming Twitter DM around twelve-thirty, just as he was finishing up a new song for his Patreon patrons. He checked it eagerly, hoping, and was super pumped when it did, after all, end up being from Sam.

Playitagainsam: Good afternoon, Dovid (I believe it's afternoon for you now? It's a bit after eight for me). I had a bit of a day at work and I thought of you.

Dovid grinned. Sam was thinking about him! His day just got one hundred percent better.

Dontlooknowdovid: Hi! Great to hear from you :) and yeah? What happened?

Playitagainsam: Nothing so unusual as a porn-filled computer. Just a few very cross clients. It was my day to be yelled at, apparently.

Dontlooknowdovid: Oh no, I'm sorry.

Playitagainsam: It's alright. I'm a bit used to it at this point. Anyway, that's not the part I meant to tell you. It was more that I had one man in particular who was very creative in his insults.

Dontlooknowdovid: Yeah?

Playitagainsam: I was called a "half-tall shortman," a "horse-pulling layabout" and, most brilliantly, a "shark-toothed walnut."

Playitagainsam: I don't particularly know what a shark-toothed walnut is, but it seems like a very ferocious creature!

Dontlooknowdovid: I can't say I love that you got yelled at and insulted, but those are pretty ridiculous insults.

Playitagainsam: Aren't they? I wouldn't mind fancying myself a shark-toothed walnut.

Dontlooknowdovid: Hahaha, yeah, I can see it.

Playitagainsam: :)

Playitagainsam: Have you got anything interesting in the cards today?

Dontlooknowdovid: I'm not sure I can live up to being a walnut, but I'm doing a livestream with Rachel later for the channel. We're opening fan mail. Which could very well be traumatizing; most of my fans send food. I've eaten a lot of weird stuff, as a result.

Playitagainsam: That sounds so interesting though! To get packages from all over the world.

Dontlooknowdovid: Hey, I mean, if you're interested in that, you're well on your way to getting popular enough for people to want to start sending you things.

Playitagainsam: Oh no, that would be a bit much for me, I think. I'll be content to just hear you tell me about it.

Playitagainsam: If you want to, I mean!

Dontlooknowdovid: I do :)

Dontlooknowdovid: And you're always free to tune in and watch! Though uh, yeah, with the time difference, I can't imagine you'd ever be able to :(

Playitagainsam: You upload them all to YouTube after the fact, don't you?

Dontlooknowdovid: Yeah.

Playitagainsam: So I can just watch you then :)

They were using an awful lot of emoticons with each other. Were they flirting? Was this flirting? If this were anyone *else* Dovid would totally consider it flirting. But he really liked Sam, and Sam was just so *nice*. Maybe Dovid was just projecting. He didn't want to say or do anything wrong by accident.

Dontlooknowdovid: Sure thing. Feel free to tell me what you think, okay?

Playitagainsam: Okay, I will.

* * *

"Hey, guys, this is Don't Look Now with Dovid and Rachel. I'm Dovid, Rachel's behind the camera, and today we're doing a livestream! So welcome, everyone. We are live, right, Rachel? Hey, guys, if you can hear us, tweet, um, tweet 'apple dumpling.'"

"'Apple dumpling'?" Rachel asked incredulously. She was, as always, standing out of view from the camera, holding their iPad to check their Twitter feed and YouTube comments.

Dovid shrugged. "I don't know, they sounded good. I've never had one before."

"Okay," Rachel said, attention on the iPad, "Tessa from YouTube says 'apple dumpling,' brianbates on Twitter says 'apple dumpling,' isabellabella from Twitter says 'apply dumpling,' I think we're live."

"Awesome." Dovid waved. "Hi, everyone! Where are you all from? Go ahead and let us know!"

"Alright," Rachel said, "We've got USA, USA, Canada, California, Colorado—wow a lot of 'C's there. Mississippi, Wales, the UK, England, Japan—geez, it's pretty late for you guys, isn't it? Michigan, Kentucky, Canada again, Mexico, Ireland—"

"Ireland?" Dovid said. "Hey! Welcome to the livestream. I've got a friend who lives there."

"You've got a friend lots of places," Rachel said exasperatedly. With, perhaps, a touch of good reason. Dovid might have been talking about his burgeoning friendship with Sam maybe a lot.

Maybe.

"Moving on," Dovid said. "Welcome again, everybody! Today we're going to be answering some questions and opening some fan mail. First off—" he picked up a box from out of view of the camera and held it up "—this one Rachel picked out. I have been assured that it's covered in a cute cat print, so I'm taking her word for it. Who's this from, Rachel?"

Rachel was in charge of opening all the boxes and taking out the letters they were sent, so Dovid could address the fan on camera. It also meant she was the one who read the letters aloud for Dovid. She usually had fun with the gushy ones.

"This one's from Diane and Matthew in Rochester, Michigan," Rachel said. "Matthew is thirteen, and he and his mom put together this package for us."

"Oh cool," Dovid said, even though inside there was that "oh no, a child is watching me" feeling he wasn't ever able to escape. "Thanks, Matthew! And Diane. Looking forward to seeing what you sent! Or feeling. Or eating. Whatever. Looking forward to it."

"It's specialties of Michigan," Rachel told him, obviously looking at the letter. "And they wrapped each item in a different color, so I could let you know what things were as you unpacked 'em."

"Awesome." It was always great when fans took his blindness into account while wanting to make fan packages fun. Color-coded packages meant Rachel wouldn't have to fumble around trying to stay out of the camera while she identified things to Dovid. Rachel would go to great lengths to avoid being on camera. "Okay, well, let's see…" He reached in and grabbed a package. It was on the heavier side, and something sloshed in it when he picked it up. A beverage of some kind? "What color is this?"

"That's red," Rachel said. "It's a pop. He said they were sending you some of Michigan's specialty pop. Open the one you've got."

Dovid ripped the package open and held up the bottle. "Okay, definitely feels and sounds like a bottle of pop. Are you going to tell me what kind it is?"

"I suppose I can. It's called Red Pop."

"Wow," Dovid said flatly after a minute. "That is so creative. Let me guess…it's red?"

"Surprise!"

"Okay, well, red Red Pop. Let me open this and give it a try." He cracked open the bottle—slowly, they'd had enough pop bottles explode on them from being rattled in transit to know better now—and sniffed it. "Whoof, that smells like artificial red. You know how sometimes something isn't a flavor, but the flavor of a color? I can't even see colors and I know when something is red flavor. This definitely is it."

"It's got a picture of a strawberry on the bottle," Rachel said helpfully.

"So I guess I'm to assume it tastes like strawberry. Okay, well…bottoms up." He took a long swallow and, well, it wasn't the worst thing he'd ever tasted, not by a long shot (here's looking at you salmiakki), but it did taste very red and very artificial.

"How's it taste?" Rachel asked.

Dovid held up the bottle. "You want to try?"

"I might be curious."

"Go ahead. It tastes like red."

"It really does," Rachel said, after Dovid handed her the bottle. "That's. Interesting."

Dovid laughed. "Right, well, next item?"

"Oh, pick the brown one. That's another pop."

"'Pick the brown one,' she says. To the blind man."

Rachel snorted. "It's a pop-bottle shape. Pick it out."

"Fine, fine…" Dovid felt around until his fingers found something the right size and shape that sloshed familiarly. He triumphantly held it up. "This better be the brown one."

"It is. Open it, open it. It's called Rock & Rye."

"Rye?" Dovid asked as he tore open the packaging and held up the bottle for the viewers to see. "Like the bread?"

"Don't look at me."

"I couldn't even if I wanted to. Anyway, here goes." He twisted open the top and took a swallow. "Well," he said after a minute. "That is…interesting. I honestly don't know how to describe that. It's…not quite root beer flavored. How would you even describe this?"

Rachel took the bottle from him and took her own drink of it. "I'd say that Faygo is a weird brand," she said. From the sound of it, she had capped the bottle. "Here, hold out your hand to take it back."

Dovid did so, and set the bottle down on the floor at his feet, before he reached into the box again. "What color?"

"Green," Rachel said.

Dovid hefted it. This too felt like a pop bottle. "And it is?"

"…also a pop, apparently. Michigan has a lot of specialty pops."

"What kind is it?"

"It's a ginger ale. Vernors."

"Oh. Can't go wrong with ginger ale, I guess. And it looks like I'm not going to be thirsty, thanks to this box." He opened the bottle and took a swallow. "Okay, that one's really good. I haven't had ginger ale in a while, but I really like this stuff."

"Gimme."

Dovid made a face. "See how she talks to me?"

"Dovid, come on."

"Here." He held out the bottle so Rachel could grab for it and stay out of the shot. "What do you think?"

"Oh yeah, I like that a lot."

"Right? It's really good."

"It is."

"Now give it back."

"You already have the other two pops!"

"Rachel, come on."

"Ugh, fine, here, hold out your hand."

Dovid took the bottle back and set it down next to him on the couch, so he wouldn't get it mixed up with the two Faygo bottles on the floor. He picked up another package. This one had something dry and crackly-sounding inside, like dead leaves rattling against each other, but the package itself was puffy, like it was covered in a layer of Bubble Wrap. "What is this? It sounds like chips. Are these chips? And what color are they?"

"Yeah they are. And yellow. It's wrapped in Bubble Wrap so the chips didn't get squashed by the pop."

"Okay. Are they...special chips?"

"Yup. According to the letter, these are Better Made chips, a brand from Michigan. That one's regular, and there's another one that's barbecue."

"Oh. Alright. Let me just...figure out how to open a bag of bubble-wrapped chips, then. I might need scissors for this."

He didn't end up needing scissors; after some careful feeling around, he found the piece of tape that was holding it all together and peeled it off. The Bubble Wrap unwound easily, and then he was opening the bag Rachel identified as the plain kind. "They taste like chips," he said after trying one. "Maybe saltier than normal. And...a little greasier, to be honest. Okay, now the barbecue."

He put one in his mouth, bit down, and immediately— "Hot! Hot hot hot, okay, bleh, no, sorry, no."

"Don't talk with your mouth full."

"I'm covering my mouth!" He was; he'd brought his hand up to his mouth—though that was in part to fan it. "I don't think I'm a fan of barbecue chips."

"Wimp."

"You want to try them?"

"Sure."

Rachel couldn't tell a difference between the Better Made chips and regular ones ("That's because I have a more refined palate," Dovid said smugly), and she liked the barbecue chips. Dovid graciously said they were hers to keep.

"One last package," Rachel said, "and so you know, it's wrapped in white. I'm excited for this one."

"Okay..." Dovid pulled out the package. It felt sort of hefty, and was about the size of his whole hand. "Are you going to tell me what it is?"

"Nope."

"Great. That means I should be terrified."

"It's a good surprise, I promise."

"Uh-huh." This too was wrapped in Bubble Wrap, probably to keep it from getting squashed by the bottles. He opened it up and took a sniff, and was immediately bombarded by the smell of chocolate and peanut butter. "Wow, this smells amazing."

"Open the rest of it so you can try it so I can try it."

Dovid grinned and took his time unwrapping the package until he was holding something that felt smooth to the touch, but soft. If he pressed a little bit, his finger indented it and it didn't spring back. The texture and feel, along with the smell... "Is this some kind of candy?"

"Eat it, eat it, eat it."

Dovid broke off a little piece and put it in his mouth. "Fudge! I think. Is it fudge? Because it's amazing." He took another piece.

"Don't eat it all," Rachel whined. "I want to try it."

"In a second. And this is great. But why's it special?"

"It's from some place called Mackinac," Rachel read. "They're famous for their fudge."

"Well, good, they should be. You're not getting any."

"Doviiiiid."

"Fine," he grumbled, handing it over. "But you better not eat it all. We'll split it after filming."

"Deal." And then, "Oh wow, this is delicious."

"Right?"

"I changed my mind, I'm eating the whole thing."

Dovid turned back to face the front, where the camera was. "See how she treats me? Anyway, thank you so much Matthew and Diane. Rachel will read me your letter after filming. This was a great package to open. You all know that I love to try new things! And feel free to send more fudge, by the way." He took another sip of the Vernors and then said, "Okay, now that we've opened a package, I think it's time to read some comments and answer some questions. Rachel, any good ones?"

"Oh yeah, quite a few," she said. Dovid could hear the wicked grin in her voice. He immediately got worried. "First one, Marissa from London: 'Love your channel! Are you ever going to tell us if you're dating someone?'"

Dovid didn't sigh aloud, but he was going to get back at Rachel for this. He had the same canned answer, but Rachel had been teasing him a lot about the fact that he was talking to Sam. "Thanks, Marissa, glad you like our show. And no, I really would like to keep that part of my life separate from YouTube. If—*if* I were dating someone, and I'm not saying if I am or not, I'd really want to keep that quiet, at least for a little while. It wouldn't be fair to bring my possible datemate into my YouTube life, especially if they weren't prepared for the fallout." Like he'd done with Sam. "It can be really overwhelming to be a popular YouTube personality, even more so when you don't have any experience with it. I wouldn't want to do that to someone before they were ready."

And it was hard sometimes. Dovid did, occasionally, talk about hookups, both the good and bad experiences. He'd had times where someone had wanted to fuck him because he was blind and it was a kink and, gross, no. He'd had people who'd been really good about working with him, so the sex was fun for everybody. He did his best to keep his channel PG-13 for his viewers, but even with that stipulation, it was important to him to share certain experiences with other people, both disabled and not. Most of his viewers really appreciated how candid he was about it.

But actually dating someone… Dovid couldn't imagine putting someone through that. He'd had people who'd wanted to date him because he was "famous" (which was nipped in the bud pretty quickly), but he had dated a few people who, like Rachel, were camera shy. He'd actually had a breakup over it once; Dovid had gotten serious enough with Brian that he'd wanted to share his happiness with YouTube. Brian was adamant Dovid never bring him into it, and, well…a lot of things were said in the ensuing fight, and the relationship couldn't be recovered.

That still hurt.

Dovid did end up making a video about why he was so down, but he'd been careful not to go into too much detail, instead talking about how much he hurt but that he was trying to get over it. The video had ended with him being very clear about the fact that he was probably going to keep his more serious dating life offscreen. But people still asked. They were going to.

"And Rachel knows that as well as anyone," he added. "So while it was great to hear from you, Marissa, I'm not sure why she chose your question."

"Because you get twenty million of those questions a day. Might as well talk about it once a livestream."

This time Dovid did sigh. "I guess that's a fair point." He tried to grin. "Okay, well, next question."

"Sergei from Russia says, 'What is favorite movie? Many people think just because blind, I don't watch. But you watch many thing. Me too! Sorry for my English!'"

"That's an excellent question, Sergei. And your English is awesome. Though I'm going to be a little boring here and say I like to watch a lot of documentaries.

It's fun to learn things; I'm a big random-facts guy. And this might seem obvious, but I like movies that actually have a lot of dialogue? Action movies are sort of lost on me. 'What happened?' 'Something exploded.' 'What happened this time?' 'Another thing exploded.' 'Why did all the things explode?' 'Because most people are *pretty damn visual*, stop interrupting the movie.' You see my point? Next question!"

"Yuki, from Japan but currently in California, wants to tell you that she really likes Sam's channel, and she wanted to thank you for recommending it."

"Oh! Well, hey, thanks, Yuki. Glad you're liking him. I hope you went ahead and let him know!" He grinned. "But I'll be sure to pass along that information to him."

"Whoa," Rachel said.

"What?"

"Comments just exploded asking you about Sam."

Oh.

Dovid hadn't actually told YouTube that he and Sam were in contact now.

Shit, shit, shit. Why couldn't he just be a normal human being when it came to Sam? He'd been on You-Tube long enough—he should be better at this! He just…he just was happy that they were talking, and his first instinct was to share that. But not at Sam's expense again, *damn* it.

"Dovid, there are a *lot* of questions and comments about Sam now." And from Rachel's tone, Dovid could tell that some of them were probably more personal than others.

Dovid cleared his throat and smiled wide. "Okay, guys, I really don't think I'll be able to get to all those, so I'm just going to clear a few things up now. We didn't know each other when I plugged his channel. That's true. And he didn't know me when he dedicated his next video to us—that was just a thank-you for the plug. But since then, we have been talking a little, yeah. He wasn't super sure about how to handle the sudden burst of popularity. I've just been giving him a little advice. But it couldn't hurt for you guys to be nice to him! And now I think we should open the next fan mail package. What do you think, Rachel?"

"Excellent. I want to eat more."

"Sounds like a plan to me."

* * *

As soon as the livestream was over, even before he took off his mic or started to help clean up, Dovid was sending a message to Sam.

Dontlooknowdovid: Hey, listen, during my livestream today someone thanked me for rec'ing you on my channel, and I said I'd pass the compliment along. So uh, there's the compliment. But it also meant that I basically told all my followers that we officially were in contact with each other, and I'm really sorry about that.

It was late for Sam now, around eleven at night, and he wasn't expecting a response so it was a little bit jarring to have one come in. Still, by then Dovid had actually listened to some of the tweets and comments fans had left asking about Sam (or speculating about Sam) and he was glad that he'd be able to at least apologize now while things were still fresh.

Playitagainsam: ? I'm sorry, why are you sorry?

Dontlooknowdovid: You're awake?

Dontlooknowdovid: Shit, sorry, duh, of course you're awake if you're talking to me.

Playitagainsam: Haha, no, you're right, I should absolutely be asleep right now. I'm in bed! But I was reading. And oh no, I didn't think to check your livestream channel because I thought it'd be later. I'm sorry, I could have watched!

Dontlooknowdovid: It's totally okay. Next time! Maybe we can coordinate :)

Playitagainsam: I'd like that very much. Live a bit vicariously through you and your fan mail packages, haha.

Playitagainsam: Oh but! Sorry, you were apologizing for something and I steamrolled you completely. What's wrong?

Dovid sighed and typed out his reply.

Dontlooknowdovid: Now that my subscribers know that we really know each other, they're going to be worse than ever, asking us about the other.

Playitagainsam: Oh that's alright. I really haven't had too many questions at all. Or none that I've noticed.

Playitagainsam: Though I, er, I do admit that I might not be reading my YouTube comments all that thoroughly anymore. I try! And I keep an eye out for the usernames I'm used to seeing but…there's just so many now.

Dontlooknowdovid: Fuck, I'm sorry.

Playitagainsam: You don't have to keep apologizing! I understand. It was nice of one of your fans to mention me :)

Dovid sighed and rubbed at his face. Sam had no idea.

Dovid should probably just bite the bullet and tell him now. Better to do it as soon as he could and soften the blow, over letting Sam find out from an overenthusiastic fan.

Dontlooknowdovid: That's not all.

Dontlooknowdovid: I mean, not all I need to tell you.

Playitagainsam: Okay.

Dontlooknowdovid: Some people think we're dating.

Dontlooknowdovid: I mean they're just fans! But there's always speculation once someone mentions someone else on a channel, and I, uh, I did, talk you up like a lot and so people are taking all the 'adorable' comments and running with them.

Dontlooknowdovid: I'm so, so sorry.

* * *

Sam blinked down at his phone. It was certainly surprising to learn that someone on the internet would come to the conclusion that he was dating Dovid. Even though he was in bloody Ireland but…long distance was a thing, after all. However, if anything, it only made Sam feel bad that Dovid felt bad. It wasn't Dovid's fault that people liked to let their imaginations get the better of them.

Besides, Sam had burned through an awful lot of Dovid's videos at this point. That, coupled with their much-more-frequent conversations, well...

Sam's little crush had definitely solidified. He had to admit that he would not be opposed to dating Dovid.

And he'd already taken much too long to reply, so he hurriedly tapped out a message and sent it.

Playitagainsam: I'm the one who's sorry. I don't want you to feel responsible for that. People will think what they think. It's not like I mind.

He stared at the words he'd just sent for Dovid to read. "It's not like I mind"? *Really, Sam?*

Dontlooknowdovid: You really don't mind?

This was getting into dangerous territory here. Sam tried to be honest without giving too much away.

Playitagainsam: Of course not. You seem like a wonderful person. Anyone would be lucky to date you, I'm sure.

This time there was a significant pause. The little "..."s by Dovid's username appeared and disappeared half a dozen times before the reply came.

Dontlooknowdovid: Wow.

Dontlooknowdovid: Um.

Dontlooknowdovid: Thank you.

Dontlooknowdovid: I really—sorry, thank you. I don't know what to say.

Playitagainsam: You don't have to say anything. It's a compliment :)

That was okay to say, right? And a smiley face emoticon was okay to use too, right? Right? Oh dear, Sam had very little experience with talking to someone like this. At least Dovid didn't seem like the type to get mad if Sam said the wrong thing.

Dontlooknowdovid: Hahaha, okay, okay. I'll take the compliment. Thank you. I mean it. Means a lot, coming from you.

Sam swallowed. Seeing those words made him come up all warm.

Playitagainsam: Oh, I'm nobody special.

Because he wasn't. Dovid was this amazing (and, well, very handsome) YouTube sensation. He was a voice for disabled and differently-abled people, incredibly clever, obviously kind, and such a special person. Sam was a nobody. He didn't have an interesting career or do anything all that exciting. He was terrible when it came to human interaction because he was so shy and it was, frankly, incredible that he was even able to cope with his sudden popularity. That he was able to at all was all because of Dovid and his advice and willingness to be an ear for Sam to talk to.

Dontlooknowdovid: You're kidding, right?

Sam frowned in confusion.

Playitagainsam: Sorry, what do you mean?

Dontlooknowdovid: I know we haven't really been talking to each other for a long time, but I've also listened to you be you in all your videos. You're like the nicest person I've ever had the fortune to interact with. Of course you're special. I don't— I wasn't kidding. About it meaning something to me, that you think I'd be worth dating.

Dontlooknowdovid: I'm sorry, I didn't mean to go all weird on you. I just, uh, I had a breakup a while ago that still sort of smarts. So it's…nice. To be told that I'm worth it by someone whose opinions I really respect. I mean Rachel counts, but she's also my sister and best friend; she's pretty much required to take my side. You don't have to. But you did anyway.

Dovid respected his opinion? That much? About something like this? Just from Sam's silly videos?
Wow.

Playitagainsam: I'm sorry to hear about your breakup. That it's still bothering you, whatever happened. You ARE a lovely person. And you do deserve somebody special who knows that.

Dontlooknowdovid: Thank you.

Playitagainsam: And I'm so sorry to cut things short, but I really should be trying to go to bed. Early morning.

Dontlooknowdovid: Right, of course. Because you've got that real-person job.

Playitagainsam: Unfortunately.

He wished he could take back the word as soon as he pressed enter. He might be unhappy with his job, and even sometimes mentioned it in videos, but talking to Dovid was mostly about positives. So he didn't like being reminded, after a lovely conversation, that he had to go back to work.

He was a little envious of Dovid, being able to just… do something he loved so much. Sam couldn't even imagine that.

Dontlooknowdovid: Okay, well, have a good night, okay? And a good tomorrow.

Dontlooknowdovid: And I'll talk to you later?

Playitagainsam: Sure :)

Dontlooknowdovid: Sleep well.

Sam wished Dovid a good rest of his own day and lay back in bed, letting out a breath. He hoped he hadn't gotten too personal for Dovid, with his own feelings. But there they were, and none too easy to ignore.

And Dovid absolutely did deserve someone special. He was kind, smart, funny, handsome and so much more.

Sam set his phone down on his nightstand, closed his eyes, and tried to will himself to sleep and to not think about how much he sort of wanted to be that special someone.

Chapter Six

Dovid and Sam continued to talk about any number of things over the next two months. They watched each other's videos and commented on them, and sometimes Sam would ask for advice and Dovid would give it, or he'd have an interesting story to tell. Sometimes Dovid was the one with the story, or he'd bring up a subject and Sam would happily discuss. They kept on exchanging book recommendations, occasionally even deciding to start one at the same time, so they could discuss it and predict as they read chapters.

Sam really looked forward to his conversations with Dovid. And he didn't know how Dovid felt in turn, but the man initiated at least as many of them as Sam did so there was something to be said for that. He hoped.

They hadn't really touched on the dating topic again, but that was okay with Sam. If Dovid didn't want to bring it up, he absolutely shouldn't have to. And alright, there was the occasional fan speculation about their relationship, but Dovid always played it off easily, with confidence and humor. Sam, to his credit, wasn't too awkward about it either; just said that he and Dovid were friends now, and that was that.

Even if he wanted more, well, they were, if nothing else, separated by the entire Atlantic ocean. And besides, Dovid could do so much better than Sam, for a partner. Sam's mother always despaired over Sam ever finding someone who'd be willing to put up with his neediness and silly little quirks. Not like his brother, Charlie, who was happily married to a wonderful woman he'd met in med school.

Sam would never want to impose on anyone and make them feel as though they were responsible for him, least of all Dovid, who he liked and admired so much. But, he thought, they were doing rather well as friends. And he hoped that, at least, would continue for quite some time.

He was walking home from his grocery store now, idly listening to some music, and looking forward to talking to Dovid when he got home. They'd pretty much figured out when were the best times to have conversations, with the time difference and their schedules. Seven o'clock for Sam, home from work and finished with errands that needed him out of the house, was eleven in the morning for Dovid. After he had breakfast and exercised, but usually before he and Rachel did any filming or started editing together, barring specific plans. It was thrilling that Dovid kept making time for him.

The crosswalk light turned green, and Sam stepped into the street.

He didn't see the car come barreling out of nowhere.

* * *

It was about eleven-fifteen, the time Sam was usually around to DM without it being too early for him (while he was at work). Dovid really looked forward to eleven-fifteen now.

Dontlooknowdovid: Hey, Sam! Just wondering how your day went.

He sent the message off and then went back to what he had been doing. It usually took a few minutes for Sam to get onto Twitter, even if he'd been very regular about it for the last couple of weeks.

After about an hour though, and no response, Dovid sent another message, just to be sure.

Dontlooknowdovid: Hey, I'm going out filming now so my phones going to be off, but just say hi whenever you've got the chance :)

* * *

Dovid went to check his DMs again, even though he knew there would be nothing. His phone hadn't made a sound. But it had been a full day, and he and Sam had been talking so regularly, it was hard to suddenly lack him.

* * *

Dontlooknowdovid: Hey, Sam! Just wanted to know how you're doing. Almost finished with The Trident Test. I can't believe the bait and switch the author pulled in chapter 19. Looking forward to talking about it with you :)

* * *

Dontlooknowdovid: Hey, Sam, haven't heard from you in a couple of days. Hope things are going well!

* * *

Dontlooknowdovid: Hey there. Rachel and I both missed your Friday video! Did something come up?

* * *

Dontlooknowdovid: Hey, Sam. How are things going? Hope you're not working too hard. DM me whenever :)

* * *

Dontlooknowdovid: Hey, Sam. Just wanted to know how you're doing. Are you okay?

* * *

Still nothing. Dovid clutched at his phone and played the last message Sam had sent almost six days ago. A cheerful goodbye, alluding to nothing negative. A promise that they'd be talking again soon. And then radio silence. Had he done something? Said something? Sam was polite to a fault, and it was clear he hated confrontation. Maybe Dovid had done something to upset him and Sam'd just decided to stop engaging.

But Sam didn't seem the type to do that.

Dovid swallowed. Narrated another message to join the others he'd sent over the last six days.

* * *

Dontlooknowdovid: Hey, Sam, um, did I do something wrong? I'm really sorry if I did. Could you maybe just please tell me what it was? I'll stop bothering you, I promise.

* * *

Sam decided he did not like hospitals very much. They smelled like hand sanitizer, and it was impossible to sleep because they came in to check your vitals every four hours.

He did not like having broken ribs even more, because they hurt so much he couldn't do anything at all, besides sit up in bed and watch television. He wasn't allowed to lie down, but even while sitting up, movement hurt. Keeping a laptop in his lap and using it seemed unthinkable, so even though his brother had gone to his flat and gotten it for him, it just sat there, lonely and unused.

He missed his phone most of all though. It had pretty

much been destroyed. His parents had ordered him a new one, though, which he was obviously grateful for, and they were waiting for it to come in.

They'd also, of course, told him how inconvenient it had been that he'd gotten hurt. Sam tried not to think too much about how his mother had said, "Really, son? Must you?" when they'd changed the wrappings on his ribs the first time he'd been awake. He hadn't meant to cry, truly he hadn't. It had just been so painful, and the medication they gave him hadn't *helped*, just made it harder to breathe.

Well. The doctor had figured out he was reacting poorly to that medication and switched him, and he was feeling a lot better in that regard, at least. So now it was simply a lot of sitting and hurting and doing nothing. He was missing his Kindle Unlimited app a lot.

And Twitter. He hoped Dovid hadn't thought he'd ghosted him. Sam wouldn't do that to anyone, but especially not to Dovid.

* * *

It was an unusual relief when Sam's parents came over to his flat, as they were dropping off his phone. He steadfastly waited to use it until they were done with their visit and then he was turning it on to get it all sorted.

First, he used the cloud to get all his contacts back, which took several minutes. The next while was spent reinstalling all his apps—happily opening his Kindle app once it was downloaded and looking through *The Trident Test*, the book he'd been in the middle of reading before the whole "hit by a car" fiasco.

Then, it was logging in to all his accounts. He'd been pretty much avoiding social media, not having the strength or energy for it. His YouTube account had, frankly, too many notifications for him to deal with, so he ignored that for the time being. Twitter was...not really much better to be honest. He scrolled through a few of his @ notifications just out of morbid curiosity. A bunch of them were wondering about his Friday video.

Of course. He hadn't missed a video upload without advance notice since he'd started his channel. No wonder people were concerned.

Suddenly remembering about Dovid, he hurried to check his DM messages too. His heart sank as he read them all, crushed at Dovid thinking he might have done something wrong, that Sam was mad at him.

The last message from Dovid was this:

Dontlooknowdovid: Hey, Sam, I know I said I'd leave you alone but I'm really, really worried. Rachel is, your fans... We all are. If you could just let me know you're okay? Please. Here's my WhatsApp number. Just call me? Please.

Sam swallowed, aching at how upset Dovid seemed to be. It was ten in the morning for him, so it'd be about two am for Dovid. It'd be madness to call, but he could at least send him a text through the app to let him know he was alright. Dovid would get it when he woke up and then he'd know things were okay.

And...and hopefully they could continue talking like normal, after all this.

He put Dovid's number into his phone and then typed out a message.

Sam Doyle: Hi, Dovid, this is Sam. From Twitter? Just wanted to let you know I'm alright. I had a bit of a

health issue that took me out of commission. I'm sorry
if I worried you.

He nodded, hoping that was sufficient, and then
opened his Kindle app to try to get back to his book.

His phone rang three minutes later.

It was from Dovid.

Utterly nonplussed, Sam answered. "H-hello?"

"Oh my god," came the voice on the other end. It
was a voice Sam had heard dozens of times in dozens
of videos.

It sounded utterly wrecked. "Oh my god, it's really
you and you're okay."

"I am," Sam assured him. "Really. I'm sorry to have
worried you."

"Fuck, sorry, I—I thought you were just mad at me.
But you missed your video upload and no one had heard
anything about you and you basically just disappeared
and I'm rambling, I'm sorry, I'm just really glad you're
okay."

"I am," Sam said again. "But goodness, Dovid, what
are you even doing up? It's near two in the morning for
you isn't it?"

"I've been checking my social media and WhatsApp
alerts," Dovid said matter-of-factly. "They're set for the
loudest ring I have."

"What—why?"

"Because I was really fucking worried about you,"
Dovid said, voice quiet and raw. "What even happened?
If…if you want to tell me. If that's okay. It's fine if you
don't, I'm just so glad you're okay and don't hate me
and—"

"Dovid," Sam interrupted, "I could never hate you.
And of course I can tell you what happened. But it…

it sounds sort of bad. But I'm better now! Mostly. So don't worry too much, alright?"

"What...what happened?"

"I, erm, I got hit by a car."

"*What?* Fuck are you *okay*? What...how—"

"I'm alright," Sam said, trying to sound as reassuring as possible. "I, well, I broke two ribs and sprained my left wrist. I've only just gotten out of the hospital, actually. They had to keep me for a few days to make sure that none of my organs had been punctured by my ribs, and then I didn't react the best to some of the medication. But things are all good on that front. Now I just have them and my wrist wrapped, and I'm on quite a lot of pain medication that isn't giving me trouble."

"Thank god. I— Is there anything you need? Not that I can do very much since we're separated by a fucking ocean, but I would definitely try my best."

Sam had to smile. "The thought is very much appreciated."

"Seriously, anything. Name it. At this point I will fucking fly to Ireland."

Sam laughed, which turned into a cough, which in turn hurt. "Ow, sorry about that. Laughing is unfortunately not the best medicine at the moment."

"Don't apologize. Fuck just—god." A loud exhale. "I'm so glad you're okay."

"Oh dear," Sam said, just realizing something.

"What? What is it? What's wrong?"

"YouTube," Sam said. "I almost forgot. I need to tell everyone I'm okay. I don't think I'd be up for making much of a video. Do you think anyone would mind particularly if I just slapped up some text and some canned sound?"

"No, I really don't think anyone would mind. They'd probably just be relieved you're not, like, dead in a ditch. Maybe tweet too? Just to cover your bases, if you wanna do that."

"That's a good idea," Sam said. "I wouldn't have thought of that." Twitter usually slipped his mind.

"Well, that's why you've got to keep me around."

"There are more reasons than that, I'm sure," Sam said, a smile in his voice.

"That's good to know." A loud yawn. "Sorry, sorry."

"Please. It's ridiculously late for you. Go back to sleep. I'll still be here in the morning. Your morning, I mean."

"Promise?" Dovid's voice was still wet and raw, just this side of pleading.

All Sam wanted to do was to never make him sound like that again. "I promise."

"Okay. And um. Could I call you? Again, I mean. When we're both free."

"I'd like that very much," Sam said with feeling.

After he hung up, he took a shaky breath and opened Twitter again scrolling back through Dovid's DMs. He couldn't get Dovid's scared, relieved voice out of his head. The...the obvious desperation that had come from his need to know if Sam was alright.

Sam tried to sort through his feelings. He knew how much he'd come to care for Dovid. He hadn't dared to entertain the idea that Dovid might care for him right back.

And that was a lot to think about.

For now, Sam opened Twitter and wrote a quick message. *Hey, everybody. Sorry to have worried you. Had a bit of a health thing. But I'm okay now!*

After a second of thought he added, *But please be patient with me, if it takes me some time to get back into the swing of things.*

* * *

"Hey, guys, this is Don't Look Now with Dovid and Rachel. I'm Dovid, Rachel's behind the camera, and today I wanted to talk about something, well, something kind of personal." Dovid let out a breath, fidgeting with his hands. "This might be something a lot of you deal with. It's the age of the internet, right? We basically live in the future, what with having the world at our fingertips. That means we also have the chance to meet and talk to people all over the world.

"But sometimes…" Dovid swallowed. "Sometimes that also means you might lose contact with someone for whatever reason. And then there's nothing you can do. You can't make sure they're okay, or ask what's wrong, or even maybe know if they're mad at you or not. People disappear all the time and that…that really sucks. I've never been ghosted myself, but I can imagine that some of you have been. I bet that hurts. Leaves you wondering why.

"Me, well… I just found out a friend had been hurt. Really hurt. Like, they're getting better now, on their way to making a full recovery, but with what happened… there was a legit chance they might not have been okay." His voice was getting thick, damn it. He hated crying; his lacrimal sacs were intact, but without eyes for the tears to travel through, it all went straight into his nasal passage, giving him the worst runny nose in the world. He swallowed and tried to fight it down. "And I wouldn't have known. I never would have known what had happened. I'd just have been wondering and waiting and worrying and—" He swallowed again, biting his tongue on the curses. *Fuck.* "And I know some of you must be experiencing that right now. Maybe you were talking to someone for a while and they just stopped replying. And you don't know if they got mad, or if they just lost their phone, or they got sick or what. And it's so, so hard and I'm so sorry."

He tried to smile. "I really hope that it all works out for you guys. And if, well, if you're the person doing the disappearing, well, maybe you're doing it for a good reason. I won't begrudge you for that. But if you're sick or hurt, please tell the people you care about. Who care about you. We'd rather know than have you try to protect us. Sorry I—I don't even know where I'm going with this." He sat for a minute and just breathed. "Yeah I—I think that's all I've got for today. Social media and stuff is all in the description box below and as always, guys, see you later. Well, I won't, but you know what I mean."

"Okay," Rachel said after a minute. "Camera's off. You okay?"

"Fuck." Dovid pushed his hands up underneath his glasses. "Fuck that was so hard. I don't even remember what I said. Shit, I need a tissue—" His hand was grabbed, and Rachel placed his box of tissues in it. "Thanks."

"No problem. Are you really sure you want to post this?"

He nodded. "Yeah. Yeah, I—I think it's important."

"Okay. If you're sure."

"I am. Let's just edit it now and get it over with, yeah?"

"Alright."

Editing went pretty easily. There wasn't a whole lot

to cut or switch around, and Dovid slapped together some simple music really quick to put as an underlying noise so there wasn't just the stark background nothing-sound of dead air.

He was up for posting it immediately after they were done, not wanting to think about it anymore, but Rachel held back.

"Dovid, I kind of want you to think this over a little more."

"What do you mean?"

She sighed. "I mean that pretty much everyone knows who you are. And a lot of our subscribers also follow Sam now. And they know he disappeared from the internet without warning. And that he just released a couple of quick messages all 'sorry I haven't been around, I was sick.'"

"Okay. So?"

"So your fans are not stupid. At least some of them are going to make the connection. That means speculation in the comments, which means a lot of back-and-forth, and then people asking all sorts of questions. Do you...really want to do that to him?"

Dovid bowed his head. "That's a point," he said. "I really don't want to make things harder for him." Sam had said several times that the attention made him a little...not uneasy, but unsure about what he was supposed to be doing. He felt that he had to keep up some sort of appearance, and then proceeded to feel like a disappointment. Dovid had always been quick to assure him that he was no such thing, but still.

Besides, if fans thought that they were dating before, there was no telling how they'd react once they got this new footage to play with.

"So what do you want to do?"

"I'll sleep on it," he said. So saying, feeling drained (and, honestly, a little hungover-tired from being jolted awake at two am), Dovid went to his room to take a nap.

* * *

Dovid Rosenstein: Hey, Sam, when you have a minute, could I call you?

It was late. After eleven, and half the reason Sam was still up and reading was because he hurt. He was waiting for his pain medication to kick in.

He got Dovid's message and was pressing down to call his number in the next moment.

It picked up on the first ring. "Hey there."

"Hi, Dovid. How're you doing?" Dovid had sounded so tired and sad and stressed when they talked earlier. Sam only wanted him to feel good.

A sigh. "A lot better. How are *you* doing?"

"Oh, I'm quite alright," Sam said, keeping his tone light. "Not in too much pain. The usual healing period is about six weeks and, well, at least it's already been one. I'll be back to work in a few more days, and just, you know, taking it easy in general. I'll be right as rain soon."

"Thank god."

"Yeah. Nothing to worry about."

A sharp laugh. "If you say so. But actually that's, uh, that's one of the reasons I wanted to talk to you."

"Oh?"

"Yeah, I—I made a video. I was just going to upload it, but then Rachel actually made me think and not just do something like an idiot and, look, long story short it's sort of about you? And I wanted to get your permission before I put it up for the public."

"Oh," Sam said again, rather taken aback. "About me?"

"Yeah, just, like, about what happened. How I was worried about you."

"I can't imagine why you'd need my permission for something like that. If you wanted to make a video about that, you're entitled to."

"Not if it means backlash for you," Dovid replied. "Because I know there's going to be."

"What do you mean?"

Dovid sighed. "With this video, um, I'm a little emotional. About what went down. I mentioned before that some of my fans think we're dating?"

"I remember." Every so often Sam got comments on his videos asking or starting threads of speculation, but Sam mostly found that he needn't even bother addressing them.

If *he* wished it were true, that was neither here nor there.

"Well, let's just say that this video would not exactly, uh, disprove that fact."

"Could I see it?" Sam asked, a little breathlessly.

"Of course. Of course, I—here, it's an unlisted file right now, I can just DM you the link. Do you want to watch it and then get back to me?"

"If that's alright."

"Oh yeah, sure. Of course. And, uh, feel free to tell me 'no' if you're against me putting it up. You're more important to me than some views. I can always make another video."

But Dovid loved sharing that part of himself with

his viewers. It was part of why Sam liked him so much. "I'll keep that in mind" was all he said.

"Okay. Um. I sent it. Actually, uh, do you...do you mind if we stay on the phone while you watch it? It's okay if you don't want to. I'd just go a little crazy waiting, but, um, whatever you want."

"I don't mind," Sam said, moving to his computer and going to his Twitter DMs to get the link. Keeping his phone pressed to his ear, he opened the video.

Dovid was sitting in his room on his spinny chair. Instead of looking straight ahead, face pointed in the direction of the camera, his head was bowed, hands clasped. Every inch of him read stiff tension. *"Hey, guys—"* he sounded so quiet and defeated, it was like a punch to Sam's stomach *"—this is Don't Look Now with Dovid and Rachel. I'm Dovid, Rachel's behind the camera, and today I wanted to talk about something, well, something kind of personal."*

Sam watched the rest of the video barely breathing, and by the time Dovid's voice got wet—horribly wet, it was such an awful sound—Sam was almost crying with him.

"I'm so sorry," he managed, swallowing around a dry throat. "I'm so sorry I made you feel like that."

A quiet laugh, not quite a sob. "It's okay. I just...you know. I'm glad everything worked out."

"Right," Sam assured him. "I'm totally fine. Just a little banged up."

"Yeah."

They drifted into silence, before Sam realized that he should probably say something. "I don't mind. You sharing that, I mean. It's yours to share. And—and if anyone gives you a hard time about it—"

"It's not me I'm worried about. I couldn't care less if they bother *me*."

"I'll happily ignore anyone being silly about our friendship," Sam said evenly. "And if anyone is, you know, hateful, I'll just block them."

"You sure?"

"Absolutely. It's a, well, it's a lovely video, Dovid. I mean it's a difficult one and, to be honest, a little painful. For me, because I know how I made you feel. But it's also important, I think. I see why you want to share it."

"Thanks," Dovid said roughly, after a long moment.

"You're welcome." Sam tried to lighten the mood. "Now then, I hope you have something happier planned for the rest of the day, at least?"

"Maybe I'll rewatch some of your videos," Dovid said. "Since I didn't get one on Friday."

"I said I was sorry about that."

"You were literally hit by a car. I don't think you have to be sorry."

Sam smiled. "Alright, if you say so."

"I really fucking do."

Sam laughed. "Ow, ow, ow, you need to stop being charming."

"I'm charming now?"

Sam swallowed again. Tried to sound lighthearted when he said, "Oh, I'm sure you have people telling you that all the time."

"Nah," and at least Dovid sounded like he was smiling. "Charming's a new one for me."

"Oh, well." Sam tried not to feel flustered. Dovid *was* charming, damn it. Not for the first time, Sam wished he were someone with a bit more personality. "Well," he said again. "Now it's not so new, as you've heard it from me. And you did say you valued my opinion. So yes." Why was he still talking? Stop talking. "Charming. It's my new decree."

A laugh now, rich and deep-throated. It had Sam smiling again. "Okay, sure," Dovid said. "I'll take that. Coming from you, I'll definitely take that."

"Good," Sam said through a yawn. "Sorry," he hurried to add. "Terribly sorry."

"Shit, no, it's okay. It's nearly midnight for you. You must be exhausted."

"The pain medication doesn't help," Sam felt the need to add. Maybe that was why he'd been so ridiculous.

"Fuck, Sam. Go to sleep. I'm sorry I called you so late."

"I called you," Sam pointed out.

"Alright, but I asked."

"Still. I was up. And I wanted to talk to you. I like talking to you," he said sleepily.

"I'm glad to hear that. I like talking to you too."

"Oh. Good. That's nice."

A chuckle. "You sound like you can't keep your eyes open. Go to bed."

"I'm in bed," Sam protested. "I was just—"

"You were just reading?"

"Well, yes." How did Dovid already know him so well? He cleared his throat. "Yes, I was."

"Are you lying down?"

He *had* managed to get more horizontal than vertical, even though he still needed to sleep propped up by pillows. "Yes."

"Eyes closed?"

And yes, his eyes had indeed drifted shut. When had that happened? "Maybe," he mumbled.

A breathy exhale. "Good night, Sam."

Sam was already drifting, Dovid's voice in his ear.

* * *

Sam had turned off his alarm, so he woke up at ten as opposed to the usual six-thirty, feeling as refreshed as he could considering he was still in pain. He got up, downed his morning dose of medication, and then wobbled through the rest of his morning routine.

When he went to retrieve his phone from where it normally sat, charging on his night table, it was nowhere to be found.

He had a moment of panic before the last night came rushing back to him and he found his phone among his pillows and blankets. When he picked up his phone, the first thing he could think of was Dovid's voice saying his name, wishing him good night.

It had been so nice.

But ten am for Sam meant two am for Dovid, so he was loath to send a text now, just in case Dovid hadn't fixed his alarm.

In the meantime, however, Sam thought of something he could do for Dovid. He could give him something to wake up to.

He had breakfast, made himself some tea, and then went over to his computer to open up his YouTube run of Dire Straits.

"Hello, everybody, I'm Sam, and welcome to another episode of Let's Play Dire Straits.

"First off, I wanted to apologize for the worry when I was out of commission, and say thank you to everyone for the well-wishes. You're all lovely people. I'm sorry that I disappeared so suddenly, but I'm back now, and will hopefully continue to be able to upload my Friday videos for some time. Today, however, I figured it was prudent to upload a video a day early. So happy Thursday everyone. And actually," he added, an idea coming to him, "I'll try to upload a video tomorrow too, if I'm up to it. No promises, but I'll let you all know on Twitter if one will be coming out.

"Now then, we last left off…"

* * *

"Sam put out a video today," Rachel announced when she came into the kitchen for breakfast.

"Why do you know that before I know that," Dovid complained, bringing the omelets he'd made to the table. "I'm subscribed to him too. I'm the one who talks to him!"

"Yeah, but you're also not the one who checks the YouTube view count first thing in the morning, and thus the one who sees all our subscription updates first."

Grumbling, Dovid took a bite of his omelet. "Okay," he said. "Watch it first thing after breakfast?"

There was the sound of something being set on the table. "Way ahead of you," she said. "Want to watch it now?"

"Oh hey, sure."

"Good."

They ate their breakfast and watched Sam's let's play, pausing when they were finished eating to move to the couch. Dovid listened with interest as usual, but also with a sense of overwhelming relief. Sam really was back, and fine (or on his way to getting there). Things would return to normal, but now, maybe they'd be able to talk on the phone and actually listen to each other's voices when it had nothing to do with video, on top of texting.

Sitting there, with Sam's voice washing over him, the memory of Sam's genuine, kind nature playing through his mind, how happy Dovid was every time they talked, how fucking worried he had been about him, and then how starkly relieved, a jumble of emotions all mixed together... Dovid realized something that he probably should have known a while ago.

He was definitely in love with Sam.

Chapter Seven

Sam Doyle: Do you mind if I ask you a business question?

Dovid Rosenstein: Never :) what's up?

Sam Doyle: There's been a lot of activity on my channel lately. More than usual. People keep asking for me to do let's plays for other games, and some of them have suggested livestreaming. Some even want to know if I have a donate button! There are people who want to pay me for doing let's plays! I don't know what to do. I don't want to disappoint anyone.

Sam had actually waited a while to ask Dovid about it, because he hadn't wanted to be a bother. But he was getting more and more subscribers every day, and it was, frankly, a little alarming. He sort of felt like he had back when Dovid had first plugged his channel all those weeks ago.

But at the same time, he couldn't help but feel a little excited about it. That there *were* people who wanted more of his content. He even found himself, once in a while, entertaining the fantasy of being more like

Dovid. Being able to have a job that didn't make him miserable. Even made him happy.

That was a scary road to even think about going down though. At least he was used to his current routine.

Sam Doyle: Viewers keep asking for more things from me. And some of that is things that would pay me. I'm already making money off ads (much more than I expected, to be perfectly honest). I'm honestly not sure where to go from here. Some part of me wants to do it, because I wouldn't be averse to a little more extra income, but I just don't know.

Dovid Rosenstein: Do you want to call me? It'd probably be easier to have this conversation over the phone.

Sam Doyle: Are you sure that's alright? You have the time?

His phone rang. Sam picked up. "Hello."

"Hey there," Dovid said, voice a calm amid the storm of Sam's mind. "So, what's up?"

"About what I said in text, I'm afraid," Sam said. "I just— I don't know what to do. The popularity I've reached is a bit alarming. I didn't do anything to deserve it. I—I just make silly little let's plays. Half the time I'm talking nonsense. I don't understand."

"Hey now," Dovid said. "You're yourself in your videos. That alone is pretty endearing. Trust me, I speak from experience. And you play the game well, so people are liking that too. *Have* you thought at all about… I don't know, getting a little bigger? You've kind of got the following now, that you could."

"I don't know. I mean, I suppose I'd like to? To try it at least. It seems like some aspects of it could be fun. But there's a lot that I don't know and don't know how to learn."

"You've got me," Dovid said. "I can help. If you'd like me to."

Sam sighed. "That would be amazing, but that's also such a commitment on your part. I don't want to take up your time."

"I want to give you it," Dovid said. Like it was *easy*. "What's your first question?"

Sam stumbled through his query on what to do about people wanting to donate to him. Dovid talked him through some different options, and then suggested Sam set up a Ko-fi account when Sam admitted that Patreon seemed a little daunting at this point.

"That way people can donate to you if you want, but you're not running a Patreon or something, which would kind of require you to put out more content than you can handle."

"I just can't imagine people would actually want to donate to me. What do I do if they *do*?"

"Thank them however you'd like. Maybe say all their names in a video while you play, or put their names in a credit at the end. That's all up to you."

"I—that's a good idea. I'd of course like to give credit."

"There you go," Dovid said encouragingly. "And I promise, if they like you that much to want to donate, then hearing their names in your video would be an awesome thank-you. Now, what's this about playing other games?"

"Oh, erm, well, a few different commenters have requested that I play various other games, such as adventure games or terraforming games, but also…the company that made Dire Straits is releasing the beta of another game, called Brightforest, and, well, someone from the company asked if I wanted a version of the beta to play on my channel."

"Hey! That's awesome!"

Sam grinned hesitantly. He'd been pretty excited over it, even if he wasn't entirely sure of what to think or do. He said as much to Dovid.

"That's pretty easy," Dovid said. "Do you want to play the game?"

"Well, yes. It looked like a lot of fun."

"So why not? You get a free copy of the game that you want to play anyway. All you have to do is record yourself playing it, do a short review, and post it to YouTube. You don't have to do a series of it or anything, unless you want to."

"You don't think people would mind that it's a change?"

"Not at all. If they're watching you now, it's either because they like the game or they like you. Or both. I'm gonna go ahead and say that, for most of them, it's both. You're a pretty popular Let's Player now."

"I suppose you're right. And I do want to play the game."

"Okay! So accept their offer. If you had the time, you could space out the videos and upload on a different day, even. That would gain more viewers. And it'd be nice for the current ones, to have like, a bonus episode."

"Alright." Sam could do that. He normally played games every night to wind down, when he wasn't reading or doing errands. It wouldn't be too much of a hardship to record himself doing that for a different game. Even if he was usually wiped after work and talking

more seemed daunting. Maybe he could do it on a weekend though, when he was a little better rested. "I'll
write them back."

"Sounds good."

"Thank you so much for talking me through this."

"Anytime. You do realize I like talking to you, right?
This just gives me another excuse."

Sam flushed, not just pleased at the words, but with
the knowledge that Dovid really *meant* them. "Alright.
That's good to know. I like talking to you too. As well
you know, I hope."

"I'm glad."

* * *

*"Hello, everybody, I'm Sam, and welcome to a review
of Brightforest. C-land, the company that made Dire
Straits, just released their beta version of this game
and I was asked to review it. So, well, here I go."* Dovid
listened with interest as Sam talked through the gameplay of Brightforest. It did sound pretty cool. He might
have to get it for Rachel off Steam and see if she were
interested in playing it with him.

*"That about sums up my review. I did, in the end,
have a lot of fun playing it. And, well, if you liked this
video or want more of me playing this game, or anything else, let me know? I'm looking to branch out a
bit, I suppose, and I'd love to hear your input. Thank
you, everybody. Have a nice day."*

Dovid grinned and had his phone out, typing a message to Sam in the next moment.

Dovid Rosenstein: Hey! Just saw your latest video on
Brightforest. It seems like a cool game! And it was a
good idea uploading it Sunday. I also liked how you
asked for input at the end. That was a good touch.

You'll probably get a lot of comments with video and gaming suggestions now.

Sam Doyle: Thank you so much. I'm glad you thought it was good. I... Apparently several people liked it a lot. I've gotten quite a few views on it. So much more than I expected. My view count has increased a ridiculous amount. Which, well, has been very nice for my income.

Sam Doyle: Also there have been quite a lot of donations through Ko-fi? I didn't expect quite so many.

Dovid Rosenstein: That's great though! And yeah, people will, actually, pay artists they like for their art. It's really cool how the internet does that. I mean, that's how I earn my living you know?

Sam Doyle: Oh yes, of course! I just never would have considered myself in the same level.

Dovid Rosenstein: You're well on your way, if you were interested. Doing a variety of videos, monetizing your view count, and setting up that Ko-fi is a good start.

Dovid Rosenstein: And hey, IT is your dayjob and you don't love it. Maybe this'll give you some ideas.

Sam Doyle: Goodness, well. It certainly is something to think about.

Sam Doyle: Again, thank you so much. I really appreciate all that you do.

Dovid Rosenstein: Not a problem at all :)

* * *

"Hello, everybody, I'm Sam, and welcome to another episode of Let's Play Brightforest. Since so many of you wanted to see me play the game, I thought that I could maybe continue to do a bit of a series for at least a few episodes. Dire Straits will still be going up on Friday as usual, but for the next few Sundays I'll be posting Brightforest let's plays too. I hope you enjoy it."

Sam cleared his throat. "Also, I, erm, I wanted to give another thank-you to Dovid from Don't Look Now. He's been an absolute wonder in helping me learn how to navigate YouTube now that a few more of you have started watching me. So thank you to him, and, of course, thank you to all of you for your support.

"Now then, we last left off…"

* * *

Dovid Rosenstein: Hey! Rachel and I watched your Brightforest let's play. I really liked the review you did (super clever, boss editing, as I told you before ;p), but it was really cool to watch you actually play the game. I like how you have to make different decisions that all affect the outcome. I'm hooked, and I'm buying Rachel the game on Steam for sure.

Sam Doyle: Thank you so much! I'm glad you liked it. The review was one thing, but I wasn't sure how everyone would take a full-on video. But overall it got a very positive response. And you telling me you liked it is, of course, the greatest compliment of all.

Dovid couldn't handle this, he really couldn't.

Dovid Rosenstein: Aw. You'll make me blush.

Sam Doyle: Oh, and I hope you didn't mind my dedicating the episode to you.

Dovid Rosenstein: Are you kidding? Why would I mind? I was honored. You didn't have to do that. I told you—I like talking to you. And helping out is just another way for me to do that.

Sam Doyle: Well either way, I appreciate it, and I appreciate you. And also I just wanted to say... I hope you don't think I'm only talking to you FOR the advice. I like all our conversations.

Sam Doyle: I just wanted to clarify that.

Dovid Rosenstein: Thank you. And don't worry—I didn't think you were taking advantage of me or whatever. If anything I kind of felt a little like I was bothering you. Because I was contacting you to just have conversation, instead of discussing YouTube.

Sam Doyle: Oh no! You've been absolutely lovely on all events.

Dovid clutched at his hair. "Absolutely lovely"? And Sam was talking about *him*. About their conversations.

Dovid Rosenstein: Good to know :)

* * *

"Are we live?" Dovid asked. "Guys, if you can hear us, the phrase of the day is 'barracuda.'"

"Why 'barracuda'?" Rachel asked.

Dovid shrugged. "It popped into my head."

"Alright then, well, Timmy from Holland says 'bar-

racuda,' Oliver from Florida says 'barracuda,' San-
deep from England says it, so does Alex, Reign47,
Theintrepidmrox—awesome name, by the way—"

"Cool! Looks like we're up and running. So hey,
guys, this is Don't Look Now with Dovid and Rachel.
I'm Dovid, Rachel's behind the camera, and today we
were going to do a review of Applebubble, a new boba
tea place that just opened up in the area, but then we
were hit by basically a monsoon—thanks, end-of-April
showers, and, frankly, Rachel and I refuse to leave the
house. So instead it's rainy-day livestream time!"

Dovid had released the information that he and Rachel would be doing a livestream around eleven, and
Twitter and chat were bustling by the time they'd got
everything set up at eleven-thirty.

Sam had even said he'd be watching. He'd gotten
out of work and was home making dinner, and texted
Dovid to say he was excited to actually be watching a
livestream live for once. It made Dovid go warm all
over, to hear that from him. Especially after watching
Sam's latest Brightforest video.

Fuck, he was so in love.

He cleared his throat and went through the motions
of asking where everyone was from, and then opened
the floor to questions.

"You look really happy," Rachel read, from Antonio
in California. "Did something good happen?"

"I look happy?"

"You are kind of beaming your head off," Rachel
said.

"Oh." Dovid felt his cheeks. He was indeed smiling pretty wide. "Let's just say that I have someone in
particular watching today. They haven't been able to

catch any of my streams until now, and we've both been looking forward to them getting to watch a live one."

Rachel sighed in exasperation. "Surprise, surprise, but the next thirty questions are all about you being in love."

Dovid rested his chin in his hand and did not stop smiling. "I will neither confirm nor deny that fact."

"Oh my god, Dovid. Just announce it to the world why don't you." Then, "'Oh, oh, is the person listening the one you're in love with?' Sam from Canada."

"Hi, Sam from Canada! And quite a lot of people are listening to me today, I think. Who knows? If I am in love, it might be with one of them."

"You're enjoying this, aren't you?" Rachel said flatly.

Dovid shrugged. "I'm happy. Hopefully that makes for good entertainment."

"You do *realize* that someone in particular, who, as we have established, is *watching*, might be making some assumptions now, right?"

"What can I say? I'm feeling brave. Hear that guys? You're making me feel brave!"

"Oh, for pity's sake—"

"Next question?"

Rachel sighed again. "*Moving on*, Natalie from the Netherlands wants to know if you're going to be doing another baking segment soon, because she really likes them."

"Oh cool, yeah, sure, Natalie, I can do that. Anything in particular you guys want to have me bake?"

* * *

Sam stared wordlessly at his screen.

Dovid couldn't possibly have meant—

No, no that was…that was ridiculous. Not Dovid. Not smart, handsome, clever, creative, successful—

He couldn't possibly be *interested* in boring old Sam. Sam was a *nobody*. He was terribly unexciting. He worked in IT. He liked quiet, and tea, and video games, and reading.

And yet...

And yet Dovid had said he'd liked that Sam liked all those things.

He'd said that he respected Sam's opinions. That he thought Sam was one of the nicest people he'd ever met.

He'd said that Sam was special.

And...

And he'd just insinuated that he was in love with him.

Sam swallowed, throat dry. He couldn't pretend that he hadn't wished, hoped it were true.

But was he brave enough to bring it up when they talked next, if Dovid didn't?

* * *

After the livestream was over and Rachel was putting away the lights and camera, Dovid helping to clean up the mess of boxes and wrappers and food—Rachel would help him sort through it all later—he eagerly checked his phone, hoping for a message from Sam.

There wasn't one.

Trying not to feel too crushed, Dovid thought about what to do next. He'd basically gone and all but out-and-out declared his love for Sam on his channel during a livestream.

Sam had said he hadn't minded the speculation.

But...

But he might have minded things now, now that they no longer were just speculation.

Dovid tried to swallow around the lump in his throat. Had he done the wrong thing? He'd wanted to come clean about his feelings, and this was one of the ways he knew how. He'd been giddy.

Shit, fuck, he'd just done the equivalent of proposing to someone in a public place. He *had* done that; the internet was as much a public place as any. More so. Fuck, fuck, fuck. He must have made Sam uncomfortable. And now there was no way to take it back. He could not put the video up on YouTube, but there were still all the people who'd tuned in, who'd be buzzing.

And Sam knew. Sam knew now, he had to know. Dovid hadn't been subtle and now—

Now Dovid might have gone and just ruined everything.

* * *

Sam picked up his phone. Put it down again. Moved to write a message and stopped. Dovid hadn't sent him anything. The last thing Sam wanted to do was assume. Assume that Dovid really had been talking about him, and not somebody else. Somebody else who was probably attractive and funny and interesting. Who was more extroverted.

Who lived on the same bloody *continent*.

He went to wash his dinner dishes, to at least give himself something to do, instead of think about what Dovid could possibly have meant. If he had meant those words for Sam. Sam wanted them to be. God, did he want them to be.

He finished his dishes and set them to dry, checked his phone. Still nothing.

Should he send a message first? Maybe that's what Dovid was waiting for. If Sam at least sent out a message, he wouldn't have to stew like this just wondering.

In the end, he tried for something simple, unambiguous.

Sam Doyle: Hi, Dovid. I was able to watch your livestream today, like we talked about. It was so interesting to see it while it was actually live! And it was nice to see you so happy :)

There. That wasn't so bad, was it?

Either way, he'd sent it off now. Nothing else to do but wait. If Dovid replied and acted normal, Sam would know he couldn't have possibly been talking about him.

If he didn't...

Sam would just wait and see.

* * *

Dovid got Sam's message and instantly got all twisted up into knots. What did Sam mean, it was nice to see Dovid happy? Did he get the message? He didn't sound upset, but it was easy not to sound upset when things were just words on a screen.

Did he know what Dovid had meant? Had he maybe thought it had been a joke?

"For fuck's sake, just ask him," Rachel said, exasperated. "He's spent this much time talking to you, he has to like you."

"Liking me is different from liking me *back*," Dovid pointed out. "And if he doesn't, I'll have ruined, like, the best relationship I've ever had."

"You're not even in a relationship with him!"

"He's my friend, Rachel. He's my friend and I *value* that."

"Yes, but you're also totally dopey about him and want to kiss his face a bunch."

"Maybe," Dovid muttered. "My point still stands."

"If you don't ask him, I will."

"Don't you dare."

"I mean it. You two need an intervention."

"If he doesn't—"

"If he doesn't what? He's mentioned being shy in his videos like a dozen times. I bet he doesn't even know what to do. I'll just ask him what he thought about the video. Bam. Easy."

"Please don't."

"Then you need to actually make a decision about what to do. Because you're driving me nuts."

Dovid took a deep breath. "Okay. Okay, I'll—I'll talk to him."

"You better."

* * *

Dovid Rosenstein: Hey, Sam! Could we talk?

Sam Doyle: Of course. What's up?

Dovid Rosenstein: I mean talk talk. On the phone. If that's cool with you?

Sam swallowed, but made himself call Dovid's number.

"Sam! Hey."

"Hi, Dovid. How're you doing?"

"Really good now that, uh, now that I'm talking to you."

"Oh."

"Yeah. I got your message. I—I'm glad you liked the video."

Sam tried for a smile. Dovid sounded about as nervous as Sam felt. Why? "I really did! It's amazing how many people talk to you from all over the world. And it's so interesting. I feel like I learn a dozen more neat facts about you every time I watch another one of your videos."

"I'm glad. And, uh, about what else you said. My being happy? Yeah, I was happy. I was really happy. Because you were watching me."

Sam's breath caught. "Dovid—"

"I was talking about you. In—in the video. I was talking about you."

Sam opened his mouth, but couldn't manage a sound. He squeezed his eyes shut, overwhelmed by those words. Dovid loved him. Dovid loved *him*. Dovid thought Sam was someone worth loving.

"Sam? Sam, please say something." Dovid's voice was small and afraid, and Sam never wanted him to sound like that ever again.

"I—" He still didn't know what to say. "I was hoping you were," he blurted out. "But I wasn't sure and I didn't want to assume."

"Well. Now you're not assuming. Because I'm telling you. It—it doesn't bother you?" A pause, followed by, "You...you were hoping I was?"

"Yes," Sam said. Easily. It was easy to say it aloud, now that he knew Dovid felt the same way. "Yes, of course. Dovid, you're wonderful. I said it before, that anyone would be lucky to have you. I meant it then. I mean it now. The thought that you like me makes me so happy. I don't—I don't know what I can say."

"Oh god, you just said so much. I'm really happy. I'm so, so happy."

Sam knew his smile was watery when he said, "I'm so glad."

"Yeah. Yeah I..."

"Yes?"

"I wish I could see you," Dovid said quietly.

Sam was about to say *you can* or offer to Skype when he remembered why Dovid couldn't.

"What else could I do?" he asked.

"What do you mean?"

"So you could see me. Without, um, actually seeing me. How would you like to—I could do something. If you wanted. I'm not quite sure what but—erm. I'd try?"

Dovid laughed. "God, I lo-like you so much. Honestly, if we were any closer it would be touching. That's one of the ways I see. Um, scent too. People smell different. Their natural odors, their shampoos, body wash, deodorant, if they wear aftershave or perfume. Rachel always smells like coconut and tea tree oil."

"I wear a cologne," Sam said. "Um. I could…send you some?"

"What, really?"

"I mean, if that's not too weird."

"No, no, that would be awesome. Actually, uh—" He cut himself off. "No, nevermind, sorry."

"Don't apologize. You haven't even asked anything. Go ahead."

"I…" Dovid sounded flustered. It was cute. "If you have maybe, um. A shirt? That you don't mind, um, parting with? Like an old one."

"I have sleep shirts," Sam said. "Would that work? I could send you one."

"Fuck, you mean it?"

"Of course I do. I wouldn't have offered if I weren't sure." He hesitated before adding, "And to be quite honest, I, ah, very much enjoy the idea of you in one of my shirts."

"Fuck."

"Was that alright to say?" Sam asked uneasily. "I don't want to make you uncomfortable—"

"You have no fucking idea what you do to me," Dovid said. "Believe me, the last thing that sentence did was make me uncomfortable. I love the idea of wearing one of your shirts. Please send me one. I'll text you my address."

"Alright."

"If—if you don't mind sharing your own address, I could send you one of mine too."

"Oh," Sam said. "I think I'd like that very much."

* * *

"I told you so," Rachel crowed. "Did I not tell you so?"

"Yes," Dovid said happily. "You absolutely did. You were right. You were so right. I can't believe it. He likes me back."

"He likes you back."

"He's going to send me one of his shirts," he said gleefully.

"Dovid." Rachel came up to him and clapped him on the shoulder. "I am very happy for you. When he eventually visits, let me know so I can say hi in person, and then go visit Mom and Dad for a week."

"What? Why?"

"Because you'll want to pound him into the mattress or vice versa, and I refuse to be around to listen to that through the bedroom walls."

"Oh my god, *Rachel*."

"What? Is it not true?"

"No, it actually *isn't*. I don't even know if Sam is sexual. I didn't ask. And it's never come up in his videos."

"Huh. That's a tricky question to ask too. Not everyone goes around wearing buttons."

"Not to mention I can't see the buttons. But no, yeah, I… It won't be an issue for probably a long time." As much as it sucked, Dovid didn't exactly have any plans to go to Ireland anytime soon, and he wasn't about to ask Sam to come to Seattle for a visit. Even if Dovid really wanted to be able to be with Sam in person. Just to touch him. Hold his hand.

Kiss him, if Sam was into that.

"Alright, I have no idea where you went," Rachel said, "but come back down to earth. We have social media to attend to."

"Fine, fine."

* * *

Sam Doyle: Good morning! I hope you're doing well. I just wanted to let you know that I got your package. Thank you so much! I wasn't expecting quite so many things, but the candies and snacks all look very interesting.

Sam Doyle: And the shirt is perfect, thank you. It obviously doesn't fit quite right (I'm afraid I'm rather tall and gangly), but it's really soft, so it's nice to sleep in.

Dovid grinned.

Dovid Rosenstein: Hey! Glad you liked the care package. I woke up in YOUR shirt this morning, which was basically the best. And that's interesting to know you're tall! I never actually asked before, what you look like.

Sam Doyle: Oh, well, I could describe myself? If you wanted.

Dovid Rosenstein: Oh yeah, please :)

Sam Doyle: Alright. Well, as I said, I'm quite tall. 189 centimeters. Long-limbed, you know. My mum always used to say I was all elbows and knees. I never quite grew out of that stage.

Dovid Rosenstein: Okay, I just googled the conversion and wow, you're 6'2"? I'm only 5'10".

Sam Doyle: Oh yes, I remember you saying. But that's still tall!

Dovid Rosenstein: Haha, don't worry, I've never cared about my height. Rachel's only 5'6", and she's forever going on about how unfair that is. Anyway, keep going?

Sam Doyle: Okay, well, um, I'm a redhead. Which I understand is so ridiculously stereotypical, but there it is. I'm clean-shaven, because I look abysmal with a beard. And I'm absolutely covered in freckles. I spend three minutes out in the sun and there always seems to be more of them. My ears stick out a bit—they're rather big.

Sam Doyle: I'm not all that much to look at, to be honest.

Dovid Rosenstein: I have a hard time believing that. But also, like, guess how much that matters to me?

Sam Doyle: It doesn't bother you? I mean, even if you can't see me, most other people can.

Dovid was suddenly furious. For Sam to react like that, someone must have obviously said something to him. Maybe when he was younger, or recently, and maybe more than once. And that was just so patently unfair.

Dovid Rosenstein: Fuck 'em. You're amazing, and you're beautiful. Am I not allowed to have an opinion, just because I can't see?

Sam Doyle: No, no, of course not. I'm so sorry, I didn't mean to imply your opinion wasn't important. Of course it is. I—you're right. Actually, your opinion is rather the most important one.

Sam Doyle: It IS important to me. I'm sorry.

Dovid Rosenstein: No, it's okay. It's okay. I'm sorry. I didn't mean to, like, come off all aggressive. That wasn't aimed at you. I'm just, I don't know, mad on your behalf.

Sam Doyle: But why?

Dovid Rosenstein: Because it sounds like someone, at some point, told you you weren't attractive. And that's just not true. Even if I cared about looks (which, surprise, I don't), I'm already attracted to you. Just because of who you are. I'm attracted to you, so you're attractive. Boom. Done.

Dovid Rosenstein: … Sorry, I didn't mean to get weird on you.

Sam Doyle: No, ah, that was beautiful. It's a little odd to hear it being said about me, but thank you. I mean it.

Dovid Rosenstein: How about I just keep telling you that until you get used to it :)

Sam Doyle: I'm blushing right now, so you know.

Dovid Rosenstein: Yeah? Oh, oh, you're a redhead— does that mean your blushes stand out more? Do your cheeks go all hot when you blush? I need to know this. For science.

Sam Doyle: I never thought about it. I... I suppose it's fairly obvious when I blush, yes. I get all red. It's very embarrassing.

Dovid Rosenstein: Nooo, don't be embarrassed! It's cute.

Sam Doyle: Haha, if you say so.

Dovid Rosenstein: I mean it. You're so cute. I kind of want to kiss your whole face.

Then he cursed. Idiot.

Dovid Rosenstein: But like, only consensual kissing, duh. And it's cool if you don't like kissing! I'm also big on holding hands. And hugs. I'm kind of hugely tactile? But if you're not that's okay too. And I guess it doesn't really matter a whole bunch right now considering we're a continent apart. Just, whatever you want and are comfortable with. Seriously, I'll be happy enough just talking to you.

Which was another example of just how much Dovid liked Sam. Because he *was* hugely tactile (and very sexual). But if Sam wasn't...

For Sam, Dovid would take that and be okay.

Fuck, he was so in *love*.

Dovid Rosenstein: Sorry, went a bit on a ramble there, haha. Feel free to ignore me.

Sam Doyle: No, no! Sorry I might have gotten stuck there, a little. I'm not entirely sure how to respond.

Sam Doyle: Also I'm blushing quite a lot now, I think.

Dovid Rosenstein: Hey, hey, it's okay. If you don't have anything to say, or don't know what to say, or don't want to say anything, that's cool. I just wanted to lay my cards on the table. Again, not that it matters super much right now but uh. I'm thinking that maybe, in the long-term, we'd meet up.

Sam Doyle: Oh, that would be wonderful!

Sam Doyle: I'd like to think we would be long-term too.

Sam Doyle: And I...about the rest of it. Um.

Dovid Rosenstein: It's alright, really. You don't have to say anything.

Sam Doyle: I want to though. I'm just unsure as to how to phrase it. But I suppose just coming out with it is the best thing to do.

Dovid Rosenstein: I'm all ears, whatever you want to say.

It took almost three minutes before Sam's next message came through.

Sam Doyle: I, um, I haven't done very much at all, I'm afraid. I don't have a lot of experience at all, really. And I know you do, that you've said as much in your videos. And that that's important to you in a relationship. And so I admit that I'm just, you know, wondering a little bit about how not to be a disappointment in the event we do meet up, because that's the last thing I'd want to be.

Oh. Wow.
There was a lot to extrapolate from that.
But first off, he wanted to nip something in the bud.

Dovid Rosenstein: Okay, one, that is not a disappointment. That would never be a disappointment. YOU are not a disappointment, no matter what your experience is. All that means is we'd get to experiment and figure out what you'd like :)

Dovid Rosenstein: If you like anything at all. And if you don't, that's okay too.

Sam Doyle: No, well, I, I do like holding hands. (Goodness that sounds so childish to say.)

Dovid Rosenstein: Hey no. It's sweet. And that can be really intimate.

Dovid Rosenstein: I pretty much like all physical contact. I'd really like to hold your hand :)

Sam Doyle: You are not making this blushing business any better, I hope you know.

Dovid Rosenstein: :) :) :)

Dovid Rosenstein: But seriously, that's a good place to start. Whatever comes after—IF anything comes after—you don't have to worry about that now.

Sam Doyle: Thank you.

Dovid Rosenstein: Of course.

Sam Doyle: I think I'd like to, you know.

Dovid Rosenstein: Like to what?

Sam Doyle: Kiss you.

Dovid bit his lip and tried to keep his breathing even.

Dovid Rosenstein: Well then. One day we'll figure out how to make that happen.

* * *

Dovid Rosenstein: Are you still awake?

Sam Doyle: Yes.

Dovid Rosenstein: Could I call?

Sam Doyle: Please do :)

"Hey you," Dovid said quietly, once Sam picked up the phone. "Sorry I called so late."

"It's okay," Sam replied. "I wasn't asleep yet, just—"

"Reading?"

Sam laughed. "I'm not going to change anytime soon, am I?"

"Please don't. I like you."

"Well then. I'll endeavor to keep at it. Anyway, how did filming go?"

"Pretty good. We decided to do the food truck tour. What with the weather getting warmer, more of them

are out. Rachel and I ate so much food. Rachel's coma-
ing it out while I talk to you. We'll be hitting the editing hard in an hour or so."

"So I get you for a whole hour?"

"How about you get me until you fall asleep. It's
eleven-thirty for you, right?"

"Maybe."

"Sam, you need to be going to bed earlier. You always say you're wiped in the morning."

"But if I go to bed earlier, sometimes I miss talking to you," Sam pointed out. "You can't always be
free at eleven in the morning. It's the middle of the
day for you."

Dovid sounded decidedly grumpy when he said, "I'd
make the time."

"Oh stop, that's not fair to you. If I weren't talking
to you on the phone, I'd be up just as late reading anyway. And, frankly, you're more important to me than a
book, no matter how exciting it is."

"Aw."

Sam smiled. "You know I mean it."

A sigh. "Yeah. How are your ribs doing today?"

"Much better! I'm only taking my pain medication
to sleep now, because lying down still hurts. But they're
well on their way to being fully healed. They barely
bother me at work, sitting at my desk."

"I'm glad."

Sam chuckled. "Me too, believe me. So that's what
your plan is for the rest of the day? Editing?"

"Mm-hm. Though a nap might be in order for me
too, honestly."

"Oh dear, why are you so tired?"

"Just woke up early after a late night, is all. Sometimes my body hates me." Right, Dovid had mentioned

that once in a while he just woke up really early for no reason, and nothing could get him to fall back asleep again. He mostly dealt with it by taking naps.

"Well then, you've certainly deserved a nap too," Sam said.

"Can I tell you something?"

"Of course."

"I took a leaf out of your book; I'm already in bed."

Sam grinned. "So if we close our eyes, we can just imagine we're lying next to each other."

There was a quiet gasp, followed by a shaky, "Y-yeah. Yeah, we could. And I don't even have to close my eyes."

"There you go," Sam said softly. The conversation felt light and easy, but with a distinct sleepy haze. Intimate, in a way yesterday's more awake conversation wasn't. "I'm just there, right next to you."

Another gasp. "Yeah?"

"Mm-hm." Alighting on an idea, he added, "You can feel it, can't you? Me reaching out to touch you?"

There was a sharp intake of breath. "Wh-where?"

"Your cheek, I think. Just softly. And then your arm, so you could feel I was there."

A noise that sounded like a whimper. "Then what?"

Sam thought about it. "I think I'd curl my fingers around yours. Pull in you close. I'd—I'd like to hold you."

"Fuck," Dovid whispered in Sam's ear.

Pleased, he continued. "You'd like that? Like me holding you?"

"Sam." The word sounded punched out. "Fuck, Sam, yes. So much."

"We'd fall asleep like that," Sam murmured. "Wrapped around each other. I'd press a kiss to your hair before we both drifted off."

A quiet sound, almost a sob. "I wish you were really here."

Sam stared up at his ceiling. He could picture it; holding Dovid close. His long limbs would actually be good for something, being able to wrap around the man he loved. Besides, touching meant so much to Dovid, and Sam only wanted to give him everything he could. "So do I."

Chapter Eight

"Hey!" Dovid said, when he answered his phone. "What's up?" He sounded a little breathless. Sam tried to push down feeling guilty at having interrupted something. If Dovid had been too busy to answer Sam's call, he wouldn't have done so.

"Nothing much," Sam told him, feeling a bit shy. "I just wanted to say hello." He'd been trying to think more, lately, about what he could do and offer on his end. They were already so far apart it was difficult to come up with ideas aside from sending mail, but Dovid enjoyed talking with him, and of course Sam did too, and thinking back over their conversations, Dovid started quite a lot of them.

So Sam had decided to reach out more often. He loved talking to Dovid anyway, so it wasn't exactly a hardship. Especially since he *knew* he wasn't being a bother. Dovid loved talking to Sam just as much. Had, in fact, made it quite clear.

It was very nice, to know that.

It made Sam feel brave.

"I'm so not complaining about you calling me just to say hi," Dovid said, sounding like he was grinning. "What were you up to?"

"Just finishing up exercising. I slept in today, so I've been moving a little slower than usual."

Sam frowned, concerned. "Did you have more trouble sleeping?"

"Nah, just the opposite. I think, you know, my body was just trying to catch up on some sleep that I've been missing."

"Oh. Alright. I'm glad you were able to get some more sleep in, then."

Dovid chuckled. "Thanks. How was work? Not too bad today, I hope?"

"Oh, it was fine," Sam said lightly.

"Sam."

"I just mean, ah, it was only the usual sort of awful. Nothing out of the ordinary."

A sigh. "You have no idea how often I wish you were able to say 'good' and not be lying about it."

"It's alright," Sam tried to assure him. "I get through it, and then I come home. It's not so bad."

It was funny though, how it had been getting harder lately. Before Sam had met Dovid, he was content to come home to his books and games. He dreaded getting out of bed, and possibly avoided going to sleep because it meant morning—and thus work—would be coming sooner, but it was tolerable enough. What else would he be doing with his life, after all?

Now he couldn't help but spend the time at work wishing he were doing other things, because he *had* other things to do. Planning ideas for his channel, making more videos, talking to Dovid. He'd become a lot more active on Twitter, and even was doing a little more fan interaction.

It was just something else that had been on his mind.

* * *

"Dovid," Rachel said, knocking on his door, "Dovid, did you check your email in the last ten minutes?"

"Um, no?" He didn't lift his head. "I've been making another song for our video? Why would I be checking my email?"

"Because it's *important.*"

"And? Care to elaborate?"

"Okay, so you know how we did that tour last year, across America?"

"Yeah…" They'd hit LA, Dallas, Chicago, Detroit, and Boston. It'd been a whirlwind of traveling and plane trips, Airbnbs and reviews, and videos. Editing it all had taken them ages, and that was with trying to release a couple videos on the actual road. "Why?"

"Airbnb offered the same type of package again, for a Europe tour."

Dovid shot to his feet. "Excuse me?"

"You. Me. Expenses paid Europe tour. In a month, for two weeks."

"Are you shitting me right now?"

"Are you kidding? Do you even know how excited I am? Do you know how much *stuff* we'll get to see? And do? And eat?"

Dovid turned to her, mind whirling, already planning out videos in his head. "What are the stops?"

"Norway for three days, Germany for two, France for two, England for three, Ireland for two. I'm not sure about the exact order but—"

"Hold up," Dovid said, freezing. "Ireland?"

The grin he heard in Rachel's voice was wicked. "You heard me."

"What—when?"

"July. So just under a month. Think that's enough

time to plan things out with Sam? I bet we could swing it to make Ireland our last stop. Maybe stay a few extra days, if we spring for the return trips and the Airbnb ourselves…"

Dovid could have kissed her. "You are a genius and I love you."

"I know, but feel free to remind me."

"Okay, okay. We've got to figure out a plan, get the full itinerary, see what they want from us in terms of plugs, start scheduling meetups and meetup locations…"

"I'm already in the living room with my laptop and a notebook. Come on."

Dovid followed her out of his room.

* * *

Dovid Rosenstein: You are not going to believe this.

Sam Doyle: What is it?

Dovid Rosenstein: I'm coming to Ireland in July.

Sam Doyle: Oh my goodness! Really??

Dovid Rosenstein: Told you you weren't going to believe it. But yeah—Rachel and I get sponsor videos every so often. Some are pretty standard, like reviewing a restaurant or a blind box, but others are bigger. Airbnb sponsored us to go on a tour last September, for meetups and room reviews and stuff, and they sometimes do "Spend a week in such-and-such" deals. It looks like they want us to do another tour, but for Europe this time.

Dovid Rosenstein: Ireland is our last stop too. So even though we're only supposed to stay there for a couple days with our hosts, Rachel and I could extend our stay. Make some more videos there.

Dovid Rosenstein: Give me more time to spend with you. If you wanted.

Sam Doyle: Dovid, of course I want to. Do you know what dates yet? I could come to your meetup and then...maybe we could spend time together after. Depending how long you stayed.

Dovid Rosenstein: For Ireland we're flying in Tuesday night, going out to dinner with our hosts, the meetup Wednesday evening after an Ireland day, having another Ireland Day Thursday, and then flying out Friday morning. But Rachel and I were thinking that we could stay through the weekend instead and leave Monday. Maybe...maybe longer, but I know you work and I don't want to have you try to take days off if that would cause trouble for you.

Sam Doyle: No, no, I could try to get Monday and Tuesday off. It's still a month in advance. I don't know if I'd be able to get it, since I was already out a week with my ribs, but I would absolutely ask.

Sam Doyle: It'd be worth it, to me. After all, it'd be my first time actually getting to meet you in person. That's a big deal! And I'd want it to last as long as it can.

Dovid Rosenstein: Yeah, me too.

* * *

"Hey, guys, this is Don't Look Now, with Dovid and Rachel. I'm Dovid, Rachel's behind the camera, and today we're going to be talking to you about our video tour!"

Dovid grinned wide and sat back in his chair. "Airbnb has been kind enough to sponsor a trip to Europe. Yeah, I know, right? If some of you remember, we went before a couple of years ago for that conference thing in Sweden, but this time we're doing a full out-and-out stay at a bunch of different places. We'll be talking about where we stay, all the food we're going to eat, and, of course, accessibility while traveling. Not to mention that we're going to have an official meetup at every place we go."

He went on to talk about the stops on the trip, the places for the meetup and meetup dates. "All the information is also going to go up on our website, and that's where you can buy tickets to each meetup. As always, half the proceeds of ticket sales goes to charity, and the charity we're supporting this trip is the Hadley Institute. We're looking forward to seeing you all! Well. Sort of seeing, duh."

"Vid."

"Rachel."

"If you're allowed to make the same dumb jokes twelve million times, I'm allowed to make mine."

Dovid sighed. "Anyway, stay tuned for more information about the trip and videos of us getting ready—because I know you like our packing videos. I am so excited to visit Europe again, and to meet all of you. Of course, we're going to be making videos the entire time we're there, and will try to release at least one or two depending on how jet-lagged we are. Anyway, don't forget to follow Don't Look Now on social media—links in the description box below. And as always guys, see you later! Well, I won't, but you know what I mean."

Rachel let out an excited squeal once she (presumably) turned the camera off. "I can't believe it, we're actually doing this."

"We were actually doing this since we found out about it three days ago."

"Yeah, but now we've filmed the video. It's really real."

Dovid beamed. "Yeah."

"I want to edit it right now. No harm in slapping it up early."

"Oh yeah, for sure. And the sooner we tell people, the sooner they can start planning too." The tickets were already up for sale on their website, had been since that morning once they'd clinched the meetup places, and it would only be a matter of time before the news spread. Better to let everyone know official details sooner over later, even though the explanations were on the website too.

* * *

The news spread like wildfire once the video went live, and England and Germany sold out in two days, Norway, France, and Ireland, not very far behind. It was really real, and it was really happening, and Europe was going to be *amazing*.

And Ireland was their last stop. Sam had gotten Monday off (not Tuesday, but it was fine, that was fine), and Dovid was so excited he could explode. He and Sam talked pretty much nonstop, in between Dovid making videos and Sam working. They texted through the day, and called each other when they could and that was amazing too.

* * *

"I bought a ticket," Sam said, smile evident in his voice. "For your meetup."

"What? Why? I—you didn't have to—I was just going to have you come. I thought you knew that."

"Well, I wanted to make sure I had one. I didn't want to take someone else's seat; they were selling out so fast. Besides, it's for a good cause. And I want to support you."

"Okay," Dovid said after a minute. "Okay. Thank you. I—you still didn't have to, because I was going to get you in, but thank you."

Sam chuckled. "You're welcome."

"So what else did you do today?"

"Oh, well, actually, I found something very interesting to read? Although a bit…erm…"

"What? What is it?"

"Did you know there's fanfiction about us?" Sam blurted out.

"What!" Dovid yelped. "You found that?"

"So you did know, I'm guessing."

"Uh, well, yeah. It's—sorry, I know it's a little weird. But people have been writing fanfiction about me for years. I get paired up with a bunch of different people. Rachel thinks it's hilarious." She also avoided stories about herself like they were the plague, which, at least, gave Dovid some revenge fodder. Especially since she had, recently, brought "Dovid (Don't Look Now)/Playit-againsam (Video Blogging RPF)" to Dovid's attention. *("Look, there's one where he's a barista at a coffee shop! Whoa, it was released two months ago and it's got like fifteen hundred kudos."*

"Please stop talking.")

"There's a website that has over four hundred stories that feature Dovid from Don't Look Now and Sam the Let's Player," Sam said. "My brother found it through Tumblr."

"Oh my god, I am so sorry."

"It's perfectly alright! Just a little odd. He promised

he hadn't actually read any of it, which I was quite relieved by."

"No, yeah, that is a dangerous road to go down. I've read a little bit, sometimes for the camera, but yeah, don't do that to yourself."

"Don't worry, I'd be much too embarrassed to read anything that starred me in it. Besides, some of them are, ah, very highly rated? In terms of graphic detail. Apparently. There's a whole rating system. They range from G to quite explicit."

"Sam, Sam, please back away from Archive of Our Own and don't look back."

"Oh, you know this website, then?"

Dovid sighed. "Yeah, I do. And I know about those stories too. Every so often I check, just to know what's been happening. And fans also *tell* me sometimes. Boundaries are kind of loose, for some of them. But really, it's a path you don't want to go down."

Besides, it was absolutely unfair that fans got to write about Dovid with Sam while Dovid wasn't able to actually do anything.

Though that would be changing in a couple of weeks.

* * *

"This is so cool," Dovid enthused. "I'm calling you at nine on a Saturday and there's only an hour time difference instead of eight. It's *morning* for both of us. I mean, I'm still jet-lagged out of my mind, so it sort of feels like I've been up way too late, but my point stands."

Sam laughed. He had such a nice laugh, and Dovid loved how often he got to hear it now. "I almost can't believe it. I see you so soon. You don't even know how happy I am. People at work think I'm absolutely manic, I've been so giddy."

"I can take a guess at how happy you are, because

I'm so excited I might pop. I mean, Norway was fantastic and Germany is amazing so far, but I am really, really, really looking forward to Ireland."

"I'm looking forward to you being in Ireland too. Funny, that."

I love you. No, it was still too soon to say it out loud. Even if they'd been talking for months, even if it had been mentioned that one time on his channel, even if Rachel already knew, Dovid didn't want to freak Sam out. Maybe he could say it when they finally met in person. That was probably for the best. He'd held it in this long.

They were just so *close.*

Dovid cleared his throat. "Yeah. So what have you got going on today?"

"Not much. Just doing some chores about the place. Cleaning up, doing laundry, you know, the mundane things."

"Making it nice for me when I come by?" Dovid teased. "You know I can't see the mess."

"Oh, I know," Sam said, "But I want to make it as easy as I can for you to get around. I've just been moving furniture about, in case you're able to pop by."

Dovid almost choked. "Sam, you—you don't have to rearrange your apartment for me." That was too much. God, how did Sam always manage to make Dovid like him more every day. "I'm sure I'll be fine figuring it out, with some help. Besides, what about your ribs?"

"Those have been better for ages, you know that. It's no trouble, really. I know how you like to be independent. And rightly so. So if there's anything I can do to make that more possible, I want to. Besides, it's actually quite fun; I haven't redecorated in a long time, and this is giving me a chance to figure out a new layout. I'm learning how to make a lot more space."

"If, uh, if you're sure."

"Oh, definitely. Now then, what's in the cards for you today?"

"It's a Germany day. We're doing the meetup tomorrow afternoon, so today our hosts are taking us around to a couple of different tourist places and restaurants. Rachel and I are making sure we get to the Holocaust Memorial. We're not sure if we're going to be making a video about it or not though. Our fans all know we're Jewish and stuff, and the memorial is something we've both been talking about for a long time, way before this tour, but it's a pretty serious topic. And we'd want to treat it with the solemnity it deserves. I'm not sure how I feel about us filming there."

"Maybe for that you could just do a talking vlog, instead of one where you film at the site," Sam suggested. "Because you're right, if it's an important topic and means a lot to you, you should absolutely share that with your viewers if you want to. Just maybe a short video of how it made you two feel?"

"Yeah, maybe. I mean…we're fifth generation on my dad's side, but only second gen on my mom's. Her parents came over to escape from the Holocaust. My, um, my grandfather survived one of the camps. He's got the numbers on his arm and everything." One of the big, few regrets that Dovid had about not being able to see. But sometimes, when he held his grandfather's hand, he could almost feel the ink, with how heavy it was.

"Wow," Sam said quietly. "That's a big, personal connection for you."

"Yeah. And we've talked about serious topics before on the channel."

"Then absolutely. And you don't even have to release it as part of the tour videos. You could always make it and put it up later on."

"That's a good idea. Maybe, like, wait a month."

"Right," Sam said, sounding encouraging. "Do that."

"I'll talk about it with Rachel. Thank you."

"Of course."

"Dovid! Come on!"

"Speaking of Rachel, I think she's about to kick my door in," Dovid said, disappointed. "We're meeting our hosts for filming at this local breakfast place."

Sam chuckled. "By all means, don't keep her waiting."

"Yeah…"

"Dovid."

"Yeah?"

"It's Saturday, and we're only an hour apart. You can call me anytime today. And we can also text, if you can't call. I'll be able to answer right away, since I won't be at work."

Dovid perked up. He'd almost forgotten. "Right! Yeah, I—"

"Doviiiiiiiid."

"Shit, I've got to go. I'll talk to you later. Love you!" He hung up. And only then did he register what he'd said.

Rachel finally burst into the room to find Dovid clutching his phone, focused on nothing.

"Dovid, you ready? I gave you ages to talk to Sam. Come on, we don't want to keep our hosts waiting."

"Right," Dovid said faintly. He'd said it. He hadn't meant to say it, but he'd absolutely meant it.

And now he had a full morning of filming, and his next break probably wouldn't be until at least eleven.

Fuck.

He hoped Sam wouldn't mind. Dovid didn't need him to say it back, just—Dovid was that kind of person. He said what he felt. It worked well for camera! And he'd said it on camera before, that he was in love. But he hadn't actually said the words *to Sam*. It was a conclusion that Sam probably had come to though. Maybe?

Sam was so, so important to him. Dovid was in deep here. That's why he kept second-guessing himself.

"Dovid? What's the matter?"

Dovid shook his head. *Knock it off.* He'd talk to Sam like an actual adult person, and they'd talk this out. Now wasn't crisis time, it was work time. "Nothing. Let's go."

* * *

If Sam didn't stop smiling, his head was going to pop off. He squeezed his eyes shut, playing the words over and over in his head. Dovid loved him. Dovid loved him. He'd *said* it. To *Sam*. Not being cheeky to an audience of viewers, but to Sam. And he'd—he'd said it so matter-of-fact, like it was natural. Like it was only natural that he loved Sam.

He went through the next fifteen minutes in a happy haze before he froze in realization.

He hadn't said it back.

Oh no, he hadn't—Dovid had hung up before Sam had been able to reply. Clearly that needed to be remedied. But should he just send a text? That didn't seem good enough. Dovid had said it aloud, Sam wanted to do the same. But Dovid was filming now, and Sam didn't know his schedule. While Sam had nothing pressing to do today, Dovid was working and it was his schedule that would dictate when they next spoke.

Hm.

Sam Doyle: Hey there. Give me a call when you can? I have something to say, and I'd rather do it over the phone instead of with text.

There now, that would work, wouldn't it? When Dovid called, Sam could tell him he loved him back.

Still beaming, Sam went to mess around with his furniture a bit more.

* * *

When filming was over for the time being and they had done their teardown, Dovid excused himself from his hosts for a minute so he could check if he'd gotten a message from Sam—or so he could send one himself. When he plugged in an earbud to hear what Sam had written, he had to swallow hard. Sam had something he wanted to say over the phone. That—that couldn't be bad, could it? Of course not. Neither had done anything to make this a bad phone call. Dovid hoped. He had, after all, used the L-word directly but...

He hadn't thought Sam would *care*.

No, he was being stupid. He was twisting himself into knots over nothing. He didn't have to wait hours to get a reply from Sam and stew, he could literally call him right now.

So, he did, waiting nervously while the phone rang.

"Dovid!" At least Sam sounded pleased. "How did filming go?"

"Really well," Dovid said trying for a smile. "I'm so full now. We tried like five different dishes. I see what the fuss is about German sausage."

"Good, I'm glad you had fun."

"Yeah. We're going to go to the next location soon so I can't talk for very long, but, uh, you wanted to say something?"

"Yes! Only I wanted to tell you that I love you too. Since you hung up before I was able to say it back."

Dovid couldn't breathe. He'd hoped, he'd *hoped* but hearing it was...

Wow, it was something else.

"Dovid? Are you there?" Now Sam sounded uneasy. "Was it alright for me to say that?"

Dovid hurried to say, "No! I mean yes. Yes, of course, god, of course it's okay. I'm—wow. Wow, um." He laughed, half nervous, half so happy he could barely think. "Wow."

* * *

"Hello, everybody, I'm Sam, and welcome to another episode of Let's Play Dire Straits. Now, I'm sure some of you are wondering about why this video is being up-loaded on a Tuesday of all times, instead of this Friday. Well, that's because I'm having some friends visit from out of town, and I wanted to make sure to have all the time to spend with them that I could. I've been looking forward to this visit for quite some time, you see, and they've traveled a long way to come to Ireland.

"Anyway, that's my explanation. Though you didn't come to my channel for that, you came for Dire Straits. So back to business, when we last left off..."

Once his video was done and rendering he turned his phone back on.

Dovid Rosenstein: Plane landed safely! Shortest plane trip of my life. Now we're out to dinner. I'll call you when we're at the Airbnb?

Sam Doyle: Please do. I'll look forward to it.

He was still a little sad that he hadn't been able to go meet Dovid at the airport, but Dovid had told him just how much of a crowd there would be and that he and Rachel would mostly be hustled to a waiting car. But it was fine. It gave him time to record his video tonight.

Dovid's phone call came just as Sam's video went live.

"Hey you," Dovid said, voice warm. "How've things been?"

"Very nice," Sam told him. "Quiet, but I like the quiet." And it was good that everything around him was relaxing, because he felt he was about to rattle out of his skin. "Did you have a nice dinner?"

"Yeah. They took us out to a pub, and we filmed. Surprise." A laugh. "We're basically always filming."

"It's your job, as much as IT is mine."

"Yeah. Well. Don't worry, being with you, the camera is definitely staying off. In part because Rachel won't be following us around the whole time. I mean you'll get to meet her, obviously, but yeah. She's pretty adamant that we get alone time."

"I'm looking forward to meeting her. But I'll admit I'm looking forward to meeting you more."

"Aw. I am so looking forward to meeting you. Tomorrow. I can't believe it's tomorrow. I get to touch you *tomorrow*."

"I can't wait," Sam told him honestly. "I wish I didn't have to work, so I could see you before the meetup."

"I know, I know. But still—you'll come and see me actually do my stuff live, and then after the crowd leaves you'll stay and we'll actually be able to *talk* and—god I can't believe it."

"Are you really sure you won't want to go out to dinner afterwards?" Dovid, instead of planning to go to a restaurant or pub, had decided to have dinner in, with Sam, at the Airbnb.

While Rachel went out on her own with their hosts to dinner.

"Are you kidding? And miss out on getting to have you to myself? Rachel volunteered to leave us alone but if she hadn't I probably would have blacklisted her."

Sam had to laugh. "Alright, if you're sure."

"I am so fucking sure."

* * *

Dovid was almost finished setting up at the meetup location when his WhatsApp rang with Sam's ringtone. Beaming, he answered his phone. "Hey, Sam! We're almost done and should be letting the crowd in soon. I can't wait to see you."

"Dovid! I'm so sorry." Sam sounded panicked. "I'm so sorry. I got home from work and tried to get ready for your meetup and I just—the thought of so many people—I—I'm so sorry. I haven't even left my flat yet. I'm going to be late. I'm sorry."

Dovid tried to shove down the disappointment, in lieu of helping Sam calm down. "It's okay. Really. I get that the crowd is a lot for you. Are you, um, are you sure you'll be able to come?"

"I…" Sam did not sound any less panicked. "I—I can. I want to. I can."

"Sam, it's really okay. There are going to be a lot of people, and it's going to be loud and a little chaotic and not at all quiet or zen. It'd be really out of your comfort zone."

A shaky breath. "Yes. Oh I *know*. But—but I still, I'm sure if I—"

Dovid desperately wanted Sam there. To see Dovid live and in his element. To be there so Dovid could see him as soon as possible.

But Dovid wanted Sam comfortable more than anything else. "Sam, don't come. It's fine."

"No, it's alright, I—I know you wanted me to come."

Dovid raked a hand through his hair. "Yeah, I did.
But not if it freaks you out. I don't want that to be how
we meet for the first time. Besides, I'll be hanging out
with you after anyway, right?"

"R-right."

"There you go. How about this: you know how we
made plans to go back to where I'm staying together,
for dinner?"

"Yes. Yes, of course."

"How about I just give you the address direct, and
you can meet me there when I'm done? You can bring
dinner, just pick whatever you want. Deal?"

"Alright," Sam said sounding, at last, much calmer.
"Deal. But I'm still so sorry."

"I know, and it's okay." It was worth it, for Sam to
feel at ease. "I'll get to see you soon anyway."

"Yes. Right." And then, adamantly, "I love you. I'll
see you soon."

Just like that, Dovid was pumped again. "Love you
too."

* * *

"Hey, guys! This is Don't Look Now with Dovid and
Rachel! I'm Dovid, Rachel is right here next to me, and
welcome to our Ireland meetup!"

The crowd roared, and Dovid basked in it, grinning
his head off as he encouraged them to make some more
noise.

In the back of his mind, he was relieved Sam hadn't
come. People in general made Sam nervous, but he'd
mentioned a few times how he was "slightly bothered"
by crowds especially, particularly noisy ones. He'd said

it in the same offhand way Sam used to downplay all the things that made him unhappy or caused him distress, which meant it was worth paying attention to. This would probably have terrified him.

And anyway, this way Dovid was going to meet him in person while also getting to have him all to himself.

Chapter Nine

Dovid was unaccountably nervous when his hosts dropped him off at the place where they were staying.

Rachel walked him inside and gave him a hug. "It'll be great," she told him. "You love him to death already, and it's obvious he's just as crazy about you."

"Right." Dovid ran his fingers through his hair. "It'll be fine."

"It'll be way more than fine. Now stop fussing with your hair. And promise me you won't change, like, twelve times after I leave."

"I won't change twelve times."

"You are allowed to change one time."

"I am allowed to change one time," Dovid repeated. "Oh my god, I'm going to meet him, Rachel. I'm going to *meet* him."

"You are going to meet him, and it'll be great."

Dovid clutched at his face.

Rachel patted him on the shoulder. "Go change and then do something productive until he gets here, okay? Now, I've got to go. I'll be back late. If he's still here when I come back, I expect to be able to meet him, unless you two are already asleep."

Asleep. Asleep together with Sam. Dovid couldn't handle this. "Right. Of course."

"And then I'll meet him tomorrow."

"Right. Yeah."

She hugged him one more time. "Have a great night," she said into his ear. Then she turned and walked away, the door closing and locking behind her.

Dovid stood in the quiet living room and tried not to freak out.

Changing. He was going to change out of the clothes he'd worn for the meetup (one of his Don't Look Now T-shirts) and into something nicer (a soft, red henley that Rachel insisted he looked great in).

He breathed out. Sam had already texted him to say that he was on his way and bringing dinner. Dovid wasn't hungry; he was too nervous. But he had to pass the time somehow.

He set the table, because Sam was bringing dinner and Dovid didn't want to have to fumble with putting out dishes and cutlery while Sam was there. But then he had nothing left to do.

In the end he got his laptop set up in the living room, plugged in an earbud, and did some social media work. Or tried to. His thoughts kept drifting over to Sam, to the point that Dovid went to check his Twitter. Mostly it was about Sam talking about his Tuesday video upload, reminding his fans that there wouldn't be one on Friday this week, and a few tweets here and there about how excited he was to have his friends visiting him. Those made Dovid smile.

And then someone knocked on the door.

Dovid shot to his feet and went over to it. "Who is it?" he asked, surprising himself with how calm he sounded.

"Erm," came a voice that Dovid recognized, that he'd listened to hours of video footage of and, more recently, had spent hours on the phone with. A voice that, this time, was simply behind the barrier of a door, as opposed to hundreds of miles away. "It's Sam. Sam Doyle. I brought dinner?"

Dovid wrenched the door open and smiled, knowing it was probably shaky. "Hey there."

"Hey." It sounded like Sam was smiling too. Dovid could hear the crinkle of plastic bags. "It's...it's good to see you."

"Come in," Dovid said, brain scattered as he backed up. "Come in, um, you can put your stuff down over here." He led Sam to the table, bumping into it with how nervous he was.

"Oh dear, are—are you okay?" Followed by the sound of items being set down.

"Yeah, yeah, I—sorry, I'm just—I'm nervous."

"Me too." It sounded like an admission. "Could I—could I hug you?"

"Please," Dovid breathed, opening his arms.

Sam enveloped him, long arms like Dovid had been told to expect. He smelled like the bottle of cologne Dovid had sitting safely on his nightstand at home, and his shirt was soft and he was so, so warm.

Dovid buried his face in his shirt and hugged back tight. "I can't believe I'm really here with you," he said.

"Neither can I. I—I can't believe it. It's amazing."

A million different thoughts blew through Dovid's mind at what to say to that, and he ended up blurting out, "I like your shirt."

"My shirt?"

Dovid nodded, stroking his hands down the front of it. "It's really soft."

"Oh good," Sam breathed, sounding relieved. "I went through half my closet trying to find the nicest thing

I had to the touch. I know you care about that sort of thing."

Fuck, Dovid wanted so badly to kiss him.

And now...now he could. If Sam wanted.

He pulled back, tilted his face up. "Could I kiss you?"

"Y-yes," Sam said. "Yes, please do. How should I— what would you like?"

"Stay still a minute," Dovid said, moving his hand to Sam's arm and trailing upward, until he reached his shoulder, his neck, his cheek. He felt Sam swallow, take a shuddering breath. "Here," Dovid said, brushing a thumb over Sam's lips. They felt just a bit wet, like Sam had nervously licked them.

Dovid moved to kiss him, slanting their mouths together. He dimly registered Sam's hands at his back, clutching tightly, like Sam couldn't do anything but hang on and kiss and be kissed.

He didn't want to stop. Kissing Sam made his head spin; it was so good, felt so *right*.

"Fuck," he ended up panting, letting his head rest against Sam's chest. "Fuck, can we just do that forever?"

A soft laugh. "I—I might be partial to that. But you should eat. If the video of your last meetup was any indication, you've just had a very exciting few hours."

"Meeting you is what's exciting," Dovid said, but he did reach for Sam's hand and tugged him towards the table. "It all smells really good. What'd you get?"

"Some things from my local pub. Champ, boxty— meat and vegetarian—and some Irish stew for you. I—I can't vouch for the meat things myself, but I've been assured they're quite good. I, erm, I hope you like it."

"Well, it smells fantastic. That's usually a good sign."

They both sat, and Dovid loathed to let go of Sam's hand, but he did what he had to do. Personally, he felt the quicker he ate the quicker he could go back to touching Sam.

"So how was the meetup?" Sam asked, after they'd served themselves.

"It was great," Dovid said. "A lot of great energy. Rachel and I talked about traveling to and around Ireland, and then we did a 'Dovid guesses the object' segment—those are always really popular. Different fans in the crowd brought stuff specifically for it, so we called on people to come on up with their stuff. Some guy brought his pet *skunk*. The crowd went nuts."

"Did that…go well?"

"Oh yeah. It was super well-trained. And really soft. He put it straight into my lap—I thought it was a cat at first. It was really cuddly. That was one of my favorite parts. And after that we did a food tasting. Again, people brought stuff and we called them up from the crowd. Rachel and I both had a lot of fun with that; there was a lot of homemade stuff, which is always cool to try."

"Sounds like it was a lot of fun."

"It was. After was the meet-and-greet. I got a lot of hugs."

"Was that nice?"

Dovid smiled. "Yeah. There were a lot of people who were disabled or otherwise special needs. It's… it's amazing to hear their stories, and to be told that I'm helping them somehow."

Suddenly there was a hand on top of his own. "I'm so glad," Sam said. "That it was so nice for you. I'm… I'm sorry I wasn't able to make it."

Dovid turned his hand so he could link his and Sam's fingers together. "It's really okay. I mean it. There was a lot of people and noise in a really concentrated area." Sam had mentioned several times in both his videos and to Dovid personally how even using public transportation sometimes made him nervous. "I wouldn't have wanted to do that to you."

"Thank you," Sam said quietly.

"Of course."

When they'd finished eating, Dovid gave Sam a quick tour of the apartment, showing him the bedrooms (Rachel had gone on about how cutely they'd been decorated), where the bathroom was, all that stuff. Then they went to sit down on the couch. Dovid was suddenly experiencing butterflies again. He was holding Sam's hand. He was holding Sam's hand and he still wasn't sure if he was really awake or dreaming.

"Hey, Sam?"

"Yes?"

"Remember, uh, that time we were talking on the phone and you—you described how you'd touch me, when we were together?"

"How I'd hold you, you mean?"

Dovid swallowed. "Yeah," he said quietly. "I've... I've been thinking about it a lot. Maybe too much, really, but I—"

"Dovid, no, here. Come with me?"

Dovid held out his hand to be led, and Sam took his arm, slowly and carefully guiding him off the couch and—oh, and back to Dovid's temporary bedroom.

And bed.

"Lie down?"

Practically shaking, Dovid climbed in underneath the covers. A moment later the bed dipped and Sam was sliding in next to him. "Here," Sam said softly. "Face me?"

Dovid turned towards Sam's voice, and then two arms were wrapping around him and pulling him in close. Dovid let out a noise that might have been a whimper and clung on.

A kiss was pressed to his hair. Just like—just like Sam had said he would. "Alright?" Sam asked.

"Yeah," Dovid managed. "Yeah. Perfect."

They lay together like that for a long time. Not even talking, just resting with each other, listening to one another breathe.

Eventually Sam murmured, "I've maybe dreamed about this."

"Yeah?"

"Mm-hm."

Dovid let out a soft laugh. "Me too. Ever since you talked me through it that one time. I went to bed a lot just…thinking about just this."

"Does it live up to expectations?"

"Are you kidding? Way, way better."

"That's gratifying to hear," Sam said, smile in his voice.

"Hey," Dovid shifted a little, moved up. "Could I kiss you? Like this?"

"I'd like that very much," Sam said quietly, hand coming up to cup Dovid's cheek.

Dovid pushed up with one arm, and leaned in, catching the corner of Sam's mouth before moving lower. He moved to kiss under Sam's chin and Sam let out a gasp, his other hand clutching at Dovid's shoulder.

"That okay?" Dovid asked, pulling back just a little bit.

"Y-yes I—it—yes."

"Could I kiss there again? Is that okay?"

"What—whatever you like."

Dovid grinned ruefully. "Don't give me that much power. What would *you* like?"

Sam stroked Dovid's cheek. "I'd like to keep kissing you."

"Okay," Dovid breathed against Sam's lips. "I can do that."

He felt Sam smile against him, and then curl his fingers around Dovid's back.

* * *

As much as Sam was loath to leave, he did still have work in the morning, which meant waking up early. And he wasn't going to do that to Dovid, especially since he had a full day of filming and editing ahead of him.

"I don't mind," Dovid insisted. "Maybe…maybe tomorrow you could bring, like, an overnight bag? And just leave from here. If you want to, I mean. If it wouldn't be like, upsetting your whole life."

Sam squeezed his hand. "I'd love to. You and Rachel won't mind?"

"Of course not. And Rachel's dying to meet you. Since you can't meet her today, it'll be great that we'll be able to introduce you tomorrow once you're done with work. We could go out to dinner together. If you wanted."

"I do," Sam said. "So much. It'll be something to look forward to tomorrow, amid the exciting world of IT."

"Okay," Dovid grinned. "Plan."

They kissed goodbye for a long time, until Sam regretfully had to pull away. "If I don't leave now, I won't at all," he said.

"Right." Dovid trailed his hand up Sam's arm again, until he was cupping his face, and pressed one last kiss to his mouth before stepping back. "Have a good night. Get home safe. Text me, okay?"

"I will. I'll see you tomorrow." He squeezed Dovid's hand. "Love you."

The last thing he saw before he left Dovid in the apartment was Dovid beaming, his whole expression directed at Sam. "I love you too."

* * *

Sam Doyle: Home and safe. Have a good night and I'll see you tomorrow!

Dovid Rosenstein: <3 <3 <3

* * *

"Are you really sure we should take the camera equipment in?"

"If we're going to do a food montage of Ireland, it only makes sense to film every time we eat out to get as much footage as we can," Rachel said. "Don't worry, I'll keep Sam out of all the shots. I'll just pretend he's me."

"But what if he's not comfortable with us filming around him at all?"

"Then we won't, obviously. But it couldn't hurt to be prepared in case he doesn't mind."

"That's true."

"Besides, he's meeting us there. We might as well get shots of you going in and getting seated. This place is kind of famous for the way it looks."

"I'll be sure to appreciate that in the video," Dovid replied dryly.

She nudged him. "Alright, camera's on. Go ahead and introduce our eatery. This would be why we showed up fifteen minutes before he's supposed to meet us."

Dovid went through the motions of introducing the show and where they were eating, trying to be calm for the camera, but inside he was buzzing with excitement. He was going to get to see Sam again. And introduce him to Rachel. With each new thing that happened, things got more real.

The host and servers were all great, and the place was easy to navigate on his own while Rachel followed behind with the camera. Since they had reservations, they were seated without issue without having to wait.

"Right," Rachel said. "Camera's off. I can't wait to meet him."

"I can't wait for you to meet him either. He's nervous about meeting you by the way, so don't be weird."

"Me, weird? Never."

Dovid nudged her under the table. "I mean it. Don't give him a hard time, okay?"

Rachel sighed. "You know I wouldn't. I like him a lot. Not nearly as much as you do, but he's cute and endearing and obviously nuts about you. I'm not gonna give him the shovel talk."

"Good. He's been getting enough of that on the internet."

"It hasn't gotten any better at all?"

Dovid shrugged. "He doesn't really mention it all that much. I think he doesn't want me to worry. But I still check his comments once in a while to watch out for that sort of thing. Then again," he added thoughtfully, "there have been a few—only a few, but still—people who've done the same to me."

"Really?"

"Oh yeah. Meganbeginagain is someone who was a fan of Sam long before me. She left a comment on one of my videos. Promptly got a lot of hate—remember when I did that mini-vid about how I wouldn't tolerate hate in my comments?"

"I didn't know it was because of that. Why didn't you tell me?"

He shrugged again. "What were you going to do?"

"Not sure. Maybe congratulated her. And also said my own piece about personal attacks. She did a good thing."

"Giving me the shovel talk was a good thing?"

"It's sort of standard. Hey, does Sam even know what she did?"

Dovid shook his head. "I don't think so. I haven't brought it up."

"Ooh, ooh, can I?"

"What would you possibly even say?"

"'Hey, Sam, so you know, one of your loyal fans gave Dovid the shovel talk. Isn't that great?' Basically that."

"I mean…if you want to. He'll probably just be embarrassed. He still doesn't really know how to deal with how popular he is."

"Well, no time like the present to talk about it. Especially since we're in person and there isn't a time difference. I mean, what, he's uploading two videos a week and attempting to make a presence on Twitter, right?"

"Yeah. I helped him set up that Ko-fi account a while back, and he's been getting donations through it. And his revenue through YouTube is not insignificant anymore. It's basically the equivalent of a second job for him now."

"Yeah…"

"What?"

"I mean, he could be doing more, if he wanted to. Have you talked to him about it?"

Dovid shrugged. "Only a little. I get the feeling he still doesn't want to bother me about it. Which I've said that it wasn't at all, but still. He doesn't like feeling as though he's a burden." Dovid wished he knew why. What made Sam feel like he had to walk on eggshells all the time?

But Sam was opening up to him more each day. Which was so ridiculously fantastic.

"Maybe we can be the ones to bring it up, then," Rachel suggested. "He's, uh, he's mentioned in his videos about how he doesn't love his job. We're as good a success story as any about how YouTube can be a viable career. And I know for a fact that there's been fans asking him to review and play more games. He might not be able to hold to that sort of upload schedule with a full-time IT job but if he maybe moved to part-time for a little while, used his YouTube and Ko-fi earnings to supplement—have you talked to him about Patreon?"

"Whoa, whoa, I think you're getting a little ahead of yourself here." Not that Dovid hadn't had the exact same thoughts. He just hadn't been sure how to bring them up to Sam.

Rachel sighed. "Probably. I just...forget you feeling mushy, *I* really like him. And I really like his stuff, and his review of Brightforest was a thing of beauty. I'd love to have more of his content out there. And I know for a fact that there are a lot of people who share my opinion."

"Yeah, I know. Did I tell you he had someone ask him to review a Loot Crate box?"

"Oh hey, no. And?"

"And Loot Crate reached out to him about starting a complimentary subscription for him to review."

"Awesome! What'd he say?"

"It was a couple of days ago. He asked if he could think about it and get back to them. I think he's nervous about showing more of himself on camera."

"That's easy," Rachel said dismissively. "He can do what Ashens does and just keep the camera in front of him and review like that. They'd only ever see his arms."

"Yeah…"

"Excuse me? Terribly sorry to interrupt but—"

"Sam! Hey!" Dovid stood and turned in the direction of his voice, holding out a hand. "You made it!"

Sam's hand slid into his. "I rather said I would." He sounded like he was smiling.

"Come on, sit, sit." Dovid tugged Sam down into the seat next to his, and then faced forward again. "Rachel, this is Sam."

"Really? I couldn't tell. It's not like you didn't just sigh dreamily and fawn all over him." Followed by, "Hi, I'm Rachel! Dovid's better half. It's really great to meet you."

"The feeling's mutual," Sam said. "I've heard so much about you. And, erm, I've watched your videos, of course."

"Awesome. I've watched yours too. I was the one who introduced Dovid to your channel, actually."

"Oh yes! I remember Dovid saying so. Thank you for that."

Rachel laughed. "Hey, you getting more popular was a gift. Now I get two videos from you a week."

"Maybe more," Sam told her. "I…maybe."

"Oh," Dovid said. "Really?"

"I've been thinking about it. Maybe we could all have a chat? About that?"

"No, yeah, of course. Rachel?"

"Oh, I'm totally in. Though speaking of videos, Sam, do you mind if we record part of this?"

The hand in Dovid's clenched, then relaxed. "O-oh, I, well, if you want to."

A pause, and then Rachel said, "It's really okay if you don't want to."

"No, no, if you were planning on it, I don't want to get in the way of that."

"Nah, it's cool. We got plenty of good shots about coming inside the restaurant. We don't have to film the whole thing. Really."

"Rachel can just get some video of the food coming to the table, close-up shots of cutlery being used, maybe me eating it. I really don't have to review the food; we were going to be using this stuff for montage shots mostly anyway. It's not a big deal at all."

"It's a tiny deal," Rachel said. "Miniscule. Not even a deal. The deal doesn't exist."

Sam laughed, and something in Dovid unclenched in hearing him more at ease. "Alright. That's fine, then. I just don't want to upset any of your plans."

"You aren't," Dovid said. "Believe me. You are pretty much my one plan right now."

A thumb stroked over the back of his hand. "Thank you. You are to me too."

"Mush," Rachel announced. "You're both so cute it's gross. Can we order food now?"

* * *

After dinner, they all went back to where Dovid and Rachel were staying to continue the night. They'd talked pretty much nonstop through dinner, Sam included, and the only part Dovid could complain about was that Sam had to split his attention between himself and Rachel.

Okay, he wasn't at all complaining that his best friend was getting along with his boyfriend. Which is what Sam was, right? Like, neither of them had actually used the word, but they were dating and had said 'I love you's so...right?

Wait a minute, had it ever actually been established that they were dating?

"We're dating, right?" Dovid blurted out.

There was sudden silence. Probably a confused one, since they'd all been talking about Sam setting up a Patreon moments before.

"Yes?" Sam said, at the same time Rachel said, "Um, duh?"

"Okay. Okay, good. I just wasn't sure since we'd never actually, like, said it. I mean, *I* thought we were dating but—"

"Dovid," Sam said, reaching for his hand and squeezing, "I'm so happy I'm dating you, and you're the best boyfriend I could ever ask for. Even if it is a long-distance relationship most of the time, I wouldn't trade it, or you, for the world."

"Wow," Dovid said after a minute. He cleared his throat, cheeks hot. "Now who's making who blush, huh?"

Rachel laughed. "Sam, I'm gonna have to shake your hand. Dovid is not usually one for flustered, but where you're concerned he has, like, no chill."

Sam laughed and he shifted, seemingly taking Rachel's hand when she offered it to shake. "I'll take that as a compliment," he said.

"Now then," Rachel said. "I'm going to my room. I will be doing work, with my headphones on, sound up. If you absolutely need me, just bust down my door but other than that, I'm out."

"Oh," Sam said, "I didn't mean to overstay—"

"Are you kidding? You didn't at all. I'd love to keep talking to you. But might as well give you and Dovid some more time together, right?"

"Right," Dovid said immediately. "Besides, overstay? I was hoping you'd stay the night with me. You brought your overnight bag, yeah?"

"Well, yes, I did."

Dovid grinned. "Awesome. You wanna grab it and head back to my room?"

"Oh! Yes, I—goodnight, Rachel. It was lovely to meet you in person."

"Same. Looking forward to talking to you more tomorrow. Sounds good?"

"Yes, definitely."

"Night," Dovid said, before taking Sam's hand and pulling him along. Sam laughed and followed, presumably swinging up his backpack onto his shoulder.

Once inside his bedroom, Dovid got nervous again. He wanted so much. He wanted so much with Sam. "Want to just get ready for bed first?" he asked, in part to procrastinate thinking too hard. "Teeth brushed, change, all that?"

"Alright."

Sam went through his bag to get his toothbrush and then they both headed into the bathroom to get ready to turn in. Back in the room though, ready to change, Dovid sort of froze. He hadn't thought this far. Shorts and the shirt Sam had sent had been Dovid's night clothes for quite a while now. Did he want to wear less with Sam there, to feel more skin? Would Sam mind that?

He cursed himself for being so weird about this. Forget his casual flings; he'd never even overthought stuff like this in any of his serious relationships. He and Olivia had dated for *months* and Dovid had barely ever second-guessed himself. Even Brian hadn't flustered him like this, and certainly not so often. Sam was just...

He was something else.

"How would you like me?"

"Sorry," Dovid said, mind blanking out. "What?"

Sam cleared his throat. "I mean, I thought maybe you wanted to go to bed together? Or not even to sleep, not right now, but to cuddle again. If you wanted. I mean, I do, but obviously it sort of is up to you whether or not we do anything."

"Yes, absolutely to cuddling," Dovid said. "And sorry I just, uh, I sort of get caught up in my head sometimes."

"I certainly can understand that," Sam said. "I do that too. Far too much, probably. My father always says I've got my head far too high up in the clouds. Not that I think you do!"

Dovid had to smile. "I get it. No, yeah, I just—how comfortable would you be if I, uh, if I didn't wear a shirt? So I could feel more of you. But it's totally cool if you'd rather I wore one."

A very loud silence.

"Uh… Sam?"

"Well, I… I can't say I'm against you not wearing a shirt," Sam said, like an admission. He cleared his throat again. "You're incredibly good-looking."

Dovid swallowed, taken aback. To hear Sam just out and out say it, like it was just fact, like he was just being honest… "Oh."

"I rather thought you knew that," Sam said. And then he chuckled. "What was it you said, in one of your videos? That just because you couldn't appreciate looks, you knew that many of your viewers could?"

Dovid covered his face with his hands.

"Hey now, what's that for?"

"Because I'm such a *nerd*."

"You're a popular YouTube sensation who's incredibly personable, smart, and quite handsome. You do all nerds a service, by ranking yourself among us."

"Okay, you're a nerd too. And I want to kiss you a lot right now."

"The feeling is quite mutual. But did you want to keep your shirt on, or take it off?"

"Fuck," Dovid said, pulling his shirt off and folding it up, leaving it on the chair by the door. He shimmied out of his pants and put those on the chair as well, then went to the bed, taking a seat and holding out his hands. "C'mere?"

The sound of quiet footfalls, and then Sam sitting down next to him, his leg brushing Dovid's own. Sam was wearing long pants made of a soft fabric. Dovid reached out to stroke it. "Let me guess," he said. "This is plaid."

"How did you even know that?" Sam asked.

Dovid grinned. "Because these feel like legit pajama bottoms. And everyone I've ever talked to tell me that men's PJs only come in plaid or stripes. And you didn't seem like a stripes guy to me."

"I marvel at you every day." Sam said, putting an arm around him and kissing his temple. Sam was wearing a shirt himself, but Dovid wasn't going to hold that against him. He was, however, going to happily hold himself against Sam.

That thought in mind, Dovid turned and pushed closer, wrapping his arms around Sam and nosing along his shirt until he reached the open collar at Sam's throat. He pressed a kiss there and was rewarded with a quiet intake of breath. "That okay?" he asked, just to be sure.

"Yes," a sigh.

Another kiss there, then, a little higher up. "Can I keep going?"

"Yes, yes please."

Dovid grinned against Sam's skin and then pressed a kiss just underneath his jaw before mouthing there, not sucking too hard to leave marks but enough that—

"Ah!" High and thready, and delicious to hear. Dovid surged forward, laying Sam down on his back before finding his mouth for kisses, hands running up and down his sides.

His fingers found the hem of Sam's T-shirt, and he dipped them underneath just a little, just enough to stroke skin. "Can I touch you? Would that be okay?"

"More than okay," Sam breathed. "I—would you— shall I take it off?"

"God, yes, if you want to." All that skin, all of *Sam.* "Fuck, please."

"Here." Sam sat up, hands brushing Dovid's own, and then he was lifting his shirt over his head. Dovid heard the soft *fwump* as it fell to the floor. "There, is that alright?"

"Can I…" Dovid swallowed. Sam was right there. He was right there. "Can I touch you?"

Sam took his hand and pressed a kiss to his palm. Dovid shuddered. "However you'd like."

Permission granted, Dovid brought his hands up to feel him, to run his fingers over Sam's bared skin. Arms to shoulders to pecs, sides, stomach, back again. He pressed Sam back down against the sheets, tucking away all of Sam's little inhales and gasps, moved to kiss his mouth and taste them as his hands stroked down Sam's body.

* * *

"I am going to fucking miss this," Dovid murmured sleepily. He was pressed against Sam's side, arms wrapped around him, and if he never moved again it would be too soon.

Sam chuckled. "Hey now, your visit only just started. We still get to see each other for several more days. And yes, well, I won't be here in the morning, but Friday night to Saturday to Sunday I'll be there to wake up with you."

"I know," Dovid said. "I can't wait. I'm with you right now and I can't wait til I get you again. I'm gonna savor, like, every moment."

"Same here. I spent the whole day knowing I'd be seeing you again. Everyone at work thought I was mad, I was so happy. Cynthia, my cubicle mate, even commented on it and asked if I'd gotten good news, and, well, you know the most we interact is to exchange pleasantries and comments on the weather. And I'll be the same way tomorrow, I assure you."

"Aw. But no, yeah, me too. At least Rachel knows why I've been so crazy happy. She's just glad I'm able to get it out of my system a little."

Another laugh. "I'm glad too."

"Ugh, I love you so much, stop it."

"I love you too." Easily.

"Hey, Sam?"

"Mm?"

"If you close your eyes, it's like I'm right here with you."

Sam shifted just a little. "You're right," he said a moment later. "It is. What are we doing?"

Dovid smiled. "I'm turning you onto your side, so I can be the one to hold you this time."

Sam obligingly moved as Dovid guided him, until Dovid's cheek was pressed against Sam's back, their legs tangling together. "Oh," Sam said faintly. "I like that very much. Being held by you."

Dovid kissed him there, because he could. "Good," he said. "I like it too."

Chapter Ten

Sam wearily sat back down at his desk, and it took him a moment to put his headset back on. Cynthia glanced around her own monitor to raise an eyebrow at him. "Office call, eh?"

Sam bit his lip. He often didn't know how to respond when Cynthia spoke to him.

"Oh, you know," he said gamely. "Sometimes they need to yell at someone in person."

She huffed a laugh. "Don't I know it."

Interaction over, they both turned back to their screens. Sam had to type up the report of his office visit, which needed to include why he had personally gone by instead of just fixing the problem with TeamViewer like he was supposed to.

He couldn't very well write "Because my father insisted," though, so he maybe fudged the trouble a bit to make it seem as though the solution was more difficult than it had been.

He was unable to stop the small sigh that escaped him as he wrote. Sometimes he wished, just a little, that his parents treated him a bit more like they did Charlie. More often he at least dreamed that he and his father worked at different companies.

He flicked his eyes over at Cynthia's monitor. She

had gotten a call and was asking a question in bright, bubbly tones. "It's the way to do it," she had told him once, after a particularly angry client had Sam needing to turn off his headset and just breathe. "If they become upset at you telling them to do something simple, just repeat yourself with more exclamation marks. Helps to just steamroll their bad mood."

Cynthia was an interesting woman. She had told him once, cheerfully, that she was utterly without ambition. She went to work, got to sit and talk on the phone all day, went home to her cat and her husband, and that was a pretty well-rounded week for her.

Sam had no qualms going home to his empty apartment of course. It was wonderfully devoid of people and their social expectations. Though lately he had come to be a touch envious of Cynthia. To have someone she loved so close by. To not mind the work she was doing, even if it wasn't necessarily her dream job.

But while Dovid lived far away, Sam wouldn't trade him for anything. He was so, so lucky to have Dovid in his life. And today, for the next *few* days, Sam did have him to come home to. As for his displeasure with work, well, with Dovid and Rachel both talking to him about Patreon, coupled with the fact that his channel really *was* doing well in terms of ad revenue...

"There you go," Cynthia said. Sam jerked his head up at the sound of her voice. "Couldn't ruin your good mood too long, with your weekend plans, hm?" When she'd asked, Sam had told her he had someone special in for a visit. She'd winked at him, which had left Sam utterly nonplussed.

Now she was grinning. And, hesitatingly, Sam grinned back.

* * *

When it was finally time to leave work, Sam raced home, filled with yet another mixture of excitement and anxiety. It seemed as though he went through a different flavor of it every day, in the time leading up to and surrounding Dovid's visit.

But tonight, Dovid was going to come to Sam's apartment after dinner. And spend the night. In Sam's bed, with him. Tomorrow Sam didn't have work, so they could wake up together at a decent hour, have breakfast together, and just enjoy the whole day.

Sam was so happy he could hardly stand it, and so nervous he felt as though he might burst. He hoped Dovid liked his flat. He'd ended up leaving the main room as it had started, just making sure everything was picked up and swept clean, but he'd moved things around in his bedroom so that his furniture was more back against walls instead of dividing it in half, and he'd found that he quite liked the change. It made things a bit more open and airy.

Sam's flat was up a set of stairs, and he shared a hall with the residents who lived below him. It was fairly easy to navigate he thought, but he hoped it'd be alright for Dovid. Then again, the Airbnb Dovid was staying at was also up a flight of stairs, so maybe Sam was silly to worry.

He gave his flat one last nervous once-over and then had to leave so that he wouldn't be late to the pub where he was meeting Dovid and Rachel for dinner. Rachel had been looking forward to talking to him too, apparently, and Sam liked her. He didn't at all mind spending more time with her. They'd decided that they'd spend the evening continuing to brainstorm with Sam about his channel, and then Rachel would go back to their

Airbnb while Dovid went home with Sam. They were going to have all of Friday night and Saturday together, for a date day.

He got to the pub and didn't see either of them, so he bypassed the bar and went over to get a table, taking out his phone to text Dovid to let them know he'd arrived.

He'd only just finished sending the text when he caught sight of Rachel and Dovid coming in.

Sam got up to meet them. "Hello."

"Hey," Dovid said, turning towards him. "Fancy meeting you here."

Rachel rolled her eyes. "Honestly. Now then, food time. We had a pretty full day of being led around and filming. I'm ready to eat again. Sam? Where did you want to sit?"

"I had thought to get a table instead of going to the bar. It's not as, ah, friendly? But it'll be a little quieter, for talking."

"Then table it is," Dovid said, reaching a hand out. Sam took it. "Lead the way."

They took a seat and Sam, at Dovid's request, read the menu aloud to him and made some suggestions on what to order. They all also got drinks, because Dublin was, if nothing else, a walking town. Sam's own flat was only about fifteen minutes' walk from the pub, and it was a beautiful evening. July in Ireland meant the sun was out til quite late, with it getting cooler as the day wore on. It would be fine to walk back after dinner. And he was looking forward to enjoying an evening stroll with Dovid.

"So," Sam asked. "How was your day?"

Dovid waved a hand. "Meh. Filmed a bunch of stuff. How was your day?"

Sam had to laugh. "Oh come, it must have been slightly more exciting than that?"

Rachel flicked Dovid on his side. "We did a lot of architecture stuff. So he's feeling a little left out."

Dovid shrugged. "It's more Rachel's thing than mine. I mean, I can feel things? When I'm allowed to touch. But the majestic beauty of buildings is sort of lost on me."

"Oh dear, I can see how that might make a dull day."

"Don't get me wrong—the facts were pretty cool and stuff. Just…we smushed a lot into the day since it was our last official day of filming. And museums sometimes make me tired."

"Did you at least go to some interesting ones?"

"Yeah, a few."

Sam smiled. "Oh good. There's that at least. Did you enjoy the National Leprechaun Museum?"

Dovid raised an eyebrow. "Excuse me? The what?"

Sam was aghast. "They didn't take you to the NLM?"

"No," Rachel said slowly. "But that sounds amazing. What is it?"

"It's a museum about Irish folklore. Hands-on. It's really quite wonderful. They have guided tours every day. And a darkland tour, Friday and Saturday evening."

"Darkland?" Dovid asked.

"Tales of the darker kind," Sam explained. "I believe it's adults only."

"Oh man," Dovid said. "Can we go?"

"Tonight?"

Dovid shook his head. "No, not tonight, but tomorrow? That sounds like a fun way to end a date day. I like being spooked. And I like stories."

Sam grinned. "Of course. That sounds like a lot of fun."

"And uh, you said they do normal guided tours?"

"Yes."

"Do you want to do that maybe Sunday? With Rachel, if she wants to and you don't mind if she comes."

"Of course I want to," Rachel said at the same time Sam said, "I don't mind at all."

Silence.

Rachel laughed. "I *like* you."

Sam smiled. "Oh good, I'm so glad. It would have been very unfortunate if you didn't like me."

"Nah," Dovid said, "I wouldn't let her not like you."

"Excuse you, I was the one who liked Sam first, remember?"

"True. I'm still grateful."

Rachel wrinkled her nose. "Oh, stop."

Dovid raised an eyebrow. "Hey, you make up your mind. Do you want me to be grateful or don't you?"

"He's this ball of mush when it comes to you," she told Sam. "Honestly, it's a little ridiculous."

"Excuse me, I'm a cool, suave YouTube star."

"That's what you hope your fans think."

"I feel he's plenty cool and suave," Sam said with a grin.

"See? Sam thinks so."

"Sam *loves* you."

"So? That just means he's the only one who really matters."

"Boys," Rachel said, managing to sound both delighted and disgusted at the same time.

"No, but really," Dovid said, "Can we make that a plan? Darkland tomorrow night with you and the regular tour Sunday all three of us?"

"Of course. I think that'd be wonderful."

Rachel clapped. "Yay!"

"Now then," Dovid said, "how *did* your day go?"

"Oh," Sam said. "It was fine. Nothing majorly stressful today, which was a nice change of pace. But otherwise quite unexciting."

"In short, you hated it?"

Sam averted his eyes, not that Dovid could see. "Well, I—I won't pretend that I loved it. But again, it wasn't too stressful today. And hardly anyone yelled at me." Only his father of course. Sam did so wish he worked sales at a different company. Only, his father wasn't all that computer literate, so these sorts of issues happened a bit more than once in a while, and he always requested Sam specifically.

Sometimes Sam even had it in him to wonder if his father made said requests so he had someone in particular to be cross at.

Then again, it wasn't his father's fault that computers weren't his thing. He was brilliant in sales, and it was no doubt frustrating to have the same issues over and over. If Sam could help alleviate some of that frustration, it was his job to do so. Both figuratively and literally.

Dovid sighed. "Hardly anyone still means at least one person did." Dovid was not a fan of the way Sam was sometimes treated in IT.

"It's really alright." Sam tried to sound reassuring. "It's just how my father communicates, I think."

"Wait, your dad? Your dad's the one who yelled at you?"

Oh dear. Sam hadn't meant to say that. The last thing he wanted was for Dovid to form a poor opinion of Sam's father. He was a good man; it was Sam's own failing that he was such a disappointment to him. He shrugged. "He was just upset about the computer bug."

"Oh." Dovid frowned. "Well then. He must've been happy when you fixed it."

Sam had to let out a self-deprecating chuckle. He

didn't think he'd ever made his father happy doing anything.

"What? What's funny?"

And that was probably another thing he shouldn't be telling Dovid or Rachel. "Nothing. Really."

"Oh," Dovid said again. "Um. Okay."

"So," Rachel said. "Did you think any more about Patreon?"

Sam was grateful at the subject change, and eager to further discuss the service. "A little." All through the work day, actually, when he wasn't daydreaming about seeing Dovid again. "And I really do like the idea of it. Though I worry about a few things."

"Yeah? Like what?"

"Mostly content," he said. "The weekend is really when I have the time and energy to record and upload videos. I thought over trying to upload a Patreon-only series, like you suggested, but I just can't think of when."

"You can't do it on a weekday?" she asked.

"I could try. I'd worry about being able to keep it up. Sometimes when I'm done at work…by the time I get home, the very last thing I want to do is talk more. I babble enough Friday night and Sunday afternoon when I record." Sam sighed and wished he were better than this. This was something he wanted to do so much, and he still had excuses. "I'm sorry, it must sound so silly to you, since you do this practically every day."

"Not at all," Dovid said. "You only have so much energy in a day, right? And with you being an introvert, working your day job saps a lot of it. I get it."

"What about doing a shorter video?" Rachel suggested. "All your current uploads are forty-five minutes to an hour. That's a lot of talking. But your Brightforest review was only about fifteen minutes long, even if your playthrough is your regular forty-five. What if you did a weekly Patreon video, that released on, oh, Wednesday evening when you were done with work, but you only played and talked for like ten or twenty minutes? It's bonus reward content, so most people wouldn't mind that it's a shorter video."

Sam considered the idea. Twenty minutes of straight talking did seem a lot more feasible than twice or triple that. "I think that might be okay," he said after a moment. "I could probably keep that up."

"Awesome," Dovid said. "Want to talk reward levels?"

"Oh yes, please." He'd been browsing the Patreon website on his phone, to get a better idea of what people did for rewards, but it had gotten a little overwhelming. Dovid and Rachel always managed to break everything down in easy, much more manageable bite-sizes.

"Cool, well, for our Patreon, we have three tiers. One dollar, five dollars, and ten dollars. One dollar is just a thank-you tier. People donate because they like us, and we post some of our brainstorming about video projects and stuff, including some polls we don't put up on social media. Five dollars and they get a link to see our videos before they go publicly live. So we upload Monday's video on Sunday, and Patreon gets the link for it first. Ten dollars and they get the video link, but also an exclusive-to-Patreon something that we release once a month."

"Really?"

"Yeah. Sometimes it's a Patreon-only video, sometimes it's a song I've written that they get the free download for. And once in a while we host Patreon-only giveaways, on top of the giveaways that we have on our regular channel. Like we said before, Patreon is a great way to supplement your income on top of You-Tube view count."

Sam nodded thoughtfully. Three reward tiers seemed to be a bit much, especially since he wasn't as creative as Dovid, but if he did a Patreon-only series for one tier, and maybe also did an early-release link for the other...

"Speaking of giveaways," Rachel said, "Dovid said that you were offered a Loot Crate box to review?"

"Yes. I'm guessing you both think I should do it."

"Should nothing," Dovid said. "Do it if you want to. But I won't lie and tell you I don't think it's a good idea."

"If you want," Rachel said, "I could help you film it. I mean, not while I'm here obviously, because you won't get the box in time, but I could give you some pointers about doing something in front of the camera while staying *out* of the camera."

"Oh! That would be much appreciated actually." Sam had wanted to do the unboxing, since it had seemed like it would be fun, but he had been nervous about letting his viewers actually see what he looked like. Dovid, for instance, was so handsome, with his curly black hair and strong jaw, the build of his body. It was no wonder he was teased about showing off. Sam was just... Sam. And he didn't *mind* what he looked like, even less so now that he had Dovid so wonderfully adamant he found Sam attractive. But he knew that media consumers tended to care about that sort of thing.

"Awesome. We can do that Sunday too, if you want."

"I'd really appreciate that. Also, ah, maybe you might be willing to look the video over, before I posted it? I just worry about sounding dull on camera, if all I'm doing is opening a present."

"Even better idea," Dovid said. "Why don't we go to

a toy store or something and buy you a couple of blind boxes? You can do a mini-unboxing with Rachel's help. Shouldn't be longer than a five or six minute video so you couldn't monetize it, but it'd be a good way to experiment. Slap on some music, throw it up mostly uncut and boom, you've got a new video. You could even use it to announce the fact that you're starting a Patreon account. I mean, it's just a suggestion, absolutely no problem if you don't want to, but it's an idea."

"No, no," Sam said, mind whirling with possibilities. "I—I think it's a fine idea. And if you two are really so set on helping me with this, I appreciate it so much."

"Sure thing," Rachel said, right as Dovid said, "Of course." They both stopped and grinned.

Sam had to smile too.

* * *

"So, if you don't mind my asking," Dovid said, as they ate dinner—it was all delicious. "And feel free to tell me to shut up, but what are the figures you're looking at, in terms of YouTube and Ko-fi income right now? I mean, from view count alone they should be getting up there depending on adblock users. But if you gave us a ballpark, or even some more long-term goals, that'd be an excellent thing to add to your plan."

"My plan?" Sam asked.

Dovid nodded. "Yeah. I mean, it sounds like you're looking to grow. Or at least are interested in it."

"I am. So much so, really. I just…"

"Hey," Dovid said, rushing to assure him, "if you don't want to talk about this, or you don't want to do anything else relating to YouTube, tell me. I'll stop right now."

"It's not that," Sam said. "It's more that…that I really do want it to work. The way you two live your lives and talk about what you do…the idea that I'd get to be independent like that but as a gamer is…it's incredibly appealing." More hesitation before, quietly, "It would be a dream come true. I just don't know if I can. I'm not… I'm not all that good at very much."

Dovid scowled. "Who told you that?"

"Wh-what?"

"Who told you you're not good enough? Because, uh, last time I checked, you were a great gamer, an interesting Let's Player, and a rising YouTube sensation. None of which would be possible if you weren't good at things."

A quiet sigh. "I'm sorry. It's a hard habit to break, you know? I've been this way all my life."

Yeah, Dovid thought. *With a dad that apparently yelled at you.* He took a breath. "Sorry. Sorry, I get… worked up. I've been told I wasn't good enough a lot in my life. People see that I can't and they make a big deal about it. So it bothers me to hear someone talk about themselves like that. Get me?"

"I do." Sam reached for his hand and squeezed. "I do. I'm sorry."

Dovid tried to smile. "Hey, nothing to be sorry for. You're right, it's a hard habit to break. I just don't like you thinking about yourself that way, is all."

"Thank you."

"Sure thing. Now back to the topic at hand, it's appealing to be self-employed, huh?"

"It really is," Sam said. "I mean, it's also terrifying and uncertain and scary, but I like gaming and doing let's plays. It seems like it'd be worth a try to make a play of it for real. I can always go back to IT if it doesn't work out."

"That's true," Rachel said. "That's really true. That you've got a backup plan is awesome."

"Thank you. And I, well, I've been saving most of my new income. Thinking about cushions, and all that."

"Even better," Dovid said. "But that also means we should talk tax laws. We haven't yet, and I'm not sure how Ireland's work, but you really want to know sooner over later how to declare your new income. I probably should have brought it up before, to be honest. Hopefully if we figure out what you need to do now, you won't get any penalties. Or they won't be so bad."

Rachel laughed. "Fun evening, huh?"

"Oh, quite," Sam said. He sounded like he was smiling. "This is all so good to know. And I'm enjoying myself immensely."

* * *

They said goodbye to Rachel outside the pub, and then Dovid offered Sam his arm as they walked towards Sam's flat. Dovid noticed how, after several minutes of walking, some of the noise died down, especially the hustle and bustle of the general evening crowd.

"It's quieter," he said.

"A bit, yes. I live on a cul-de-sac, just a touch out of the way. I think it's very nice."

Dovid smiled. "Well, it sounds nice."

"So here it is," Sam said, as he put a hand on Dovid's shoulder to stop them from walking any farther. "This is my building."

"It looks great," Dovid said, tilting his face up.

Sam chuckled. "It is actually a rather nice building. It's old brick. Here, the door is just this way. And then I'm up the stairs and down the hall."

"Lead the way."

Sam was an excellent leader. He didn't walk too fast,

kept making sure that Dovid was following along, and kept up a steady stream of chatter that was easy to follow as well. Soon enough they were at Sam's door. Dovid swallowed, suddenly nervous, and grabbed the straps of his backpack. He'd brought enough for an overnight or two. Because this was it. He was at Sam's *house*.

"Let me show you around," Sam said, as he ushered Dovid inside. "The layout is actually fairly open so, erm, so hopefully it won't be too hard for you."

"You sound about as nervous as I feel," Dovid laughed.

"You're nervous too?"

"Oh yeah. Butterflies in my whole body, not just my stomach." He reached out for Sam's hand, giving it a squeeze. "Every time I'm, like, reminded I'm here with you, I get nervous all over again. I just want you to like me so much."

"I do like you so much," Sam said. "You're as wonderful as I thought you were before we even started dating."

"Yeah?"

"I thought you were wonderful when I saw your video where you plugged my channel. And then in all the videos after that." Sam laced his fingers through Dovid's own.

Dovid grinned. "Same here. But I knew about you before you knew about me, so I get extra points."

"Points? What are we going for, here?"

"Not sure yet. But it'll be something cool."

"Whatever you say," Sam said, sounding amused.

"I do say. Now then, you were showing me around?"

The layout of the apartment did end up being super simple to navigate. The kitchen/living space was one big open, airy room with the kitchen setup taking up one length of the wall, a kitchen table opposite the fridge, a couch dividing the rest of the room up, and a desk setup tucked away on one side.

"Is this where the magic happens?" Dovid asked, running his hands over the wooden table.

"I suppose it is," Sam said.

"What kind of setup do you have?"

"Nothing too outrageous. I've a computer, two monitors, speakers, and my mic headset."

"Perfect for gaming. Not so much for opening blind boxes, but you could always do that on your couch. It's a nice couch. In terms of feel anyway. If it's covered in lime green polka dots it might not be the best for camera."

Sam laughed. "Nothing that ostentatious. It's just light blue."

"Oh, light blue is good! Pale colors make good backgrounds. Things stand out more. Or so I'm told, anyway."

"You're the expert," Sam said. "Now here, let me show you to the bedroom and bathroom."

"Good idea. Need to be able to navigate both those places."

"And we can set your bag down too."

And maybe have fun together on the bed, Dovid thought. What could he say? He was an optimistic guy.

"Here's the bedroom, and the bathroom is just through here," Sam said, leading Dovid to another door. Dovid took stock of it, then went back into the bedroom where Sam was.

"Bathroom's connected to your bedroom, huh? Bet that means you have to keep it tidy."

Sam laughed. "I'm prone to tidiness anyway; it was

sort of beaten into me by my parents." Dovid went cold. What…was that just an expression or— Sam had *laughed* but—

Should he say something? Sam kept letting little things about his parents slip that were rapidly making Dovid inclined to hate them, but weren't you like, not supposed to bring stuff like that up?

Sam had laughed.

"Anyway," Sam said, since he was still talking, "it's not as though I have guests over all that much."

"As long as the floor is clear for me to navigate, I'm happy," Dovid said, focusing back on the now. He shrugged off his backpack.

"Here," Sam said. "Where would you like to set your bag?"

"On the floor at the foot of the bed is good. Easy to find." So saying, Dovid went to do just that. When he stood again, he turned and held out a hand to Sam. Sam obligingly took it, stepping closer.

"I had a nice time tonight," Dovid said, running his thumb over Sam's knuckles. "I'm still having a nice time."

"Me too," Sam said, before lifting Dovid's hand to his mouth and kissing his fingers.

Dovid's hand flexed, pleasure washing through him, and then he was reaching for Sam to kiss him properly.

When they parted, Sam said, a little breathlessly, "I feel bad."

"Why?"

"Because you're here, and there's so much we could be doing or I could be showing you, and instead all I really want is to curl up with you and not move."

"That honestly sounds like the best idea," Dovid said,

before adding, with a wicked grin, "But maybe we could move *some*."

"Really? You don't mind that you're not…out there? Exploring?"

Dovid went to sit on the bed, leading Sam to it to sit next to him. He took both of Sam's hands in his, still reveling in the fact that he was able to. "Not really? I mean, first of all, it's like nine at night. Most of what we could do is go out drinking. Choosing between that and staying home with you, I'd definitely pick staying home with you. Second of all, traveling and exploring and filming and editing is all Rachel and I have been doing these last few days. These last two weeks! It's nice to be able to slow down a little and get some relaxing in. And third of all, I'm only going to get you in person for so long. I want to take advantage of every minute we have. Until you get sick of me, I mean."

"I don't see myself getting sick of you anytime soon," Sam said.

"Aw, thanks. Right back atcha." Dovid laughed. "Rachel's been teasing me since we started the trip, about how we'd be in the honeymoon phase for the entirety of it. I was more nervous about meeting you in person because sometimes an online presence is different from an in-person one. I was worried we wouldn't get along or that we even might not like each other face-to-face."

"I had the same fears. I mean, I know you saw my videos, and of course we spoke and I loved those conversations but… I'm not the easiest with my words. When I text you, I can always take the time to go over things before I send them, to a point."

"Yeah, I get that. My videos are the same way. I fix a lot of what I do in editing. So unless we put up a blooper reel, people don't see my goofs."

"I like your goofs."

Dovid wasn't going to stop smiling anytime soon.

* * *

True to Sam's word, he did end up pulling Dovid down until they were both lying flat on top of his bedspread. Dovid made a pleased noise and shifted so that he was nestled into Sam's side, his face pressed into the crook of Sam's neck. Sam wrapped an arm around Dovid's shoulders and closed his eyes, simply basking in Dovid's presence, about the fact that they were still with each other, could still touch.

He did so love being able to just *touch* Dovid.

As the minutes passed, Sam drifting happily, Dovid's fingers started stroking down his chest until they reached the hem of Sam's shirt. He pressed a kiss to Sam's neck and dipped his fingers underneath the fabric to stroke along Sam's skin. "Okay?" Dovid murmured.

"Of course," Sam said. Though he was a little surprised. Especially once Dovid moved against him and Sam could feel him, hard against his leg. "Oh."

"Oh?"

"I—nothing, sorry—"

Dovid pulled back, braced himself so that he wasn't lying on top of Sam anymore. His eyes were closed—Dovid had told him they normally were when he wasn't wearing his glasses—but with anyone else it would have been a position to maintain eye contact. "You sound confused. What—did I do something—what did I do?"

Sam swallowed. And look at him, making such a nice time awkward. "Nothing! Really. Sorry, I—I guess I just wasn't expecting…"

"Yeah?" Dovid prompted, when Sam trailed off.

"Sex," Sam blurted out, feeling like a teenager. "I

wasn't, um, I wasn't thinking about it, but I don't mind that you were, of course I don't, so—"

"Sam, it's okay," Dovid said, moving completely away until he was lying next to Sam again, but not touching him. Sam missed him at once. "It's okay. I didn't— I'm sorry if you…thought I was pushing you. You can always, always say no to me. Okay? Please do, if you need to. Please."

"I wasn't saying no." Sam tried not to sound too desperate. "I just wasn't thinking about it. Like I said, I really don't mind. I just… I wasn't… I don't…" He reached for Dovid's hand, curled their fingers together, pressed a kiss to Dovid's knuckles.

Dovid exhaled shakily, clutching at Sam's hand before relaxing a little. "Sam, wait. Wait. Not minding something and wanting to do something are two *really* different things."

Were they? But Sam didn't… "But I *don't* mind," Sam said again, grasping for the words he wanted. "I… it's just not something I think about. I want to. I do. It just—it just—"

"You weren't thinking about it," Dovid finished, frowning.

Sam hated to disappoint him. "I'm sorry. Please don't be upset."

Dovid sucked in a breath, then quickly said, "I'm not upset. Don't be sorry. Don't ever, ever be sorry for telling me how you feel. Communication, right? That's ridiculously important to me. Especially since I can't get most visual clues."

"Okay," Sam said quietly.

Dovid squeezed Sam's hand. "Sam, have you…ever thought about sex with another person before? Like, you know, wanting to do it?"

Sam swallowed. He was going to be honest, but here he was, about to disappoint Dovid again. "Not really. It never really crossed my mind. In passing sometimes, growing up with everyone else making such a deal of it, but I never…" He sighed. "Not until you. And it's so important to you, I know it is."

"Do you…does it bother you?"

"Oh no! No, not at all. I really do mean it when I said I don't mind. It—it does feel nice. I *do* like what we've done so far. I'd like to continue learning about things with you. I…my favorite part is just being with you. Touching."

Dovid squeezed Sam's hand again, smiling fondly. "So you really like the cuddling."

"Yes. So much."

"Great. Me too. And kissing?"

"I—I like that."

"But you could take or leave the sex?"

"Um."

"Sam," Dovid sounded careful but not angry. "Are you asexual?"

That brought Sam up short. "What?"

"Asexual," Dovid said again.

"What—what's that?"

Dovid stroked his thumb over the back of Sam's hand. "It can mean different things to different people, but the general base is that an asexual person doesn't feel sexual attraction to others. It often also means a low sex drive, though it doesn't always. You can still like sex, or even want it, but in the end, for a lot of people…"

"You could take it or leave it," Sam said reeling with disbelief. There was a *word* for him?

"Yeah. I mean, again, everyone sort of defines themselves—it's a spectrum, you know? But Rachel's asexual. She's sex-repulsed though. It grosses her out."

"It doesn't gross me out," Sam said slowly, working through his thoughts. "I quite enjoy being with you. The thought of continuing to be with you. And I really mean it when I said I don't mind. I like being *with* you. And I know it makes you happy. So having sex with you is a way to make you happy that I also, um, enjoy."

"But?" Dovid prompted, when Sam fell silent. "It sort of sounds like you have more you wanna say. Seriously, this is good. It's great we're talking about this. Please don't worry that I'm going to be upset."

Sam worried his lip with his teeth before saying, "I suppose it just comes down to the fact that you're right. I love the cuddling and the kissing. I don't often think about more than that."

"And that's okay."

"But I—I want to be able to be more, for you."

Dovid scooted forward again until he could rest his head on Sam's shoulder. "All I want is for you to be happy and comfortable with what we do. I want you to feel safe. I want you to enjoy yourself. If you like sex, even if it doesn't cross your mind to start something, I'd be *so* down for experimenting. And, you know, initiating stuff. But that also means you've got the right to tell me if you don't feel like it."

"That won't bother you?"

"Nah."

"Oh." Sam wanted to believe him. That he wasn't being a bother by…being the way he was. "Alright."

Dovid pressed a kiss to Sam's shoulder. "Sam?"

"Yes?"

"I love you. All of you, and all the ways you are. Okay?"

Regardless of how else Sam was feeling, that made him sigh happily. Dovid was only ever honest with him. If nothing else, Sam couldn't doubt Dovid's feelings.

And he had a word for himself now. There was a word for it, which meant there were other people like him. Including Rachel. And just like Dovid was sexual and happy, Sam was…was asexual. And still happy.

And Dovid loved him just the way he was. "Okay," he said, and meant it. "I love you too."

* * *

Dovid woke up to an empty bed, and felt very put out about it. He got up anyway, because he needed to use the bathroom, and then, since he was already up and didn't know where Sam was, got ready for the morning.

He was grabbing up the jeans he'd left folded on the floor at the foot of the bed when he heard footsteps and then, "Oh," from Sam. Who sounded disappointed. "Good morning."

"Hey." He stood up, holding his jeans. "What time is it?"

"It's about nine," Sam said. "I'm sorry, I didn't think you'd be up. I went to start coffee, so it would be ready for you later but…"

"Oh," Dovid said. "Sorry I ruined your plans."

"It's alright. I was just, ah, looking forward to getting back into bed with you."

"Hey, no," Dovid said quickly. "That sounds great. I am totally down for getting back into bed for a little bit longer."

"Are you sure? I mean, if you're up—"

"C'mere," Dovid said, making grabby hands.

Sam obliged and let Dovid situate him so that they were curled around each other under the covers again, Dovid stroking lines up and down Sam's arm.

"What would you like to do today after breakfast?" Sam asked. "I'm yours, and so is the day. We can do anything you'd like."

Dovid had made a whole bunch of plans in his head already, so he was ready with an answer. "I do want to eat breakfast with you," he said. "And then, uh, I was wondering if we actually couldn't go grocery shopping? I like exploring different grocery stores, and I thought I'd make you lunch. I kind of had a menu in mind."

"Oh! Of course. We can do that. But surely you wanted to do something else besides just go grocery shopping and making me lunch?"

"Well, yeah, I want to cuddle with you a *lot*. Maybe we could watch something together? That documentary about Egypt I talked to you about—it's on YouTube, if you haven't watched it yet."

"That sounds lovely. And no, I'd been saving it for after your visit."

Dovid grinned. "Awesome."

"Anything else?"

"Actually yeah. But it's totally cool if you don't want to."

"What is it?"

"I was thinking maybe we could play some Brightforest together. Since it's more of a puzzle and building game, I can interact with it on a level I can't with Dire Straits. I thought it'd be fun to play with you. We don't have to record or anything of course."

"Would you want to?"

"Want to what?"

"Record," Sam said, sounding hesitant. "I mean, I don't think I'd mind. If you wanted to."

"What, really?"

"Yes. I think it'd be nice, actually. To record with

you. Have that little moment set into a memory in that way. Obviously I wouldn't have to post it online—we could play one of my non-YouTube runs, or even start a new game. But I quite like the idea of having a recording of us playing together."

Dovid did too. Oh man, Dovid did too. "No, yeah," he managed, "I'd love to. And if you're cool uploading it, I would honestly love that. It means I'd be able to have it to listen to even after I left."

"Alright," Sam said, smile clear in his voice. "Let's do that."

"Cool." Dovid sighed. "That means we should get up, huh?"

Sam shifted just enough to kiss his cheek. "Only if you want to. I'm enjoying the lie-in."

Dovid moved to kiss Sam back, a little more thoroughly. When he pulled away he said, "No, okay, we need to get up now or I'm never going to let you out of this bed."

Sam laughed. Dovid smiled.

* * *

"Hello, everybody, I'm Sam, and welcome to another episode of Let's Play Brightforest." Sam adjusted his headset and grinned. "I wanted to thank you all again for your support in this series. As many of you know, I gained a lot of popularity when my channel was, unbeknownst to me, plugged by Dovid and Rachel from Don't Look Now. Well, Dovid and Rachel happened to be in town for their European tour. I was lucky enough to meet Dovid in person and, well, here we are."

Which was Dovid's cue. "Hi, guys! This is Dovid from Don't Look Now and today I am without Rachel. She's probably going to writhe with jealousy after she finds out what I'm doing, because I'm going to be playing Brightforest with Sam. I'm really excited about this because I've never done a let's play before. But Sam is willing to work with me and my inexperience, which I'm really grateful about."

"There's nothing to be grateful for," Sam said. "I'm just pleased to be recording with you."

"Aw. Aw, guys, listen to this guy. Isn't he great?"

"Just don't say 'adorable,'" Sam said, nudging him.

Dovid laughed, so happy he thought he might burst. "Okay, I won't say it."

It was actually really easy to do, on top of being fun. Since Sam was a Let's Player and thus used to talking aloud and narrating while he played a game, it wasn't hard to follow along with him and offer suggestions and ask questions.

"Alright so we've reached another chasm, with the option of going across a creaky rope bridge, or a fallen tree. The problem with these options is that, if you all will remember a few episodes ago, the fallen tree was rotted and we fell through it into the water."

"And everyone knows rope bridges can't be trusted," Dovid said. "Huh. So what do you think you should do this time?"

"I was actually going to ask you that. Either way, it'll probably end with our character getting a mite waterlogged though."

"Rope bridges at least make for better dramatics?"

"That's a fair point. The rope bridge it is. Alright everybody, wish us luck. We're going to try it."

There was a moment of silence, only broken by the music from the game, Dovid waiting with bated breath, and then, "Look at that, we did it! Mind you, the—" there was a creaking, sound, followed by a splash. "Ah. Well. Alright, so we got over the bridge but we'll have to find another way back in the event we ever want to go back to that base. Oh dear."

Dovid laughed. "I'm sure you'll figure it out."

"I will, but it'll have to be next time. We've just about hit the hour mark."

"Oh no, what? You mean I'll have to wait til you do another episode to see what happens?"

Sam patted Dovid on the knee. "Sorry."

"No, no, I get it. Okay, well, guess that's it, guys. I want to say thanks again to Sam for letting me play with him. It was awesome."

"And thank you for playing with me. So for now, that's it, everybody. Thank you for watching."

Dovid waited quietly until Sam said, "The recording is off. We're not live anymore."

He sighed and pulled off his headset and mic. "Man, that was so much fun. But I'm genuinely bummed now. I want to keep playing."

Sam laughed. "We could always start a new game, like I said."

"Yeah, but half the fun was playing it with you."

"Well, I—we could keep playing, when you went home. Time differences allowing, we could Skype or chat on the phone while I played. It would be like me doing a let's play, but just for you."

"Just for me," Dovid repeated faintly.

"It sounds like you rather like the sound of that," Sam said with a laugh.

"I really, really do. And I'm definitely up for playing more. Oh man, Rachel is going to die that I got to do this with you. She's way more of a gamer than I am."

"Well," Sam said after a beat, "maybe she and I can play another time. But this was just for you."

Dovid's breath stuttered. "Fuck, okay, no, I need to kiss you right this minute, come here."

* * *

The Saturday passed altogether too quickly for Dovid's liking, and soon enough it was evening again, Dovid back in Sam's apartment to spend another night together with him. He and Rachel had an evening flight Monday night to get back to the States, and Dovid was fully prepared to get in as much Sam time as he could until then. Which, as Dovid explained to Sam, pretty much meant staying in Sam's apartment with him, watching things together and playing games, and maybe going out for a walk, weather allowing.

"In less than forty-eight hours it's back to only getting you as a voice in my ear," Dovid said, from where he was happily snuggled into Sam's side on Sam's couch. "I'd rather spend all of that with you, instead of going out. With maybe the exception of the Leprechaun Museum with Rachel tomorrow. If that's okay."

"It's very okay. This way I get to have you all to myself."

Dovid smiled. "Same here."

They got ready for bed early, but not with any intentions of using that time to actually sleep. It was more bare skin on bare skin, hands and mouths exploring, reveling in each other's sounds.

Eventually their kisses turned sleepy and they rearranged a little, Sam on his back, Dovid's head resting on his chest to listen to his heartbeat.

"Let me know if I'm squishing you," Dovid said.

"Alright," Sam said quietly. "But even if you were, I wouldn't want you to go anywhere else."

They drifted together, just listening to each other's

breathing, until a thought popped into Dovid's head. "What's your family like?"

"My family?" Sam asked, sounding surprised. Which made sense—after all, the question had come from seemingly nowhere.

"Yeah. I was just wondering. You've met Rachel and get along with her. I was wondering about your side of things. You said you had a brother, right?"

"Yes," Sam said. "Charlie. He's a few years older than me."

"What's he like?"

"Oh, he's very nice. And quite successful. He's a doctor over in Cork. He was wonderful when I was hurt; flew over to help me for a few days. Even brought me some things from my flat. His wife, Anna, is a dear too. She came with, and tidied up a bit for me. Even made a few meals so I didn't have to worry about that when I'd just gotten out of the hospital."

"That sounds great. It's nice that you have them as a support."

"It really is. You know, Charlie's the one who suggested I try making a let's play. Bought me my first headset mic. It was nearly a year later that I actually felt brave enough to do it, but still. The credit's all on him."

Dovid smiled. "I'll have to thank him, if I ever meet him."

"I hope that you do! Or… I'd like it if you did. I've never really had someone to introduce to him before. Maybe the next time you're in, we could go to Cork for a visit."

Next time. "I like the sound of that."

"As for my parents," Sam said, "my mother is a seamstress and my father works in sales. We get along alright. They were very nice to me after my accident, even though it was quite an inconvenience for them. Even bought me a new phone."

Dovid frowned. "An inconvenience? That you'd been hit by a car?"

Sam shrugged against him. "Well now, it was inconvenient for everyone involved, really. Me especially I think."

"Um, right." Sam just kept saying this stuff about his parents that pushed all of Dovid's buttons, but he was always so flippant about it that Dovid wasn't sure how to react. "Yeah."

"And they're fine people. Just, you know, Charlie was the real standout, being so book smart and handsome and in medicine and all. I was always a little too loud for them."

Too loud.

Sam.

Too *loud*?

"What?" Dovid asked faintly. And suddenly he was struck with a vivid thought of a much smaller Sam taking a criticism to heart and walking around on eggshells because he was "too loud" for his parents. *"What?"*

"Erm, sorry," Sam said, clearly confused. "What?"

No, this…it wasn't his business to ask. That was Sam's, and maybe one day Sam would be comfortable broaching the subject himself, but it wasn't Dovid's right to push. "Uh, nothing. Just, uh, just me wondering if maybe they wouldn't like meeting me then." He tried to smile. "I'm definitely louder than you are."

"But you're so interesting! And it wouldn't be a problem that you're a man either, as they know I'm gay."

"Oh. Yeah?"

"Mm-hm. They have for ages. They weren't angry about it, which was nice. I've been, you know, told I was a disappointment, but in the end I feel I was quite lucky."

Dovid, already a little on edge, went white-hot with fury. "Excuse me? No. No, absolutely not."

"Sorry?"

"You're not a disappointment," Dovid spat. And now that he had started, the dam burst. "Fuck them for ever making you think you were." His parents had always been nothing but supportive. Of the being blind, sure, and then the YouTube thing, and the being-bi thing...

But he also knew he was lucky. Not everyone got parents like he and Rachel did.

"Dovid?" Sam asked, sounding hesitant.

"Sorry." Dovid moved to take Sam's hand in his own and lace their fingers together. "Sorry. I'm just...fuck. That's not fucking fair, for them to treat you like that. For them to make you feel like that. I know my parents would love you. Let's just... I'll let you borrow mine, okay?"

Sam squeezed his hand. "Okay," he said after a moment. Dovid wished he could see his face. His voice didn't betray any particular emotion.

"Sorry," Dovid said again. "I didn't mean to...go and ruin the moment." He rubbed his free hand over his face. "Fuck, I'm not even tired anymore, I'm just riled up."

"Would you like to get up? I could make some tea."

Dovid buried his face in Sam's shoulder and groaned. "Ugh, no. Maybe."

Fingers began to stroke through his hair and Dovid sighed into the feeling of it. But part of him was upset over the fact that Sam was the one offering comfort to him.

"I'm sorry," he said yet again. "It's not my business,

unless you want it to be. I just…you're so great. You're like one of the best things that has ever happened to me. I have been so, so happy talking to you these last few months. Dating you is something else entirely, being able to *be here* with you—I love you so much. I just want everyone else to know how great you are. To treat you how you deserve to be treated."

"Thank you," Sam said quietly. "I… I won't pretend that sometimes I wish things were different. That I was better than I am." *You don't have to be,* Dovid thought furiously. *Don't do that to yourself.* "But it's—" He cleared his throat. "It's a great pleasure, knowing you, and knowing that you like me the way I came."

Dovid opened and closed his mouth a few times before he eventually settled on, "Yeah. Hard same. So just…remember that, alright?"

The fingers in his hair never faltered. "I'll do my best."

"Um."

"Yeah?"

"Is it…do you feel okay being kissed right now? It's cool if you don't, I just… I just want to," he said, feeling foolish.

"I think I always feel like being kissed by you," Sam said, voice colored with amusement.

Dovid had to smile at that.

* * *

Sam stared up at the ceiling for a long time once Dovid had fallen asleep, a warm, comforting presence curled into his side. He couldn't help but replay the words Dovid had had to say while he had been awake.

"That's not fucking fair, for them to treat you like that. For them to make you feel like that. I know my parents would love you."

Sam had never questioned how his parents interacted with him. He had only wished to be better, so that maybe one day they would…would like him more. But he hadn't doubted that he'd deserved their displeasure. He had been a bothersome child, what with being so clumsy and gangly, and had grown into a disappointing adult who they knew would never have a standout job or bring home a person (wife) they approved of or…or any number of things.

And he knew all of that because…

Because they had told him so.

"I just want everyone else to know how great you are. To treat you how you deserve to be treated."

Someone as wonderful as Dovid loved him, and Sam had changed nothing about himself. Rachel liked him too, as did his viewers. He couldn't even pretend to doubt that; he was making *money* because people liked him. Because strangers on the internet (and not-so-strangers he had started to interact with more regularly) liked who he was. His personality, his way of speaking, and he often did talk about his day-to-day life in videos, just for something to say. Mentioned his shyness, his fears, had his silly little asides. And they *liked* that. Told him so in comments, talked about their own insecurities, asked genuine questions.

For the first time in his life, Sam considered the possibility that, well…

That maybe his parents were wrong.

* * *

Sunday morning, Sam had another bit of a lie-in with Dovid before they got up and went out for a proper Irish breakfast. They met Rachel afterwards and went to the museum together, going through the tour and then the gift shop. Sam felt a bit bad, because a lot of the visuals were lost on Dovid, especially the tunnel of optical illusions, but they all had a good time regardless. Dovid cracked a lot of jokes.

It was drizzling slightly when they emerged into the daylight, so Rachel decided that the next order of business was to track down a toy store and buy some blind boxes for Sam to review. In the end, she and Dovid picked some out for him and purchased them without him seeing their choices.

"So it can be a real blind bag," Rachel explained. "This way everything gets to be a surprise, both for you and the viewers."

"Alright. That sounds good."

They went to lunch next, and after, made their way back to Sam's place. He gave Rachel the cursory tour, and then told the two to make themselves at home while excusing himself for a moment to set his Brightforest video to public. Dovid had suggested they upload the video Saturday, after they'd finished filming it, but not to put it live until Sunday afternoon, just to give Sam some experience in doing staggered videos.

Something buzzed a moment later.

"Hang on," Rachel said, pulling out her phone. "Sam! You just posted something?"

Sam rubbed the back of his neck. "Yeah. It was Dovid's idea. We recorded something together yesterday."

Rachel turned to Dovid, aghast. "You did not!"

Dovid grinned. "Sorry."

"You're not sorry in the least bitty bit, shut up. I'm so jealous," she moaned. "You got to watch him play."

"Not just watch," Dovid said, grin turning wicked.

Rachel let out a sound of deep betrayal before pausing, expression coming up all thoughtful.

"Okay," she said steadily, "how'd you present it to the class?"

"What do you mean?" Sam asked.

Dovid shrugged, seeming to know what Rachel was asking. "We said I was visiting Ireland, which, true, and that we wanted to do a collaborative. Also true." He tilted his head. "There might have been some very gentle flirting."

Rachel pinched the bridge of her nose. "So the fact that you two are dating is going to be all over the internet in about thirty seconds." She didn't sound upset though. More resigned.

"We figured it'd be safe. People do collaboratives all the time. And they all know for a fact that we're friends now."

"Sam? You don't care?"

"Not really," Sam said easily. Because this, at least, was easy. "I'm very happy to be dating Dovid. I'll just be reacting to any questions the same as I did when we first started talking and say that we like our privacy."

Rachel nodded. "Works for me. Now, let's go ahead and get set up for your blind bag unboxing, while I resist the urge to drop everything and watch your Brightforest update."

* * *

"Dovid?" Sam said, breath catching as he checked his current view count for the latest video.

"Yeah?"

"I…it looks like the collaborative was a hit."

"Oh yeah?" Dovid leaned forward and grinned. "What's up? Spill."

"One hundred thousand hits and counting," Rachel crowed, looking up from her phone. "Man, I am *so mad* I'm not watching it right now."

* * *

Monday was still wonderful. It carried a haze of melancholy, but Sam did his best to push it aside and embrace the now. Right now; the moments Dovid was still with him.

They lazed in bed for ages, and, upon finally getting up, Dovid expressed his disappointment that Sam's shower wasn't big enough for them to share it. Instead they both hopped in and out quickly so as not to waste time, and brushed their teeth side by side while the mirror was still clouded from steam.

They stayed in for breakfast. Sam got the coffee started while Dovid prepared the tomatoes for frying, and then Dovid set the table while Sam got things cooking in the skillets. They stood together at the stove, sipping from their mugs while they waited for the food to be ready and then got it all plated. They sat down across from each other, knocking legs accidentally, and then much more deliberately while they ate. Dovid leaned against the counter while Sam did the dishes, drying whatever Sam handed to him and keeping up an easy, winding conversation.

It was all very soft and incredibly domestic, and Sam only wanted for more time. More days like this one, where they could just be in each other's space. Reach out and touch whenever they wanted to.

Dovid and Rachel's flight was in the evening, but with it being an international flight, they still needed to be at the airport three hours before. On top of needing time to get to the airport, early afternoon drew closer altogether too quickly.

Rachel was going to come by Sam's apartment to pick Dovid up. They'd be getting in a car and going to the airport. Dovid was going to board a plane and go back to being hundreds of miles away, to being just a voice in Sam's ear.

It struck Sam then, just how much he would miss being able to simply *see* Dovid. See the facial expressions that went with the rest of him. His wide grin and constantly moving hands. The shy little curve of his mouth when Sam said or did something Dovid found immeasurably sweet.

He would have to see if maybe he couldn't do something about that.

For now, Dovid was all packed up, and he and Sam were tucked up against each other on Sam's couch, simply holding hands and being with each other, trying to soak up the last moments they had.

Dovid sighed heavily when his phone beeped, followed by him playing the text Rachel had sent to let them know she was on her way over.

"Fuck, I don't want to go. I don't want it to be over yet." He swallowed. "I don't want to leave you."

Sam reached out to cup Dovid's cheek, turning him so they were facing each other. "We have a little more time."

Dovid closed the distance, an edge of desperation to their kisses now, Dovid touching him as though he was trying to memorize the feel of Sam underneath his fingers. Eventually they were just clutching at each other, unable to do anything but hang on and wish they weren't about to be parted.

"I'm going to miss you so much," Sam murmured, holding on tight.

"Fucking hard same," Dovid replied from where his face was pressed into Sam's neck.

Chapter Eleven

"Hey, guys! This is Don't Look Now with Dovid and Ra-chel. I'm Dovid, Rachel's behind the camera, and today we're going to eat the entirety of Norway!"

Sam watched, smiling, as Dovid proceeded to intro-duce him to a variety of Norwegian eateries and baker-ies and took him on a tasting adventure—with Rachel behind the camera, of course, eating too and doing just as much exclaiming.

Dovid and Rachel were on a plane back to Seattle at this very moment. Dovid had texted Sam before he'd gotten on the plane, just for one last communication while they were in the same time zone.

He already missed him so much.

But watching his videos was another sort of way to experience Dovid. Sam hadn't gotten a chance to watch most of the footage Don't Look Now had released dur-ing their trip. Mostly because he had actually been sav-ing up to watch them for when Dovid had gone. And somewhat because, for some of the time during uploads, he'd been lucky enough to get Dovid in person.

Dovid was going home with another one of Sam's shirts and a bunch of memories, some documented both for themselves and the internet.

In the meantime, Sam still had the rest of Monday

off and he had work to do. Dovid had sat down with him and helped him plan out his Patreon tiers, uploading schedule, and some ideas of how to explain it to his subscribers. Now Sam had to make a video introducing it all.

In the end, Sam had decided he would only have two tiers to start with, a one-dollar and a five-dollar tier. One dollar would be a general thank-you for providing regular content, in the same way Don't Look Now's tier worked, and he would do his best to record his regular Sunday videos on Saturday, to give those first-tier patrons an early release link, at least once in a while. Five dollars and patrons got unlisted links to an exclusive Patreon-only series. Sam was going to put out a poll on which game he'd do the series of—Dire Straits or Brightforest. He was most known for Dire Straits now, and that was what was still his more popular series, but Brightforest was also getting popular, especially since it was still in beta. The link itself would be posted, as Rachel suggested, every Wednesday. However, just like he had done with the video he'd recorded with Dovid, the video itself didn't have to be recorded actually on Wednesday.

Originally, Dovid had suggested recording for an hour and breaking the video into twenty-minute chunks, so Sam could film all his extra content for the month in one session. But that would have meant Sam wouldn't be able to take suggestions or answer questions from his viewers. It had been the deciding factor, in the end; Sam wanted to interact with his audience. So he'd record an extra twenty minutes sometime in the week when he felt up to it and then put the link up on Wednesday. It didn't seem too daunting anymore, not after all the prep and planning and talking. He was actually sort of looking forward to embarking on a new project.

It took several stops and starts, and a few judicious edits, but eventually he settled on the audio he wanted.

"Hello, everybody, I'm Sam. Now, usually this is the part where I introduce the game I'm going to play for you. However, today I'm actually going to be introducing something else entirely.

"After some cajoling from some good friends, I've decided to try out making a Patreon. The links to it can be found here, or in the description box below. If, well, if you like my videos and would like to support me, there are two reward tiers. The first, a dollar, is just a thank-you for my work if you are so inclined. The second tier is a five-dollar donation. Patrons at this tier will get access to a patron-only let's play series, for either Dire Straits or Brightforest. I've a poll up right now that will stay up for a week where you can vote on which series you'd like me to start, and then you can expect new, exclusive videos every week.

"I really do appreciate all of your support so very, very much and wanted to say thank you for watching my channel. I'm hoping that my channel will continue to grow with content and what I can do with it, and this will help enable me to do so. I'd love it if you all came along with me for the ride."

After playing the video over altogether too many times, Sam took a deep breath and just uploaded it, set his Patreon to "live" and determinedly left his flat to go take a walk so that he wouldn't dwell too much about what the internet as a whole might think. He did take his phone, but he kept it turned on silent and refused to check it during said walk.

It took a great deal of wandering and a stop at his

local grocery store to pick up some ingredients for dinner, but by the time he was home again and preparing a meal, he had calmed down a lot. Enough that he was able to pull out his phone and open the book about the history of Cadbury he and Dovid had decide to read together next. He was able to get lost in that while he ate.

It was only after he'd put away his leftovers and washed up that he allowed himself to go back to his desk and check the views on his video, and his Patreon alerts. Since it had only been up for about two hours, he wasn't expecting very much at all.

Which was why the ten thousand views was a surprise, especially since the video had been specifically titled "Patreon Campaign" to keep people from watching what was, essentially, a commercial if they didn't want to.

Which was why the fifty-seven, forty-six of whom were second-tier, new patrons were even more of a surprise, good god.

And that was just in two hours.

Sam swallowed. The idea that he might be able to subsist on just gaming alone seemed like a much more possible concept now.

Wow.

* * *

Dovid Rosenstein: Hey, just wanted to let you know we arrived home safe and sound. You're probably asleep right now, hopefully having good dreams. Talk to you tomorrow? I'll be jet-lagged out of my mind but definitely up and around at eleven o'clock <3

* * *

"Dovid! How was your flight?"

"Hey, you." Dovid leaned back in his chair. "It wasn't too bad. No crying children, which is always a plus.

Mostly we tried to sleep. There was plenty of sleep we needed to catch up on. There isn't a whole lot of editing possible to do in the air, but we got a few things figured out."

"Wonderful. I'm glad it wasn't too miserable."

"The only real miserable thing was that I was leaving you behind." He was gratified to hear Sam laugh. "What? I thought that was smooth."

"Smooth and suave," Sam said, teasing grin clear in his voice. "But of course I miss you too. So much."

"Yeah…" Dovid shook his head, refusing to dwell. Sam in his ear was still *Sam*. "Anyway. How'd your day back at work go?"

"It was alright. I thought a few people would be cross with me that I took Monday off, because those are usually quite busy, but no one mentioned it. And the day was really quite mild."

"That's good. That's great."

"Also, erm…"

"Yeah?"

"I don't suppose you checked my Patreon since you got back, have you?"

Dovid's eyebrows shot up. "I honestly forgot all about it. Hey yeah! How's it going?" Even as he asked, he was moving to his computer to pull up the website.

"Quite…quite well," Sam said.

"Yeah?" he paused, waiting. It sounded as though Sam wanted to tell him himself. "Anything you wanna share with the class?"

"I've two hundred and seventy-six patrons as of right this very moment. One hundred and ninety-three of those are second-tier."

"Holy shit! Sam, that's incredible. That video's been up for how long?"

"Just over twenty-four hours."

"That's so amazing. I'm so proud of you." Dovid did the math in his head. "If they all stick around for another week that's over a grand for you!"

"I, well, yes."

"Fuck, that's— Sam. *Sam.*"

"I know," Sam said, with a nervous laugh. "I'm afraid I—I don't know quite what to do. I wasn't expecting this many, and certainly not so soon. I—Dovid, I—"

"Yeah?"

"I don't want to get ahead of myself but—but if some of these people actually stick with me, I…there's a very good chance I could actually leave my job."

"Fuck yeah," Dovid said. "I know! And you sound super nervous, so I'm going to keep being excited for you but also what's wrong?"

"Nothing's wrong, not really. I just don't know where to go from here? How to keep from disappointing everyone. This is…this is more than just putting videos up on YouTube for fun. This is people actually wanting to pay me money for those videos."

"You can start by giving your patrons what they're donating for; more of your videos. How's the poll doing?"

"Skewed rather heavily for more Dire Straits. A new character was released as a DLC and a lot of them are requesting that I play as her."

"Sounds like a plan to me," Dovid said. "And that's all you need right now. If people don't like what you do, no one is going to make them keep donating or subscribing. If they do like your stuff, they'll stick around. If there's like, an overwhelming amount of people who aren't happy and say so, that's when you might want to step back and reconsider a little what you're doing and putting out there, but really… Sam, I said it before and I'll say it again: I might have helped get people watching you, but viewers have stayed this long because they like you and what you're doing. And almost three hundred people liked what you've done so far enough to donate to you for future work. I think the only way you're really going to disappoint anyone at this point is if you get a personality transplant."

"Thank you," Sam said quietly. "That you have so much faith in me means the world."

"No, yeah, of course. Of course I do."

"Thank you," Sam said again. The sound of a throat being cleared. "So, what's on the schedule today?"

Dovid twisted back and forth in his chair. "Editing more footage, once Rachel and I fully wake up. I actually only got up a little while ago, in part because it was getting close to our phone time."

"Oh. You didn't have to do that. You could have slept in."

Dovid laughed. "We got home around three and I slept til ten. That's still seven hours of sleep. I'm a little wired right now to be honest; technically it's seven-fifteen for me too, and I just slept the day away. Jet lag's gonna be weird the next few days. Talking to you on a set schedule helps. Means I've gotta be up and doing stuff."

"Whatever works," Sam said. "I'm glad to be talking to you."

"Right back atcha."

"So more editing?"

"Yeah. A lot more. People know we were on a tour so our video uploads would be erratic, and we were able to get a little bit done while we were abroad—that's why we were able to release that video of Norway—but we've still got pretty much two weeks' worth of footage to get through and edit. The next few days we're going to be holed up at home or in coffee shops crunched up over our computer screens."

"Good luck with all that. I, for one, am really looking forward to watching your whole trip, or whatever you care to show us."

"Hey, you heard about it plenty while I was over there. Damn near talked your ear off."

"And it was lovely. But this way I'll get to experience it all again. Especially Ireland."

"I'm still pumped we did that let's play together. I didn't really pay attention to the comments on it yet, but I *might* have downloaded and saved the audio file you sent me so I could listen to it again on the plane."

A chuckle. "I'm glad you enjoyed it so much."

"I really, really did."

They chatted a little bit more about Sam's day and Dovid's plans, and Sam suggested a new documentary, this one about Vikings, for Dovid to watch when he got a chance.

"Sounds like a plan," he said with a yawn. "Sorry. I'm awake, I promise."

"You've had a busy few weeks," Sam said, sounding amused. "I think being tired is allowed."

"Yeah, yeah. Speaking of, I should probably check on Rachel and make sure she isn't dead," Dovid said forlornly. He didn't want to stop talking to Sam but—

"You have a lot of work to do," Sam said easily. "Go get started on it. I'll be up for a few more hours yet, if you'd like to text me."

Dovid smiled. "I love you."

"I love you too."

* * *

Dire Straits, with its new player character Mindy, won the Patreon poli. By the time Sam was ready to record his first Patreon-exclusive episode, he had nearly three hundred second-tier patrons, all willing to pay him five dollars a month for four twenty-minute episodes. It was all still a little surreal.

Even more so after August sixth, when the money was deposited directly into his bank account.

Sam Doyle: I can't believe it. I still can't believe it.

Dovid Rosenstein: I can! And it's GREAT.

Sam Doyle: This is really happening. It's really possible.

Dovid Rosenstein: See? I told you you could make it happen. Your audience just wants more of you. You keep giving it to them, well. Stuff like this only gets easier and easier.

Sam swallowed. He hadn't told Dovid the kicker yet.

Sam Doyle: Dovid, my flat is 1,200 euros a month including utilities. Food, transport… Between Patreon and YouTube, my entire month's bills were paid through August.

Dovid Rosenstein: Holy SHIT, Sam, that's fantastic!

Dovid Rosenstein: I'm so proud of you and happy for you and fuck just—I'm giving you the biggest invisible hug right now.

Dovid Rosenstein: God I wish I could hold you right now. Maybe jump up and down with you. Definitely buy you a drink.

Sam Doyle: I'd be happy enough with the hug. But I suppose words will have to suffice.

Dovid Rosenstein: Listen, I'm about to leave for a shoot, but we should be done and home in a couple hours. Maybe three. Would you still be awake by then to talk-talk?

Sam Doyle: Of course. I'd love to. Just call me when you can :)

Dovid Rosenstein: I can call tomorrow at eleven. I don't want you to stay up too late.

Sam Doyle: I'll be reading <3

Dovid Rosenstein: Okay, I'll talk to you soon then. Love you.

Sam Doyle: Love you too.

* * *

"Hey, you," Dovid said, slinging off his backpack full of camera equipment to deal with later and making his way to his room.

"Hello." Sam sounded sleepy. Dovid'd have to make this short, even though he was bursting. Rachel had wanted to know what the hell was wrong with him to be so happy. When he'd told her about Sam, she'd damn well near shrieked with glee though. "It's good to hear your voice."

"Right back atcha," Dovid said. "And I won't keep you, because you need to *sleep*, but I just wanted to tell you in person how super-duper happy I am for you. And proud. And fuck, I love you so, so much. I'm so glad this is starting to work out for you. That you're doing it. That this is something you can and are doing."

"Thank you so much," Sam said. "I...thank you. I love you too."

"So what are you thinking? Taking the gaming world by storm?"

Sam chuckled, making Dovid smile wider. "Oh nothing like that. But I've gotten my Loot Crate box, so I'm going to film that unboxing like Rachel showed me."

"Good, great. And when do you think you'll be able to put that up?"

"That's the other thing. I'm doing Dire Straits Friday nights still, and Brightforest Sundays, because it became so popular I'm still playing it. And then Patreon on Wednesday. I don't want to overwhelm my viewers? Or put out too much content all at once?"

"That's a good point. Even Rachel and I usually keep it to three videos a week, spaced out. And you're right that you don't want to put too much out at once; not only for your viewers, but it's easier to burn out like that."

"Right."

"I'd suggest doing the unboxing video on Sunday, then. Your Dire Straits series on Friday is kind of a staple now, but you've only been doing Brightforest a few months. Maybe this Sunday add a note at the end of your video that you'll be doing something different next Sunday, and post the video then?"

"Okay," Sam said. He sounded like he was drifting. "I'll do that, then."

"Awesome. And this is awesome, and you're awesome. So proud of you. Love you so much."

"Love you too."

"Now are you going to sleep?"

"I don't want to stop talking to you," Sam murmured.

"I'll talk you through it then," Dovid said, smiling softly. God he loved him so much. "Lie down?"

The sound of fabric moving around, and then Dovid heard a breathy "Alright. There we are."

"Which side are you sleeping on this time?" Sam tended to curl up on one side when he slept. It was nice, when they slept together, because it made him easier to hold—and Dovid loved it when Sam wrapped around Dovid's back to hold him.

"Left side."

"Good. Your eyes are closed right?"

"Mm-hm."

"And I'm right there, next to you."

"Are you?"

"Yeah. See? You can hear me. I'm right there."

"Mm."

"I'm the big spoon this time. Holding you from behind. Our legs are tangled up, a little, but it's okay."

"Yes…"

"Drift off with me, Sam?"

"Love you." Mumbled. Sam was probably barely awake.

"I love you too."

* * *

September was a whirlwind of activity for Dovid. Aside from YouTube, he also did some side-work as a public speaker, both volunteer and paid. With school sessions all starting up, he was often brought in to speak to student bodies about things like personal power, growth, acceptance, and success. Sometimes he was an example of what anyone could grow up to be. Other times he was a minor-celebrity getting to speak out against bullying.

Whatever the reason, he enjoyed the work, but there was a lot of it and it was draining, especially with travel time; he went all over the country. Not to mention that he and Rachel still had to keep up with their usual filming and editing schedule. And while most of August was just them putting up videos from the July Europe tour, September was a new month that needed to be filled with new content.

No matter what though, he made sure to make time for Sam.

Sam, who was continuing to be a rising success in his own right in the gaming community. His YouTube subscribers only continued to grow, his view count remained high, and his Patreon was a continued success. Like Dovid had suggested, Sam continued with Dire Straits let's plays on Friday nights, but switched it up on Sunday. He finished his run of Brightforest and started a new game, Dew Meadow, which was also offered for him to review first. He liked the game so much and the review was so popular that he started it the next week. Some Sundays though, he posted other reviews or opened blind boxes instead. He'd been sent a few different ones now. And Wednesday nights Dovid and Rachel got to watch more of the Mindy Dire Straits one (because of course they were patrons).

Dovid did spend a lot of time either working like crazy or asleep, so phone calls were sporadic and texts happened throughout the day as time allowed. They missed each other, missed the closeness they got to have back in July, especially with it nearing October. But being a voice in each other's ears was good too.

* * *

Ready, Dovid typed to him through Skype. Sam grinned and made the call. After a moment it connected, and he found himself staring at Dovid's beaming face. Rachel was just next to him, looking exasperatedly fond. "Hello," he said to the both of them.

Dovid, if possible, lit up even more. "Hey, you." Then, "So? Am I in the shot? Facing the right way?"

Sam couldn't tell if he was talking to him or Rachel, but he nodded just the same. "You are," he said happily.

"Awesome." Dovid tilted his head in Rachel's direction, without moving too much aside from that. Probably in an effort to stay within view. "That's your cue, thank you for your help, now go away."

Rachel rolled her eyes. "Yeah, yeah. Hi, Sam. Bye, Sam."

"It was nice to see you too," Sam told her. "And oh, I'm almost done with that walk-through you asked for."

"Oh my god," Rachel said. "Thank you *so* much. I can't find any hints anywhere, since the game is still in beta."

"Happy to help."

"Yes, okay." Dovid flapped a hand. "Are you done taking up his attention now?"

Rachel grinned. "Yup, don't worry. I'm going." She walked out of the shot.

"Close the door behind you!" Dovid called, still without turning his head from facing the monitor.

"Like I want to hear you two anyway!" followed by a near-slam.

"There now," Sam laughed. "You didn't have to be mean."

"Please. Do you know how much shit she's given me in, like, the last week alone about our date night plans?

Even if they're date afternoons for me. Because seriously, so much shit."

There was a time, not even all that long ago, where that would have made Sam feel guilty, for taking up Dovid's time. But Sam knew just how dearly Dovid enjoyed his time being taken up by Sam. Since Sam wanted Dovid just as much, they both won the more they managed to be in each other's pockets. It was why he'd suggested regular, planned out Skype dates in the first place, on top of the phone calls whenever they could manage. Sleepy good nights were wonderful, but: *"I know you can't see me but, well, I can see you. And I'd like to, as often as I can."* Dovid had made some flippant, teasing remark, but his obvious delight at the suggestion made it worth it for that alone.

So now Sam simply grinned, in on the joke. He and Charlie didn't quite have the same relationship Dovid and Rachel had, but he understood sibling love. "How silly have you been about our plans, to have her give you so much trouble?"

Dovid pinched his fingers together. "Oh, you know. The usual amount."

* * *

Dovid pushed his hands up underneath his glasses to cover his face. He was so tired. They'd just gotten home from a full day. A shoot with Rachel and then a bunch of editing and then an afternoon speech at a special-needs school which was always great but always so draining…

Kids who just wanted validation, to know that they *could* go out and do things they wanted to do. Kids who got stepped on and bullied and sneered at and Dovid had been one of them once, in some ways, before he grew up a little and learned to take some of his own back. Before he got good-looking enough that most people saw that before they saw his glasses. And even then, only sometimes. Sometimes the comments were worse because of that, like they didn't realize he was a thinking, feeling person, as opposed to a nice body that came with a white cane.

"You look totally beat," Rachel said. "Why don't you take a nap or something?"

"It's like five pm. That is not the ideal time to nap."

"With our schedules it can be. If you're not up by seven, I'll just make dinner myself."

"Don't you dare try to make dinner," Dovid said alarmed.

A sigh. "I mean I'll order dinner myself. Chinese? I'll get your favorites." It was a good comfort food for both of them.

"Yeah, thanks. That sounds good." He yawned, unable to stop it.

Rachel poked him in the shoulder. "Go. Take. A. Nap."

"Okay, okay, I'm going."

Dovid went to his room and flopped down on his bed. Eventually he wiggled around, pulling his phone out of his pocket and crawling under the covers.

After a minute of wondering why he still wasn't comfortable, he took his glasses off and folded them up, setting them on the pillow beside him next to his phone. Then he proceeded to make himself a blanket burrito.

He sighed and closed his eyes. Five o'clock, meaning it was one in the morning for Sam. Way, way too late to call. Or even text; Sam might be doing that thing where he stayed up until ungodly hours of the morning reading, and if Dovid texted him, Sam would text back and deny he was too tired to keep up the conversation and Dovid wasn't about to chance that. He loved Sam just the way he was, but sometimes Sam acquiesced to things too easily, not wanting to make waves. He was getting a lot better about it as his self-confidence grew; saying "no" to fans, sponsors, and extra hours at work when he felt he needed to. He even said no to Dovid sometimes. But if Sam knew Dovid was feeling this shitty, he'd stay up all night trying to help ease that. And Dovid was feeling so down, he'd probably take whatever Sam would be willing to give him even *with* being aware Sam was losing sleep over it.

So he needed to wait. He knew he needed to wait.

Dovid wished he could talk to Sam now. That they were closer.

Well. He'd have tomorrow.

Yeah.

* * *

"Hi," Sam said when he called, smile in his voice. "How are you? How was yesterday?"

Dovid, still tired, bit down a yawn. He felt he hadn't slept at all. He'd only gotten up half an hour ago, and that was mainly because he didn't want to be late in talking to Sam. "I'm okay," he said. "Tired. Yesterday was…draining."

"Oh no, that doesn't sound good. Do you want to talk about it?"

Dovid shrugged, not that Sam could see. Sleep had at least helped dull the ache. "It's not a big deal. I just was doing another pep-talk speech thing yesterday. I love doing it but it can get hard. I… I had a lot of people try to kick me down when I was growing up. It's sometimes hard to go to these schools and *know* that's how these kids have been treated. To know that there are so many others I can't help."

"That does sound hard," Sam said. "I'm sorry." A

pause. "If it helps… I think you are helping. You're there for people to find, to reach out to. You helped me, you know."

"Sam—"

"No, I don't mean with YouTube and my channel or anything like that. Well, I sort of do. You helped me with my confidence. To start really being my own person. I don't think I would have ever tried what I'm doing now without you. You gave me all the pushes I needed. That's something. It's something to me."

Dovid pressed a hand over his eyes. He wasn't crying, and he absolutely refused to get a runny, snotty nose while on the phone with Sam. "Wow, um. Thanks."

"You mean so much to a lot of people, Dovid. You're so very special and good."

"Thanks," Dovid whispered. It was exactly what he needed to hear.

He knew Sam'd be able to give that to him.

Chapter Twelve

Sam Doyle: I am very glad you and Rachel brought tax law up to me back when you visited.

Dovid Rosenstein: Yeah? I mean good! But why?

Sam Doyle: Because it gave me time to start figuring out what I owe for the self-employed part of my income. It's all due by the end of October and I'm SO glad that I was given the heads up about when I'd have to pay and an idea of how much I'd have to pay. And when it was all due.

Sam Doyle: If I hadn't known how much to put aside, I, well, I wouldn't be in a bad way because I'm still fully employed and mostly I've been saving all my new income, but the amount I did have to pay wasn't insignificant.

Dovid Rosenstein: Hahaha, I guess the wonders of self-employment and the government's cut is the same pretty much everywhere. I hope it wasn't too much of a blow.

Sam Doyle: Thankfully not! Especially since, after Patreon, I have to declare...significantly more than I was expecting to before Patreon.

Dovid Rosenstein: I like the sound of that :)

Dovid Rosenstein: That things are doing well, I mean.

Dovid Rosenstein: Not that you have to pay more in taxes, because that sucks.

Sam Doyle: I got what you meant :)

Dovid Rosenstein: <3 <3 <3

Dovid Rosenstein: Have you uh, thought anymore about what we talked about?

Sam Doyle: My moving the gaming to full time, you mean?

Dovid Rosenstein: Yeah, that.

Sam Doyle: I have. A lot. I think that waiting is still a good idea—maybe see how things are doing after all the holidays are over. If people still want to be my patrons through Christmas.

Dovid Rosenstein: That's really smart.

Dovid Rosenstein: And gives you a chance to get your Christmas bonus too ;p

Sam Doyle: Hahaha I hadn't even considered that, but it's a good factor to keep in mind.

Sam Doyle: But no I'm thinking about it. Seriously. And I thought I could maybe give myself a time period to work towards. I was thinking February.

Dovid Rosenstein: Yeah? That's a good solid few months to wait it out and see where things go and if they keep getting better for you.

Sam Doyle: Right!

Sam Doyle: And it's also the month we met and everything really got started.

Dovid Rosenstein: Holy shit, you're right. I just counted back and...oh MAN

Dovid Rosenstein: Do you realize

Dovid Rosenstein: We started actually talking

Dovid Rosenstein: On Valentine's Day

Sam Doyle: What, really? I knew it was February but I didn't...really?

Dovid Rosenstein: Yeah, yeah, I just pulled up the video I plugged you and that was February 12th of this year. YOUR video went up on the 13th, I saw it, agonized over sending you a message, and finally did at like nine am on the 14th.

Sam Doyle: You agonized? Over sending me a message?

Dovid Rosenstein: Uh yeah? Of course? I was half in love with you just from watching your videos. Voices do me in. That plus the actual content—I said adorable and I meant it, and continue to mean it to this day.

Sam Doyle: Oh. Wow.

Sam Doyle: Well! I suppose we'll have to do something special for Valentine's Day. As well as the anniversary of when we first met.

Dovid Rosenstein: Awesome. Four months is a lot of time to prepare!

Dovid Rosenstein: Maybe...maybe we could swing a visit?

Sam Doyle: I was just about to say!

Sam Doyle: Actually I was wondering if maybe you wouldn't mind my coming to see you. I've never been to the States.

Dovid Rosenstein: Are you kidding? Yes, yes, and more yes.

Sam Doyle: I'll start looking at plane tickets :)

* * *

Nine o'clock on a Saturday and Dovid's phone pinged with a text alert. When he checked it, he was surprised, and a little worried, to see Sam's name.

Sam Doyle: Hi, Dovid. Is it alright if I call you?

Dovid was telling his phone to "call Sam" immediately, retreating to his room for privacy.

"Evening," Sam said, voice quiet and tired.

"Hey, you," Dovid said about as quietly. "It's like

five in the morning for you. What are you doing up? Are you okay?"

"I couldn't sleep. Something happened last night and… I've been thinking about it. I wanted to talk to you, but I also wanted to make sure it was a decent hour. You know, that I wasn't being a bother and interrupting a day. I know you've been so busy lately."

"Never," Dovid said. "If I can't answer I'll tell you, but you're never a bother. Okay?" And fuck, what had happened? Sam had gotten so much more confident in just the last few months, and that had included initiating a lot of their frequent conversations without voicing worry about causing inconvenience. Dovid knew people didn't get over self-esteem issues that quickly, and he would happily encourage and reassure Sam until his dying day, but…

At least he *had* reached out, while he was feeling badly. That was so important.

"Okay," Sam whispered.

Dovid swallowed. "Sam, what…what happened?"

At first there was just silence. Dovid waited, trying to be patient. But the silence stretched and stretched and then there was a tiny sound, just barely audible. It sounded so like someone stifling a sob. Dovid's heart leapt into his throat. "Sam? Sam, please, please tell me what's going on."

"I was telling my brother about how things are going," Sam said in a rush. "Because—because things are going so well. I—I wanted to share that with him. He…he said he was happy for me."

"That's great," Dovid said softly. And it was. That was good news. So what was the problem? "That's great," he said again, not quite prompting. More trying to sound encouraging.

"My parents and I don't talk too often," Sam said, still sounding shaken. "They checked up on me a few weeks after I got hurt, and of course I help my father whenever he has computer troubles, but aside from that we don't talk too much, past holidays. But Charlie... they talk to him quite often, and I suppose he might have brought me up—or maybe they did. Either way, someone brought me up and it—it came out what I'm doing. With YouTube, and gaming, and Patreon, and... and you."

"Okay."

"Charlie... I suppose Charlie probably thought it was helping. To tell my parents that things were going well for me. But they asked details, since they know about the IT work and...some...some things were said. To me. About my...my worth in general and what they thought I ought to be doing with my life, over what I am doing with it and—and—" His voice cracked. Dovid *ached*. "The thing is that I—I quite like my life the way it is now. I do. Work is more bearable knowing that I get to come home to you, even if I've started to get more impatient with it, and I'm enjoying my games, and what I'm earning is helping me see that there...there might be a light at the end of the tunnel. That I have a future in something that isn't just getting yelled at on the phone, or in person or by...by certain people." He stopped speaking, going horribly silent.

Dovid wished he knew what to do, what to say. He wished he could pull Sam close, stroke his hair. "I'm sorry" was all he was able to do. "I'm so sorry."

"I guess I just... I just needed to tell someone," Sam said, sounding exhausted. "I, you know, I can't tell Charlie. He meant so well." The *and I have no one else to tell* wasn't said, but Dovid felt it like a punch.

"Sam," Dovid said, voice dry. He swallowed, tried again. "Sam, you deserve so much more than whatever you're thinking. You deserve a life you love. And not to be yelled at. You *never* deserve to be yelled at. You deserve a future in something you like, and for you that isn't IT, that's gaming. And you're doing it. You're so successful already, and you're on your way to being even better. I'm *so* proud of you. Rachel is proud of you. Your viewers are proud of you. Charlie's clearly proud of you. I—I wish there was more that I could say. That I could do."

Silence.

"Sam?" Dovid asked hesitantly.

"I… I wish they were proud of me," Sam said, voice small. "I—I was proud. Of myself. Of what I've been able to do to. Of what I'm doing."

"You should," Dovid rushed to say. "You should be so proud. As for *them*—" Dovid clenched his teeth, trying to hold back the venom he wanted to spit about Sam's parents. That wouldn't help anyone, certainly not Sam. "As for them," he said again, calmer, "I don't know why they can't see the beautiful, wonderful, kind, and special human being you are. I don't know. But you *are* all those things. To me, to Rachel, to Charlie. To any-one with *sense*, you're all those things. I… I know it's hard. To be told something over and over again until you have to fight for it to be not true." *Look at the blind kid. Freak, missing his eyes. Stare because he can't see it, gawk and gape and point—* "But it isn't. You're worth *so* much. I'm so sorry they're not proud of you. You deserve it. It's not your fault they can't see that. I wish they did. But it's not your fault that they don't."

"Thank you," Sam said, after a while. "Thank you for talking with me. For—for being with me."

"Sam, you have no idea how lucky I am."

"Lucky?"

"That you're with me. I basically count my blessings every day."

A wet laugh, barely an exhale, but it was a start.

"No, really," Dovid said, "I mean it. Every day. Wake up, exercise, shower, make breakfast, bother Rachel, count blessings about having Sam in my life, proceed with rest of day."

"Oh, stop." Sam was starting to sound like himself again, thank god. "That's a bit much, don't you think?"

"A bit much? Are you kidding? Never. It's not enough! And then we get to text every day *and* I get to talk to you on the phone. Plus our Skype dates? Even with the ridiculous time difference. I still get you. It's amazing."

"You're amazing."

"And you're—" Dovid let out a breath, grinning. "And you're overtired. What time is it for you now?"

"Half past," Sam said after a moment.

"Think you could try getting some sleep?"

"I don't know," Sam said. "I could try. Would you... would you stay with me? Is that alright?"

"Yeah, of course." Dovid wished he were holding him right now. "Of course."

* * *

Sam Doyle: I got the week off work! Flying over February 11th, leaving the 17th, but that's still five days with you. You'll have to show me around.

Dovid Rosenstein: You will see all the sights. Though with me that also means eating all the food.

Sam Doyle: I can't wait.

* * *

Christmas Day, Sam's phone rang at eight in the morning. When he saw it was Dovid, he hurried to answer it, terrified something was wrong.

"Dovid?"

"Hey! Happy Christmas." Followed by a yawn.

"Thank you! I...what are you even doing up? It's midnight for you, isn't it?"

"Yeah, it's not so bad. I stayed up. I'm going to bed right after we're done talking."

"But why did you stay up?"

"I wanted you to have a good start to the day," Dovid said matter-of-factly.

And oh.

Oh.

Sam was spending the day with his parents. Charlie and his wife were coming in from Cork for the holiday as well, which usually helped act as some sort of buffer but still. It was a full day of immediate family. And dealing with Sam's parents could be...difficult. Especially since he and his father worked at the same company, albeit in completely different roles.

Not to mention that Charlie would probably ask how things were going, and Sam wasn't going to lie but... but he already knew that telling the truth was not going to work out so well for him.

"Well, thank you," Sam said, smiling, knowing the expression would carry over in his voice. "Thank you so much. You know, it *is* a good start to the day."

"Good. You'll have to tell me what you thought of my present! You didn't unwrap it early, did you?"

"No, Dovid," Sam replied, amused, "I did not, in the last twenty-four hours, tear through the wrapping like a madman."

"Good. I hope you like it."

"I'm sure I will. It's from you."

"Hey now, maybe I got you something awful. Like a horrible, itchy sweater. In puce."

"Do you even know what color puce is?" Sam asked, curious.

"Nope. But it sounds like an ugly color."

Sam laughed. "I'd still love it, even if it were a puce sweater. Which, I'll have you know, would clash horribly with my hair. But I'd wear it just the same."

"You love me," Dovid sing-songed.

"Of course I do. Though now I'm worried. I got you a sweater for your Chanukah present."

"I mean okay, yeah, but it is literally the softest, most comfortable thing I now own. And I've been assured that it isn't puce, since you said it was grey and then Rachel also said it was grey. Whatever grey means."

"It means I thought it would look good on you."

"And? I sent you that picture of me wearing it."

"Obviously I was right, of course."

Dovid laughed. "I love you so much."

Hearing that still made Sam come up all warm. "Look at us then, loving each other."

"Yeah, it's almost as if it's one of the things lasting relationships are built on."

"What are the other things?"

"Communication and collaboration, I think."

"Well then. I think we're doing a pretty good job so far."

"Aw. Yeah, I think so too." Another yawn.

"Get some sleep," Sam said fondly. "I'll text you as soon as I open my present and give you my exact emotional response."

"I think it's annoying how so many of our conversations end with one of us falling unconscious," Dovid grumbled. "S'not fair."

"Just a month and a half," Sam said. "And then they won't, for a little while."

"Are you kidding? *All* of our conversations will end with us falling asleep. Together, on account of you will be with me, in my bed."

Sam smiled. "I'm so looking forward to it."

"Me too," Dovid sighed into the phone.

"Alright, off to bed with you. Thank you so, so much for calling. It was a lovely surprise."

"G'night. Love you."

"Good night."

* * *

Sam Doyle: A snowball mic and pop filter?? DOVID REALLY.

Dovid Rosenstein: Hahaha, too much? I just thought it was about time for you to move to a better mic. Get rid of some of that audio fuzz.

Sam Doyle: It's lovely, thank you.

Dovid Rosenstein: Glad you liked it!

Sam Doyle: How are you doing, now that you're a little more awake?

Dovid Rosenstein: I'm good! Rachel and I are taking the day off. Though we both get restless when we do, so probably we'll do some filming tonight anyway. I've been in the mood for brownies, so clearly that means I should make some.

Sam Doyle: That sounds very good!

Dovid Rosenstein: Yeah, it does. Okay, plan. Gonna make some brownies. I'll get Rachel to send you a picture when they're done.

Sam Doyle: That'll only make me sad that I'm not eating them :(

Dovid Rosenstein: Well, I mean, you could wait for the video then.

Sam Doyle: I love watching your cooking videos, but I will admit that sometimes they do make me want to eat whatever it is you're making. I've made those chocolate chip cookies you filmed a while back two or three times now.

Dovid Rosenstein: Oh cool!

Dovid Rosenstein: And I'll tell you what—we will bake all the things when you come to visit. I've decided.

Dovid Rosenstein: Maybe not ALL the things, because there's only so much food even Rachel will want to eat, but several things. We can make several things.

Sam Doyle: I'd love to :)

Dovid Rosenstein: Yay!

Dovid Rosenstein: So how did the rest of the day go for you? You're home now, right?

Sam Doyle: Yes, I'm home now. The day was...fine. I enjoyed talking to Charlie and Anna.

Dovid Rosenstein: And things were okay? With your parents?

Dovid Rosenstein: Though if you don't want to talk about it, just tell me to shut up.

Sam Doyle: No, it's alright. Again, things were fine.

Sam Doyle: They're usually much more pleasant when Charlie is around. It was just little things.

Dovid Rosenstein: Little things?

Sam Doyle: Well I

Sam Doyle: I was thinking about what you said before. About trying to separate what they say about me and who I actually am as a person. That I'm...better than what they think of me. So I've been trying. And the more I do, the more I notice all these little things. Jabs and digs and stuff that I never registered before. They just hurt. I think now I'm a bit more aware of why they hurt.

Dovid Rosenstein: I'm sorry. You know how I feel about the situation. And how I feel about you.

Sam Doyle: I know. And I love you for it.

Sam Doyle: I've been trying not to let it all get to me. It's as you said: sometimes people are just mean without purpose. I think my parents just. Might be like that, with me.

Sam Doyle: But here I am, being mopey. It really wasn't too bad a time. It was nice to see Charlie and Anna again, especially since the last time I saw them was right after the accident back in April.

Dovid Rosenstein: God, April. Can you really believe it's been almost a year now?

Sam Doyle: Just a bit over nine months!

Dovid Rosenstein: That's a BABY. Sam, our relationship is as old as a baby!

Sam Doyle: Hahahaha. You know, I wouldn't have thought of it that way, but it is true.

Dovid Rosenstein: That's why you've got me ;p

* * *

"Sam! Sam, over here!" Sam searched for where Rachel's voice was coming from, quickly finding her waving. And next to her...

There was Dovid, standing with his cane in one hand and holding a bouquet of flowers in the other, beaming his head off. Videos were one thing, but in person... Sam was so lucky and so happy to be where he was now.

He went over to them, pulling his roll-on luggage behind him.

"Hi." He suddenly felt shy. "I'm, well, I'm here."

"Hey, you," Dovid said, turning in the direction of Sam's voice. "Welcome to the States." He held out the flowers. Sam took them, touched, and then handed them to Rachel before going in for a hug.

"Oof," Dovid said for show, even as he curled his

hands over Sam's back and held on tight. "I'm so happy you're here."

"You and me both," Sam murmured before tearing himself away and saying hello to Rachel, as was only polite.

Rachel laughed. "It's great to see you. And maybe now Dovid will stop pining for the week that you're here."

"Oh stop," Dovid said. "I don't pine. Unless Sam is into that. In which case I might pine a little bit."

Now it was Sam's turn to laugh. "I'm just happy to be here." Away from his parents, and their disappointment. They hadn't been pleased to find that Sam was leaving the country for a week. *"To visit a boy? Really? You're flying across half the world for a boy? Is he the only one who'd have you?"*

They hadn't been pleased with a few other decisions Sam had made recently either.

But Sam was decidedly not thinking about it. He was focusing his attention on the people he loved dearly, and he was going to make the absolute best he could of his time.

Besides, his parents had been the only people to voice negatives about how his life was going as of late. That counted for something.

And it further emphasized how little Sam should try to care.

Dovid felt for Sam's hand and squeezed. "C'mon," he said. "Let's go home."

* * *

"So here it is!" Dovid said, opening the door and leading Sam inside. "Casa de Rosenstein. Here, let me show you to my room. You can put your bag down."

"Way to be subtle," Rachel said, closing the door behind her. "'Oh, let me show you to my room.' Are you sure I won't have to relocate for the next five days?"

"Why would you have to leave?" Sam asked. Innocent Sam.

"No reason!" Dovid said, grabbing his arm. "Come on, this way."

Sam obediently went where Dovid led him, across the living room and to the first door, Dovid's room. Rachel had the "master" bedroom in their two-bedroom, with her own personal bathroom. Dovid said it was because it would be way easier to keep a smaller room clean—which was true. But also because he wanted Rachel to have the best he could give her. He owed her a lot, not that either of them were keeping score.

That also meant she stored her share of equipment in her room. They had to put their lights and camera stuff *somewhere*. "Here we are."

The room was as clean as it could be, and, Dovid knew, pretty sparse. His walls, he'd been told, were white. He didn't have much wall decoration either. Rachel fairly papered her walls with fan letters and pictures. Dovid kept his favorite letters in a filing cabinet, organized by "subject" and the pictures were sort of lost on him. He did have a few pieces that he loved; people having taken the time to print in braille for him in all sorts of creative ways, including puffy paint. Those were what went up. Aside from the walls, there was a bed pushed in the corner of the room, a nightstand next to it (no lamp), and a large desk with said filing cabinet. The desk came with a computer, some *nice* speakers and sound equipment, his mixing board, and his guitar stands and keyboard. All his clothes were put away in his closet and a small chest of drawers, carefully organized by color and texture.

There was a pause, and Dovid got suddenly nervous. Did Sam not like his room? Was he uncomfortable with how little there was in it?

"Ah," Sam said, "sorry, could I turn on the light?"

Oh. "Fuck, sorry, yeah, yeah, uh—" He didn't actually know where his light switch was. Rachel always turned on the light herself when she came into his room. He waved a hand in the direction of the doorway. "Go ahead, sorry."

There was a small "click" sound and then, presumably, the lights came on. "Your room is very nice," Sam said. "And so neat!"

Dovid laughed. "Yeah, haha, kind of needs to be. Which, I mean, you made your entire house neat for me."

"It was no trouble at all, I told you. Where would you like me to set my bag?"

"That corner works, if you're cool with that," Dovid said, pointing in the general direction. "Keeps it out of the way?"

"Of course, sure." Dovid felt cold as Sam left his side, going over to the corner.

"You're probably beat," Dovid said quickly. "Do you want to change or shower or eat something or—" He stuttered to a stop as something touched his shoulder. A hand, Sam's hand. Because Sam was really here.

"I'd love to kiss you first," Sam murmured. "I've been waiting a long time."

Dovid gasped and reached out, letting out a noise that might have been a whimper as Sam moved to kiss him. He curled his hands into Sam's shirt and hung on, giving back as good as he got.

When they broke apart, they were both panting, and Dovid didn't go far, keeping his hands fisted in Sam's shirt. "Fuck, I missed you," he said, leaning in to rest his head on Sam's chest.

Sam's arms came up to encircle him. "I've missed you too. So much. There were so many days that I just wanted to hold you or be held by you. That was when I really felt the distance."

"Yeah," Dovid whispered. "Yeah, exactly."

They met again for the next kiss, and Dovid could have happily stayed there forever, standing in his room kissing Sam, re-memorizing the smell and feel of him.

But Sam had just gotten in from a super long flight, and no matter what he said, he had to be dead on his feet.

"Here," Dovid said, taking Sam's hand. "I love you and I love that you're here, but I don't even want to do the math for what time it is for you right now, considering how long your flight was and when you had to leave and all that. What would you like? It's late enough that if you wanted to go straight to bed—"

"Actually, since you mentioned it before, I wouldn't mind a shower. That might help refresh me too."

"Of course. And maybe after that food? I'm always starving after a long flight."

"I could eat," Sam said, sounding like he was smiling.

"Great." Dovid pulled him in for one kiss before he stepped back. "How does baked mac and cheese sound?" Sam had mentioned how much he liked it, but that he didn't make it often because there was only so much one person could eat at a time.

"It sounds lovely."

Dovid grinned. "I'll show you where the bathroom is."

After Sam grabbed a change of clothes and closed

the door behind him, Dovid went to the kitchen. Both to pull out the mostly-prepared mac and cheese he had in the fridge and stick it in the oven to fully bake, and to distract himself from thinking about a naked Sam who was literally a room over.

Thinking about something else. Right. Cooking. Right.

"So?" From Rachel, who sounded like she'd poked her head into the kitchen. "How's the reunion going?"

Dovid sighed. "I am so in love with him."

She laughed. "We knew that months ago."

"Yeah," Dovid said, feeling dreamy. "And he's *here*. With me. In my apartment! Rachel, he's *here*."

"And I'm really, really happy for you. Also happy for this mac and cheese I'm going to be able to eat. Want me to set the table?"

"No, it's okay. It'll give me something to do."

"While he's using your shower, you mean?"

"Rachel!"

"What? Do you deny it?"

Another sigh, this one defeated. "No."

"I mean it, if you're loud tonight—" a short pause "—well, I'll give you a bye since it's the first time you've seen him in person in like half a year—"

"More than that," Dovid said knowing his face was on fire. "And you can please, please stop talking about it like that. At least while he's here. Please. Because it's…" He swallowed. "It's not funny."

Sam meant so much to him. Dovid was honestly more happy holding his hand than he had been having sex with Olivia or Brian. And sex was something important to Dovid yeah, and something he'd been light-hearted about with Rachel before…

But the idea of Sam hearing about that and thinking maybe Dovid was joking was awful.

"Okay," Rachel said. "Hold up. What's really going on?"

"What do you mean?"

"You stopped me from making a joke that we literally have been making since we were like fifteen years old and then got all quiet and broody. What's going on?"

Dovid moved away from the oven and turned to lean against the counter. "Sam's homoromantic asexual," he said.

"What?" Rachel squeaked. "But he—but *you*—"

Dovid saved her. "Yeah I know. He's not sex-repulsed like you are, and he really likes kissing and cuddling and stuff, but it came up back when I visited. Sam hadn't had any experience because he didn't really care one way or another. Figuring out what he liked…stuff, uh, stuff feels good for him and he enjoys what we do, but he doesn't, um, need it like I do. And he's kind of self-conscious about it. So I'd appreciate if you didn't joke so much about it while he's in a position to actually hear you."

"Okay, yeah," Rachel said, because she wasn't an asshole. "Yeah, of course."

"Thanks," Dovid said. "It just… He already deals with feeling like a disappointment so much. We've talked about this in particular through a whole lot. And everything I can do to keep him from feeling horrible is kind of, uh…"

"I get it," Rachel said quickly. "No problem. I'll keep a lid on it. Or I'll try to. If I do anything out of reflex— but I'll work really hard on keeping a lid on it."

"Thanks."

"And...and you're really happy? With, um, with that?"

Dovid nodded immediately. It wasn't even a question. "So, so happy. You have no idea. If he were sex-repulsed and hated being touched and stuff it'd be...harder. But I would have dealt. The way things are like this? Not a problem. Not even remotely a problem."

"Okay. Okay, well good. Cool."

"Yeah. So go away. I'm setting the table. You're not getting any food until Sam's here."

"Technically he *is* here," Rachel wheedled.

"Nope."

"Ugh, fine, fine."

Her footsteps moved away from the kitchen, presumably her going into the living room with her laptop. Dovid, true to his word, busied himself with taking out dishes and utensils and setting a table for three (three!). Then he went to check the mac and cheese before proceeding to pull together an easy salad.

When he heard footsteps again, they were heavier than Rachel's. "Hey, you," he said, turning to throw a smile over his shoulder.

"How did you know it was me?" Sam asked.

"You're heavier than Rachel and you walk differently," Dovid explained, taking the completed salad and moving to set it on the table. "Easy."

"Oh," Sam said. And he didn't say anything like "wow that's amazing" as if Dovid had some weird superpower. "That's very interesting! Though it makes sense. I tend to clomp down stairs for instance, and Charlie walks much more deliberately."

"Yeah, exactly. But clomp down the stairs?" Dovid thought back to when he'd been in Sam's apartment. Sam hadn't gone up and down the stairs any louder than anyone else. "I mean, you use the stairs kind of fast, but not super heavily."

"Really! My mother always said—" And then Sam stopped. Cleared his throat. "A-anyway, going down fast has led to some accidents actually. I've tried to be more careful in recent years."

"Accidents?"

"Oh, I didn't tell you? I split my head open a few years back."

"What!"

Sam laughed. "It's nothing so exciting. I was going up and down the stairs in a building that had a fairly low cement overhang. And, well, as you know, I'm quite tall. The third time I was on my way down I, well, I forgot to duck."

Dovid winced.

"Yeah. I slammed my head into the overhang. And then proceeded to fall the rest of the way down all of the stairs."

"Oh my god!"

"Mm-hm. It wasn't all that bad really. There was a lot of blood, but I was assured that head wounds bleed a lot. I only needed about four stitches."

Dovid reached for him and Sam obligingly walked forward until Dovid could grab his sleeve. "Glad you're okay," Dovid mumbled.

Sam chuckled. "I've been okay for about four years now, if we're talking about that particular incident."

"Any other horrible injuries I should hear about?" He was trying to sound casual but there might've been a hint of real fear.

"Nothing since the car accident," Sam said gently. "Nothing to worry about. And I would have told you if there had been."

"Good to know."

The timer beeped, startling them both, and Dovid grinned ruefully. "Dinner's ready,"

The sound of quick steps. "I heard beeping!" Rachel announced. "Is it ready now?"

Both Sam and Dovid laughed.

* * *

After dinner, all of them went through the motions of getting ready for bed, with it being about eleven. It was even later for Sam, who was eight hours ahead. Dovid was really looking forward to crashing; it'd been a day filled with nervous-happy anticipation. He was also looking forward to having Sam in his bed with him. Falling asleep *with* him, being able to touch him, and not just as a voice in his ear.

He might have been thinking about this particular moment a lot over the last few months.

"Ready?" he asked once Sam walked out of the bathroom smelling like mint toothpaste.

Sam dropped a kiss to his hair, and Dovid sighed into it. "Ready," Sam said. "Only…"

"Yeah?"

"I have something I'd like to show you first."

"Oh, okay. What?"

"Want to go sit on the bed?"

Yes. Yes he did. Dovid went, and he could hear Sam rustling through something in his bag in the corner. Then Sam was sitting next to him again. Dovid immediately cuddled into his side. "So?" he asked.

"It's this," Sam took Dovid's hand and placed a piece of paper in it.

"Uh," Dovid said, feeling a little taken aback, "you… know I can't read this, right?"

"I know, sorry. I just wanted to give you something

a little concrete before I told you. I was going to wait til actual Valentine's day, but I decided on something else while on the plane and, well, I wanted to tell you as soon as possible."

Dovid licked his lips. "Tell me what?"

"It's, um, it's my letter of resignation. I gave in my two weeks. Erm. Two weeks ago."

Dovid shot up so fast he almost smashed into Sam's chin. "You what? What—you—really?"

"Really."

"Oh my god," Dovid said, throwing his arms around Sam. "Oh my god, oh my god. You quit!"

"I did quit."

"Fuck," Dovid breathed. "Oh my god. Can I kiss you? Is that appropriate? Is this a kissing moment?"

"It could be a kissing moment," Sam said, smile in his voice.

Dovid wasted no time, pulling Sam in and then pressing him down to the sheets. "I am so proud of you," he said in between licks and nips and more kisses. "Fuck, you are so amazing. I'm so, so proud."

"You know," Sam said breathlessly, "I'm rather proud of myself too."

Dovid hugged him tight, tight, tight, planning to never let go.

Chapter Thirteen

"Hello, everyone. My name's Sam, and welcome to another episode of Let's Play Dire Straits. Today might be a bit of a boring video I'm afraid, as I have an awful lot of harvesting to do. I've fallen quite a bit behind in keeping up with my resource collection, and I really do need to build up my supplies before winter rolls around again. My third winter in-game too! Can you believe I've managed to play this long without dying a grisly death? I feel like some congratulations might be in order, for the third-year anniversary." Sam tilted his head, considering. "Actually, I do know a way to celebrate! We could make a brookie. For those of you who don't know, a brookie is a dessert in-game food item that we are able to mix together and cook up in our oven. I just have never made one before myself, as the ingredients are all tricky to get. That being said, it seems like a good quest to set out on. So yes, I've decided. After I'm done with harvesting, it will be brookie ingredient collection time."

Sam continued to gather his resources; first huge bundles of grass, then twigs, moving on to the dried fruit and meat, as he continued to chat with his viewers. He did narrate gameplay as well, but since he was primarily doing repetitive work, he had to fill a lot of in-game activity with other talking.

"If you don't mind," he said, after glancing over at the notes he had started writing up to prepare talking topics for his videos, "I might get a bit more serious here, for a moment.

"My in-game anniversary isn't the only accomplishment I have to share. As some of you might know, today is also the first month anniversary of me leaving my job and moving to YouTube full time. It was an incredibly scary, exciting endeavor, and it's because of all of you that I was even able to do this in the first place. I wanted to say thank you for that, from the bottom of my heart. I'm so much happier in general nowadays, and making gaming and YouTube my job—my career is a large part of that. Of course, as many of you are aware, my channel first started getting popular when Dovid, from Don't Look Now, plugged it, unbeknownst to me.

"It was incredibly overwhelming at first, but, well, this is how it turned out so I can't complain! Dovid and I struck up a friendship soon after; another fairly well-known fact, I should think. I remember quite a few of you who were pleased by the first collaboration we did, back when Dovid visited Ireland last July for his Europe Tour. Sorry about only doing a couple more since then, by the way. It's a little more difficult to sync up, what with the time difference, and if we're talking to one another, we prefer to focus on each other and less so on recording. And, well, this has been a bit of a ramble so far, I suppose, but I assure you I'm getting to the next point."

He looked back down at his notes. "The long and short of it is that Dovid so enjoys sharing himself with his viewers. It's a part of him, being able to let you all into his life. But he's mentioned to me, just in passing, how things had ended rather poorly the last few times he tried to be open about his more personal relationships. People will speculate all the same, about someone who is in the public eye the way he is, and, well, lately he's been more self-conscious of it, I think. Not wanting to cause trouble for, ah, the one he cares about. So I thought, you know, maybe doing this might relieve the pressure somewhat. And he has utterly no idea about what I'm saying now. Though he will once I upload this video. So he'll find out around the same time as all of you do. Though I might send him the release link early, just so he has an idea of what to expect once the video goes live."

Sam shook his head, smiling ruefully. "Goodness but I've been going on, haven't I? I'll just come out with it then. Dovid and I have been dating for quite a while now. It's, ah, it's quite serious, and it's certainly been long enough that I feel comfortable speaking about it, especially as I know it's something he's been keeping from you strictly for my benefit. I'm utterly, completely mad about him, and I know there's an even split between people who are scared to use the word, and people who use it every chance they get, but I'm firmly in the latter camp. I love him so very, very much. And, well, I just wanted to share. And also give him the option to do so as well, if he wished to.

"And look at that, I've prattled on long enough to get everything all tidied away and reach the end of this video. I'll have to keep that in mind for the future; if I ever feel stalled on something to say, I'll just talk about Dovid." Sam chuckled. "Though you might get sick of that. Anyway, another huge thank-you to all who have watched me play, and next time we'll start farming for those brookie ingredients. As always, I'm Sam, and this was Dire Straits."

* * *

Rachel Rosenstein: What did you DO?

Sam frowned at his phone, puzzled. Though they had each other's numbers, he and Rachel didn't often text back and forth, instead mostly sticking with emails. It was a better medium for how they discussed things, which were often in-depth explanations of games, or editing, or some such like that.

Sam Doyle: Sorry? What do you mean?

Rachel Rosenstein: He's actually crying with happiness?? He got a video link from you and is IN ACTUAL TEARS.

Sam couldn't help his grin, at that.

Sam Doyle: I'm glad he liked it, then.

Rachel Rosenstein: Am I going to be allowed to watch this video??

Sam's grin only got wider.

Sam Doyle: Oh sure! You along with everyone else.

* * *

@dontlooknowdovid: Hey, guys! Figured this would be faster than doing a video. B/c I couldn't wait. For those who haven't heard or just want the confirmation: Yes. Yes, I'm dating @playitagainsam & I am SO HAPPY & in love. Still baffled that I get him?? He chose ME??? But eternally grateful <3<3<3

* * *

"Hey, you," Dovid said, when he picked up.

"Hello," Sam replied, as he went to sit on his couch. He tended to pace while he waited for a phone call to connect, if he was able to move around. Nervous energy, along with the general social anxiety he never quite managed to shake, even when he knew it'd be Dovid on the other end. "Good morning."

"Back atcha. Happy Monday! Though I was kind of surprised? I thought you were going to your family's Easter Monday dinner thingie."

Sam cleared his throat. "Actually, I decided to skip it. Though I did make plans to meet Charlie and Anna for drinks later this evening, since they're in town."

"Wha—really?"

"Charlie was a little taken aback when I told him I wasn't coming, and I think a touch disappointed, but he didn't kick up a fuss, which was nice." Sam had been most worried about Charlie's reaction. Charlie did have a good relationship with their parents, and so sometimes it was difficult to make him understand that Sam…didn't. And Sam had never out-and-out decided to miss a family event before.

"Oh wow," Dovid said. "Um, okay. Wow. How, um, how are you feeling?"

"My heart's in my throat a bit," Sam said honestly, voice starting to get a little shakier. "I, erm, it—it was a difficult conversation to have. To tell them I wasn't coming."

"I'm sure," Dovid said quietly. "I'm sure it was really hard to do that. God, you're so brave. I'm so proud of you."

"Thank you. I don't… I don't regret doing it. Though I suppose I regret having to have done it."

"I get that. Yeah, of course."

"It's only, since I left my father's company, it's…you know it's been so much worse. As though since I'm not there for him to summon at work, they need to make up for the missed time. With, um, with the nastiness. And I suppose I just got fed up to the back teeth with it. So I—I decided it was time to maybe…not give them the chance. To do that to me."

"I am so fucking proud of you. God, Sam. So proud. You have no idea."

Sam smiled hesitantly. "I think I might have some idea of how proud."

"I dunno. Multiply that idea by about a billion and maybe you'll be getting close." Sam had to laugh a little at that, feeling lighter. "So okay, um, do you have plans today then? Besides the drinks thing later?"

"No. I wanted to call you, of course. And after we're done I figured I'd record my Wednesday Patreon video. Read. Maybe go for a walk. It's a lovely day."

"Just look both ways before you cross the street," Dovid said affectionately.

* * *

"—Taiwan, USA, New Jersey, Canada, Canada, Boston, Hertfordshire, man, we're pretty global today."

Dovid grinned. Global included Ireland. Sam got to catch a lot more livestreams now that he wasn't employed at a nine to five. He'd already texted Dovid to say he was watching this one, which was great considering the topic of the day. "Perfect." Dovid waved at his livestream viewers. "Hey, guys! This is Don't Look Now with Dovid and Rachel. I'm Dovid, Rachel's behind the camera, and today you're in for a treat, since I'm starting the stream by opening a care package from the love of my life." He heard Rachel snort, plenty audible for all the viewers too. "Rachel doesn't have a romantic bone in her body—"

"Probably because you commandeered them all yourself."

"—so she's going to give me a hard time throughout this entire opening, but watch me utterly not care, because I am ridiculously excited. Sam's been dropping hints for weeks about the contents of this box. I have absolutely no idea what's in it, so I'm going to be as surprised as you are no matter what it is. Reactions one hundred percent genuine here." He breathed out. "Okay. Gonna open it."

He turned a little to the side, to the giant cardboard box sitting next to him on the couch. Rachel had already cut open the tape as was their usual routine, so there was nothing stopping him from pulling back the cardboard flaps and reaching inside for the first item. It was on the heavier side for a package, so he was really curious as to what was going to be in it.

The first thing he pulled out was soft cloth, long sleeves, and a neck hole. "Oh awesome! Another shirt. Thanks, Sam." Dovid laughed. "You're not going to have any left, with how you send me yours all the time. Can't say I mind though. Rachel? What color is it?"

"Green," she said, sounding as though she was grinning.

"Cool. I've been told that green goes with my lack of eyes." He set the shirt down and reached in again.

"Okay, uh, heavy, first off, but bulky too." The slick, quilted plastic-y sound of water resistant fabric. "And… this has sleeves, and a hood? A furry hood. Is this a jacket?" He lifted it up. "Oof, more like a winter coat. Um. Okay. It's a little heavy for June weather, but sure, I'll take it. Thank you!"

The next item was another long-sleeved shirt, then a couple bulky sweaters, what felt like a scarf, a pair of heavy gloves, a hat, and then, most baffling, a pair of winter boots that would most definitely not fit his feet, wrapped in a plastic bag. Each time Dovid asked Rachel for a color description, or clarification of what he pulled out, her voice got more and more amused.

"Okay," Dovid said, after it was all spread out and the box was empty. "That was…not exactly what I expected. Still fun though! Although, Sam, I'm going to be calling you like right after this for an explanation, because I know for a fact you didn't include a letter with—"

Music blared out, cutting Dovid off. A sound he recognized immediately, because it was Rachel's cell phone ringtone. "Rachel," he said, mortified, "How the fu—the hell did you forget to turn off your phone?" The only reply he got was a faint beep sound.

"You're not actually answering it?" he said, aghast.

"Hey there," Sam's voice sounded out, on speakerphone.

Dovid's mouth dropped open, but he recovered quickly. "Hi! I, uh, I guess you've been watching the stream, huh?"

"Oh yes," Sam said, voice colored with laughter. "It was a treat to watch you open the package, really it was."

"Hey, it was fun to get it. Though I've gotta say I'm definitely confused. Are you going to explain things to me?" Dovid made a face. "Especially since, whatever this is, Rachel's clearly in on it."

"Oh, you know," Sam said lightly. "Thought I'd get a head start on packing and moving my things."

Dovid registered the words and his heart legitimately

skipped a beat. "Really?" he breathed. "You—you mean it? You decided that you—you mean it?"

"Yes," Sam said simply. "Dovid, really, it wasn't even much of a choice in the end. I can work anywhere now, as long as I have my gaming and recording setup. And, well, we can always fly in together to visit. I do, after all, want you to meet Charlie and Anna in person as opposed to video chat, but there's...there's a lot more for me in Seattle than there currently is in Ireland."

"Right," Rachel said, while Dovid struggled to speak against the rush of emotion. "For instance, I'm here."

Sam chuckled. "Yes, exactly. I'm looking forward to gaming with you in person, in the same time zone."

"Yeah, me too!"

"And Dovid?"

Dovid licked his lips. "Yeah?" he managed.

"I love you." Said so easily. To Dovid, but also to Rachel, and to all the viewers currently watching, because they were *live*. Sam had specifically planned this out so that Dovid could share this moment with the world. "And I can't wait to hold you again."

"Same here," Dovid said hoarsely.

He couldn't wait to hold Sam again, but he'd be able to *soon*.

Every single night.

* * * * *

To find out about other books by Aidan Wayne or to be alerted to new releases, be sure to sign up for their newsletter at eepurl.com/cO6OGL.

Acknowledgments

Thank you to Morgan, for being my beta reader and putting up with me during the research and writing process, and to my editor Kate Marope, for both giving my story a chance and helping me work to make it better.

About the Author

Aidan Wayne lives with altogether too many house-plants on the seventh floor of an apartment building, and though the building has an elevator, Aidan refuses to acknowledge its existence. They've been in constant motion since before they were born (pity Aidan's mom)—and being born didn't change anything. When not moving, Aidan is usually writing, so things tend to balance out. They usually stick with contemporary romance (both adult and YA), but some soft sci-fi/fantasy has been known to sneak in as well, and they primarily write character-driven stories with happy endings. Because, dammit, queer people deserve happy endings too.

Website: aidanwayne.com
Twitter: twitter.com/aidanwayne
Facebook: www.facebook.com/AidanWayneWrites/
Mailing list: eepurl.com/cPDl4X

Also available from Aidan Wayne:
His Two Leading Men

On the surface, he's living the New York Dream—acclaimed by critics for his stunning debut, playing to packed audiences every night.

They don't know the truth.

Battling crippling anxiety, every show is a struggle for Skye. Only one thing gives him the courage to step into the spotlight every performance—the steady, calming support of costumer Russell. But Skye can't burden Russell with all his demons…

When wealthy patron Brent takes an interest in Skye, everything the actor knows is turned upside down. Charismatic and confident, Brent is everything Skye isn't…and just what he needs. But how can he choose between gentle Russell and magnetic Brent? Russell means so much to him, but the chemistry between Skye and Brent is undeniable.

Or does he have to choose at all…?

To purchase and read this and other books
by Aidan Wayne, please visit Aidan's website at
aidanwayne.com/wp/index.php/adult/.